THE MOON
OF MASARRAH

FARAH ZAMAN

The Moon of Masarrah
Second Edition

For information, please contact the author: Zefarah@gmail.com
https://www.farahzamanauthor.com

First edition 2006
The Treasure at Bayan Bluffs
ISBN: 978-1-945873-10-2

Design by Book Power Publishing
www.bookpowerpublishing.com

Praise and Gratitude to
the One who made all things possible.

I dedicate this book to my family
for their unswerving support,
and to my beta readers
for their invaluable insight and input.
And for all bookworms,
who have long discovered the greatest treasures
are buried in the pages of a book!

Happy reading!

Prologue

THE NIGHT WAS dark, yet full of shadows. The Captain stood still in the great hall of the house, a canvas bag clutched in his hand. His heart hammered in his chest, overwrought with fatigue and fear. Not that he was a man given to fear easily. Many were the times he had looked death in the face aboard his ship, tossed and turned mercilessly upon the wrathful seas. Through somber storms and smiling suns, he had passed endless days and nights, and had come to love the sea with a fierce affection.

The fear that gripped the Captain now was of a different kind. It was fear that came from finding an empty house, one that was usually bustling with the life and laughter of his loved ones. Where was his family?

His ship had sailed in on a strong wind that evening as the sun had set upon a calm and gentle sea. Standing on deck, he had leaned over the rails, the crimson hues of the dying sun causing his red beard to glow like fire as he had stared at the mass of land looming on the horizon. When he had bowed his head during the sunset prayer, his heart had overflowed with gratitude that once again, the Yuhanza had returned safely to land.

But his joy had been short-lived. No sooner had they dropped anchor when they found themselves in the midst of a nightmare. The distant sound of gunfire and the rising plumes of dark smoke over the city had quickly filled their breasts with horror. The Captain had run frantically all the way to his house, desperate to make sure that all was well with his family. Cold silence greeted him now when so many times before it had been joyous smiles and a warm welcome. What had become of his family?

As the Captain placed the bag upon a nearby table, he recalled the precious package and the sheet of paper within. He should conceal them before venturing out again. Lighting a candle, he first hid the precious package before turning his attention to the sheet of paper. It bore the words he had carefully composed during his sojourn at sea and as he stashed it away, he fervently prayed that his family was safe, and would once more enjoy their customary game.

He returned to the great hall, his feet dragging wearily and the solitary candle flickering in his hand. Setting the candle on the table next to his bag, he was about to extinguish it and go outside when the door of the great hall suddenly creaked open. He spun around, wondering if he would see the face of friend or foe. In the light of the candle, he saw a tall man wearing a mask that covered his face, leaving exposed his dark, burning eyes. The Captain felt a flicker of unease as the intruder closed the door and entered the house.

"Who are you?" he demanded. "And what do you want?"

"I want the diamond," the man hissed, his eyes glittering fierily above his mask. "Where is it?"

The Captain stared at him in shock. "How do you know of the diamond? I haven't told a soul about it."

"You're not as clever as you think you are," the masked man sneered. "Now give it to me."

"I will not be coerced into giving what's mine," the Captain replied. "If you want it that badly, you can buy it from me."

"I have no time for games, you arrogant fool," the masked man snarled. The next moment, he pulled out a curved bronze dagger stained with blood and pointed it at the Captain. Betrayal felt like bitter medicine on the Captain's tongue as he stared at the familiar weapon. His own dagger, an exact replica of the one that the man brandished, lay inside his bag on the table. Cold fingers of fear crept down the Captain's spine as he realized his danger. He was entirely at the mercy of the masked man unless he could get hold of his own dagger somehow.

"Not so brave now, are you?" the intruder jeered. "Now where's the diamond?"

"In my bag," the Captain replied as inspiration came to him. "Let me get it."

As he reached into his bag and grabbed his dagger, the intruder gave a ferocious snarl and sprang at him like a beast of prey. The two men grappled together, each trying to wrestle the other's dagger away. Across the floor they struggled, desperation lending strength to their limbs so that neither showed any signs of yielding. Like a wild animal, the masked man leaned forward and dug his teeth viciously into the Captain's forearm. As the pain radiated up his arm, the Captain's grip on his dagger loosened, sending it clattering to the ground, and causing his adversary to finally gain the upper hand.

With a cry of triumph, the masked man lifted his blood-stained dagger high into the air. Then he brought it down, thrusting it forcefully into the Captain's breast. The Captain staggered from the sheer savagery of the blow, crying out in agony as the sharp blade bit deep into his flesh. He swayed unsteadily for a few moments before his legs buckled beneath him and he fell to the ground, clutching at the hilt protruding from his chest.

As the strength left his body, he was powerless against the

invading fingers that searched his cloak and his bag, seizing his dagger and leaving the murderous one buried in his chest. He knew he was dying as he felt his life's blood slowly ebbing out of his body. Hovering between light and darkness, he listened to the masked intruder searching for the precious package. At last, he gave up the search, kicking the Captain in a rage before storming out of the great hall.

The Captain's lips moved silently as he affirmed the faith he had embraced as a young man. He was not afraid of death, but he hated to die all alone, worrying about the fate of his family. In a fog of agony, he saw a sudden light coming towards him. *It must be the Angel of Death*, he thought, *coming to seize my soul.* He steeled himself for what was about to come but as the light drew nearer, he heard a piercing cry.

"Papa!" the voice shrieked. "Papa!"

It was the voice of Yusuf, his young son, carrying a candle in his hand. It was not the Angel of Death as yet. Filled with a sudden urgency, the Captain took an invigorating breath and spoke in his mother tongue.

"Yusuf," he gasped. "Where is…mother…and…sisters?"

"They're hiding in the woods, Papa," the boy replied, as he set the candle on the ground. "But you…what has happened to you?" he asked in a frightened voice as he crouched beside his father.

"Going…to…die," the Captain whispered as he fought against the descending darkness.

"Die?" Yusuf repeated in bewilderment. "No, you can't die. You mustn't die," he broke into painful sobs, unmindful of the blood that soaked into his clothes as he threw his arms around his father.

"Take…care…of…mother…and sisters," the Captain's voice became fainter as he struggled for breath.

"I will, Papa," the boy wept, his tears mingling with his father's blood. "I will."

Gathering the last of his strength and with the bitter taste of blood in his mouth, the Captain clutched Yusuf's hand and told him where he had hidden the precious package.

"Diamond... hidden...in...house?" Yusuf repeated, unable to grasp the significance of his father's words.

The Captain opened his mouth to speak again but he was now beyond the power of speech. The encroaching darkness closed in on him and a rattling sound emerged from his throat. His eyes became fixed before closing slowly as he passed into the realm of the unseen. Then he was still and silent in the arms of his son.

Chapter One

Bayan House

Z AID ALKURDI CAME awake slowly in the back of the silver
Mitsubishi Outlander. In the midst of his jumbled
dreams, he had heard his mother's voice. He straightened
up in his seat, wincing as his stiff muscles protested against the
sudden movement. Picking up the book and the half-eaten bag
of chips lying beside him, he crammed them into his backpack
before staring out at the traffic-laden corniche and the long
stretch of blue water adjoining it.

"Are we there yet?" mumbled his younger sister Zahra, as
she too sat up and blinked sleepily.

"Not yet," their mother replied from the front passenger seat
where she was sitting next to their father, Professor Alkurdi, who
was at the wheel. "But we're almost there."

We're finally arriving at Bayan House, Zaid thought. It was
the childhood home of his father's close friend, Dr. Adil Horani.
The two men, both hailing from the country of Midan, had
become good friends while studying in the United States many
years ago. After completing his degree, Professor Alkurdi had
gone on to pursue a doctorate in history at one of the foremost

universities in England while Dr. Horani had remained in the United States to study medicine.

Both men had gotten married around the same time, Professor Alkurdi to a young Midanese woman born and raised in England and Dr. Horani to a young Egyptian woman raised in the United States. After fifteen years in England, Professor Alkurdi had finally returned to Midan two years ago with his family, having accepted a position as head of the history department at Crescent City University. Dr. Horani had remained in the United States and though they had kept in touch from time to time, the two men had not seen each for over sixteen years.

It came as a surprise to Professor Alkurdi when his old friend emailed that his four children were coming to spend the summer vacation at their grandfather's home in Bayan Bay, and it would please him greatly if his dear friend's children were to join them there. Zaid and Zahra had been delighted at the prospect, especially after learning that the oldest boy was fourteen like Zaid, and the only girl thirteen, like Zahra. Professor Alkurdi had accepted the invitation on their behalf and had worked out the details with the children's grandfather, Yusuf Horani.

And here we are, Zaid thought, as the Mitsubishi exited the corniche and turned onto a winding tree-lined road . They had left their home in Crescent City that Saturday morning, expecting to arrive in the seaside city of Bayan Bay in the mid-afternoon. They had stopped twice along the way to eat lunch at a small roadside café and to offer the midday prayer at a mosque. After traveling halfway across Midan, Zaid was bored of being cooped up in the car. He had read a little along the way, but the motion of the car had soon sent him to sleep. *We sure made good time,* he thought, as he glanced at the clock on the dashboard and saw that it was almost three.

"We should see the house anytime now," said Professor Alkurdi, and Zaid and Zahra peered out the windows eagerly as the van climbed up a sloping road. Dense rows of trees lined the sides while yellow wildflowers carpeted the edges. Halfway up the road, Zaid's eyes widened as he stared upwards. Against the backdrop of deep blue skies in the afternoon sun, birds were circling in slow motion high above an imposing structure perched atop the bluffs. With its rectangular shape and square turrets, Zaid thought it looked more like a fortress than a house.

"Is that Bayan House?" Zahra stared at the impressive sight. "It's very grand."

"It sure is," Zaid agreed.

"I didn't realize it would be so high up on the cliffs," Mrs. Horani commented. "It's breathtaking."

"Yes, it looks out into the Bayan Bay," Professor Alkurdi remarked. "Most seamen like to live close to water. Both Adil's father and grandfather were sailors. In fact, his grandfather was a famous captain in his time. He was born an Englishman and because of his red hair, became known as Captain Red Rafiq."

"I bet there's old *jinns* floating around here at night," Zahra murmured dreamily.

"You've been watching too much *Jinns of Jeopardy*," Mrs. Alkurdi chided, naming a popular television series. Zaid grinned. He knew that although she scoffed at it, his mother enjoyed looking at the creepy show.

The sloping road ended at wide-open iron gates set in a weathered fence cast of the same brown stone as the house. Professor Alkurdi drove through the gate and into a plain flagstone courtyard where a gray Toyota Land Cruiser, a black Honda pickup truck and a blue Land Rover were parked. After stepping out of the Mitsubishi and helping his father to unload their suitcases, Zaid glanced curiously around. The house was two stories high, the brown stone lending it an austere air. The courtyard was bare of trees and vegetation and was protectively encircled by the stone fence. Unfortunately, the fence also obscured what would have been a spectacular view of the bay to the right.

The front door of the house swung open and a tall, imposing man strode out. *That must be Yusuf Horani, the grandfather,* Zaid thought. They had learned that he was a widower in his late sixties and had no other children besides Dr. Horani. He came towards them, his stern-looking face weather-beaten, with lines crisscrossing at the corners of his eyes and mouth. With his pale green eyes, graying red hair and matching beard, his English ancestry was apparent.

A smile broke across his face as he greeted them. He shook Professor Alkurdi's hand and embraced him warmly before turning to Zaid and doing the same. Nodding respectfully to Mrs. Alkurdi and Zahra, he said, "Welcome to Bayan House. I hope you had a good journey."

"Thank you, we did," Mrs. Alkurdi replied.

"Come, let's go inside," he beckoned, helping Professor Alkurdi with one of the suitcases. "I'm sure you must be tired and hungry."

As they headed to the front door, two young boys came dashing out from the side of the house. Above their heads flew a large bird which Zaid recognized as a seagull. The boys were identical twins about six years of age. They both had red hair and green eyes like their grandfather, with a sprinkling of freckles across the bridge of their noses and across their cheeks. They were wearing T-shirts and jeans and had identical cheeky grins on their faces. Zaid guessed that they must be the younger Horani children. He had not known that they were twins.

"This is Hassan and Hakeem," Mr. Horani introduced them. "And that's Gul, their new pet."

The bird gave a loud squawk and one of the boys giggled and said, "Gul is saying hello to you."

"You can hardly tell them apart," Mrs. Alkurdi shook her head in wonder as she looked at the delightful pair.

Zaid was watching the seagull. It stared right back at him, its head tilted to the side. Its plumage was white in color, with an unusual sprinkling of gray dots at the base of its tail feathers. With its webbed feet and stout black-tipped bill, it looked like a typical seagull.

They continued to the front door, Mr. Horani shooing Gul away, who flew off with an indignant squawk. They entered a great hall which had a comfortable, lived-in atmosphere that belied the bleak appearance of the outside. Sunlight filtered in through sets of casement windows at the front and side, softening the dark wall panels and spilling onto the thick Persian rug covering the wooden floor. In the center of the room were several comfortable sofas surrounding a long coffee table. A few pieces of calligraphy adorned the walls while an ancient light fixture hung from the ceiling. At the back was a grand staircase leading to the upper floor and at its base, a passageway leading to the left wing of the house.

After placing his sneakers on the shoe rack, Zaid watched with interest as a boy dressed in jeans and a blue striped shirt came through an archway at the back of the great hall, a young girl behind him. The boy was a tall, handsome youth with unruly black hair, a square determined jaw and twinkling black eyes. He and Zaid were of similar height and coloring, though Zaid's face was longer and more prone to solemnity.

After the youth greeted them, Mr. Horani said, "This is Adam, my eldest grandson."

"Welcome to Bayan House," Adam smiled. "We're glad to have you here," he said in flawless Arabic.

The youth exuded such self-assurance that he seemed much older than his fourteen years. As he and Zaid sized each other up, he winked covertly and Zaid immediately knew that he was in the presence of a kindred spirit.

"And this is Layla, my granddaughter," Mr. Horani said next, placing an affectionate hand on the young girl's shoulder.

Layla smiled and greeted them in Arabic too. She was wearing a black floral dress with a pink scarf and had green eyes like her twin brothers, and a pair of charming dimples in her cheeks.

A couple in their early fifties came through the archway next and greeted them. The woman was wearing allover black and was short and plump, with a smiling countenance. The man was muscular and heavyset, with curly dark hair and a small trim beard. Mr. Horani introduced them as Maymun and Luqman, who served as live-in housekeeper and handyman respectively.

"Come, come," Maymun fussed. "You will join the family for afternoon tea. Don't worry about your suitcases. Luqman will take them up."

Through the archway at the back of the great hall, the Alkurdis were ushered down a long passageway. After washing off the dust and grime of travel in a bathroom, they sat down at a table in the dining room loaded with refreshments. They soon made short work of a large meat pie, a selection of sandwiches and a semolina cake, served with both hot and cold beverages. Afterwards, they moved across to the living room, which was furnished with several comfortable sofas and a television set. As Mr. Horani conversed with Professor and Mrs. Alkurdi, the teenagers smiled tentatively at each other.

"My dad told us a lot about your dad," Adam said.

"We've heard a lot about your dad too," Zaid replied.

"Is this your first visit to Midan?" Zahra asked.

"Yes, it is," Layla nodded.

"How do you like it?" Zaid asked.

"We've only been here for five days but it seems like a nice place," Adam said. "I was kind of surprised."

"I'm glad to hear that," Zaid replied. "What were you expecting?"

"I guess more chaos and confusion," Adam grinned. "From what you hear in the news, you'd think that everyone in this part of the world is uncivilized and crazy."

"Well, from what *I* see in the news, I used to think that all Americans are obnoxious and rude," Zaid shot back and they all laughed.

"I guess we have to get to know each other," Layla said. "Then we wouldn't think so bad of the other."

"You both speak Arabic very well," Zahra spoke in English with a distinct British accent.

"Oh, Mom and Dad made sure we learned it right along with English," Layla replied in English too. "I supposed you learned Arabic while you were living in England as well."

"We did," Zaid replied. "I guess we can speak to each other in English while we're here."

"Both Grandpa and Aunt Hafza speak excellent English too," Adam said. "With everyone else, I guess we'll stick to Arabic."

"Who's Aunt Hafza?" Zaid asked.

"She's Grandpa's twin sister," Adam replied. "Our great-aunt, actually. It's too much of a mouthful to say great-aunt, so we simply say aunt. She's resting now. You'll meet her at dinner later."

Shortly after, Professor and Mrs. Alkurdi took their leave. Zaid and Zahra hugged their parents in the courtyard and stood watching until the Mitsubishi went out the gates. When they re-entered the house, Mr. Horani said, "Adam and Layla will take you up to your rooms now. You can rest there until dinner."

Zaid and Zahra followed their new friends up the grand staircase to the floor above. At the top of the staircase, was a hallway which dissected that floor into two wings.

"Your room's this way," Layla said, steering Zahra towards the right wing.

Adam turned into the left wing and pointed to two doors which stood on opposite sides. "Those are Grandpa and Aunt Hafza's rooms. This wing is smaller than the other one but the two rooms here are larger, with their own bathrooms. Your room is next to mine in the eastern turret."

At the end of the hallway, Adam showed Zaid the bathroom the two of them would share. Opposite it was a flight of stairs that led to the turret. At the top was a narrow passageway with a room on each side.

"That's my room," Adam pointed to the door on the right. "And this is yours," he opened the door on the left. They entered a small but cozy room with a double bed, a dresser with a mirror, and a small closet. To the left was a single casement window, with a built-in window seat. It stood open to let in sunlight and air.

"The view from your window is spectacular," Adam said, beckoning Zaid over. "That's Bayan Bay, the watery version out there," he indicated the wide expanse of blue water surrounding the bluffs upon which the house sat. "And that's Bayan Cove down there," he pointed left towards an almost circular body of water secluded by towering cliffs that rose protectively on each side. It had a narrow opening leading out into the bay and verged a small, curving strip of rocky beach almost at the foot of the bluffs. "When the tide is in, the beach is covered with water. It's a beautiful spot, isn't it?"

"It is," Zaid agreed. "Have you swum in the cove yet?"

"Oh, no," Adam said emphatically. "Grandpa doesn't want us to go there. He said the bluffs are too risky to climb down and the cove is filled with dangerous undercurrents. Well, I'll leave you to settle in," he headed to the door. "Dinner is at seven so I'll see you later."

Zaid sat on the window seat, admiring the breathtaking view. From his vantage point, he looked down upon the craggy bluffs, which were jagged and steep and would certainly be a difficult climb down, though not impossible. He listened to the peculiar mewling calls of the seagulls and watched the white-tipped waves breaking against the cliffs, sending spray shooting upwards. It was like being in a whole different world. After unpacking his luggage and taking a trip to the bathroom to perform ablution, Zaid offered the mid-afternoon prayer before sprawling on his bed and taking a nap.

WHEN ZAID AND Zahra went down to dinner later, they found the family gathered in the living room along with several unfamiliar faces. They were introduced to Aunt Hafza, who was dressed in allover black and was frail-looking with vague black eyes. Other than the same nose and mouth, she did not look at all like her twin brother. Abbas, who was the gardener, had been specially invited to dinner to meet them. He was a short, stocky man in his late fifties with bushy eyebrows and a thick, well-kept beard. He greeted and welcomed them with a deep, resonant voice.

Last of all, they were introduced to the Ahmeds, who were friends as well as neighbors. Mrs. Ahmed was a tiny woman with soft brown eyes and a warm smile. She was wearing a peacock-blue gown with a fringed black scarf. Her husband was a stout, balding man wearing a tan robe. Their son Basim, was the same age as Adam and Zaid. He was a rather chubby youth with his mother's eyes and his father's large frame.

"Nice to meet you," Mrs. Ahmed smiled.

"How do you do," Mr. Ahmed squeezed Zaid's hand, showing rather large teeth as he smiled.

"Hello," Basim gave a friendly nod.

Shortly after, they all trooped into the dining room for dinner. The first course was cucumber soup, which Zaid enjoyed immensely. Next was the *musakhan* – tender roasted chicken garnished with pine nuts and served with bread. The boys, who were seated next to each other, conversed as they ate.

"You have to come visit us at Ma'ab Manor," Basim said,

crunching on his pine nuts. "You'll enjoy the tennis court and swimming pool."

Lowering his voice, Adam said, "I wouldn't mind trying out the swimming pool since Grandpa wouldn't let us swim in the cove. Honestly, he thinks we're still babies."

"Well, the bay is known for its dangerous undertow," Basim said seriously. "Lots of people have drowned in it."

"But I'm a good swimmer," Adam protested.

"So were many of the people who drowned," Basim said. "Believe me, it can be very risky."

As Zaid was eating his custard, his attention was caught by Aunt Hafza, who seemed to have spilled her tea. Mr. Horani came to her aid and swiftly wiped up the spill.

"Poor Aunt Hafza," Adam continued in a low voice. "She's deaf in one ear and very absent-minded. The other day, she misplaced her dentures and Grandpa had us looking everywhere for it. We finally found it stuck to an apple which had rolled under her bed."

Basim snickered and Zaid could not help grinning at the image of dentures sticking out of an apple. "Your grandpa seems to take very good care of her," he observed as Mr. Horani poured a fresh mug of tea for his sister. "They're not identical twins like Hassan and Hakeem though."

"No, they're fraternal twins," Adam said. "Aunt Hafza is older by a few minutes. She's been living here ever since she became a widow ten years ago. She has just one daughter and two grandkids who live in Canada, but she prefers to remain here rather than go live there."

After dinner, they gathered for the sunset prayer in the prayer room, which was located down the passageway on the left side of the great hall. It was a spacious carpeted room with several shelves of religious texts and a row of windows overlooking the courtyard. A cool evening breeze drifted in through the open windows as Zaid took his place in the row. After the prayer ended, Abbas and the Ahmeds left and everyone went their separate ways.

Zaid had stayed back to help Adam close the windows. After they were done, he peered with interest at the books on the shelves, recognizing some of the titles that his father had at home.

"Do you like to read?" Adam asked.

"Oh yes. I like science fiction and mysteries."

"Then you must check out the library in the next room. Grandpa has tons of books there. There is religious literature, Arabic poetry, some old English classics and lots of young adult fiction which belonged to Dad. There are even some old editions of *Tintin*. Have you ever read them?"

"Oh yes, I read a few when we were living in England."

"Aren't the characters hilarious?" Adam chuckled. "Professor Calculus reminds me of Aunt Hafza when she's not wearing her hearing aid, and Abbas definitely looks like Captain Haddock."

"Speaking of captains, my dad told us that your great-grandfather was a famous sea captain."

"Yes, he was," Adam said proudly. "He was Captain Rafiq Horani. Everyone called him Red Rafiq because of his red hair and beard. He had all kinds of adventures traveling to different lands."

"Your grandpa must have heard some great stories from him."

Adam nodded. "Oh, yes. Grandpa too, has his own stories from his days as a sailor. In fact, he's been working on his memoirs ever since he retired. There is one story that Layla and I are very interested in." Lowering his voice, he said, "How would you like to help us look for a hidden diamond?"

Chapter Two

Hidden Diamond

A FTER THE DAWN prayer the next morning, Zaid recited some verses from Qur'an before seating himself at the window and watching the sun rising slowly over the bay. Never having such an unencumbered view of the sunrise before, he was transfixed by the brilliant orange and purple hues that streaked across the horizon, spreading over the waters in a dazzling kaleidoscope of colors. *It is truly a wonder of creation*, he thought, as little by little the great orb crested over the horizon and the entire bay was engulfed in the fiery aftermath.

As he listened to the early morning clamor of the gulls and stared at the white-crested waves breaking against the cliffs, he recalled what Adam had whispered to him the night before. *A hidden diamond? At Bayan House?* It sounded quite exciting. He glanced at his bedside clock and saw that it was still too early for breakfast. Adam had told him that Maymun began serving the meal at eight. Since it was over an hour away, he pulled out a book from his backpack and settled down to read.

Zaid must have dozed off, for he woke up at the sound of feet shuffling by. *It must be Adam going down to breakfast*, he thought. His stomach rumbled, reminding him that it was time he too went in search of sustenance. After changing out of his pajamas, he donned a sky-blue cotton shirt and navy pants. He dragged a brush through his thick mane of black hair and dabbed a bit of jasmine attar on his neck before heading downstairs.

Zaid knew that the kitchen was located at the back of the house, beyond the great hall. Following the fragrant aroma of coffee and the enticing smell of food, he walked down the long passageway, past the living and dining rooms, and several other utility rooms, which included the bathroom, laundry room and a storeroom. The kitchen was the last door on the left, while up ahead was an archway leading to a spacious vestibule at the very back of the house. He paused in the doorway of the kitchen, taking in the room at a quick glance. It was quite large with surprisingly modern appliances and lots of cupboards and countertop space. In the middle was a large island, while in the right corner was a square table and four chairs. Alongside the table was a door in the wall which Zaid guessed must be a storage closet. A thick wooden door stood slightly ajar at the back.

Adam was standing by the island and had just picked up a mug with one hand and a plate of food with the other. Maymun was busy washing dishes in the sink. They both looked up as Zaid greeted them.

"There you are," Adam said. "Did you sleep well?"

"Like a log," Zaid replied. "I could hear the waves from my room. The sound was very soothing."

"Well, help yourself," Maymun gestured to the covered dishes on the island. "There's hot water in the kettle for tea and coffee. You can use the microwave if you need to warm anything up."

As Zaid began to load scrambled eggs, stewed sardines and toast onto his plate, the girls and twins soon made an appearance, and they all went into the dining room to eat.

AFTER BREAKFAST, ADAM and Layla showed Zaid and Zahra around. They went out the back door of the kitchen and onto a tiled patio in the shape of a semicircle. On the patio stood a white wicker table with eight matching chairs. Beyond it were a profusion of almond trees, with a path leading into the grounds at the back of the house.

"We'll show you a bit of the grounds this afternoon," Adam promised.

They re-entered the house through the vestibule and Layla pointed to a closed door. "Beyond that door is Maymun and Luqman's suite," she told them. "That little wing was added about eight years ago."

As they crossed the vestibule into the central hallway and made for the great hall, Adam said, "We're going up to the western turret now. We'll come back down and end the tour in the library."

On the second floor, they veered right into the western wing, passing by Layla's room which looked out into the grounds at the back of the house, and Zahra and the twins' room which faced the courtyard. Their bathroom was also at the end of the hallway, opposite the stairway that led up to the turret. Unlike its eastern counterpart, the western turret had no rooms. It was just a large circular area, filled with old and broken furniture and an assortment of boxes and trunks. Natural light poured in from large casement windows on both sides. Layla turned on the light switch and the area became even brighter.

"There's a lot of old stuff here as you can see," Adam told them. He pointed to a dilapidated rocking horse sitting in a corner. "That horse was Grandpa's when he was a child. Dad used to ride it too until it got broken."

Zahra reached into a box and pulled out a doll with black hair, a light olive complexion and glassy black eyes, which was missing an arm and a leg. "Look at this pretty doll," she exclaimed, holding it up.

"It must have belonged to Aunt Hanifa or Hafza," Layla remarked. "They were the only girls living here."

"Is Aunt Hanifa your grandpa's sister too?" Zahra asked.

"Yes, she was the eldest child," Adam replied. "She died ages ago. We never knew her."

"Are there any other twins in the family?" Zaid asked.

"Great-Grandma Saffiyah had twin brothers who died in infancy," Adam said. "She grew up as an only child."

"Does your grandfather and Aunt Hafza have any other family here?" Zahra asked.

"Oh, yes, they have several second cousins," Layla replied. "They have a few English ones as well in England."

Easing through the clutter, Adam made for the window on the right and said, "Come look here."

Zaid and Zahra followed him and peered out the window with interest. A dense wooded area stretched out for miles beyond the fence around the house.

"That's Bayan Woods," Adam said. "According to local folklore, the woods are filled with *jinn*, vampire bats and other scary creatures."

"Really?" Zaid said, intrigued. "It does look very mysterious."

Layla was looking out of the window on the left. "You can see the bay from here," she called out. "Come take a look."

Zaid and Zahra stood next to Layla and stared out the window. From this angle, they saw the blue curve of the bay, framed under a clear, sunny sky.

"Can you see the bay from your rooms?" Zaid asked the girls

"You can see a little bit of it from all the windows on that floor," Layla answered.

"Yes, I can catch a glimpse of it from my room," Zahra said.

Looking across at the eastern turret, Zaid realized that the window in Adam's room faced away from the bay. Touched by the other boy's consideration, he said, "Thanks for giving me the room with such a great view, Adam. That was very generous of you."

"It's no big deal," Adam said modestly. "I see the San Francisco Bay all the time back home, so you're welcome to this one."

"I'm really glad that we're finally in Midan," Layla remarked. "We've always wanted to see Dad's childhood home."

"Why didn't you come before?" Zahra asked.

Layla replied, "Dad was busy building his medical practice and Grandpa was always sailing away on one voyage after another. We never seemed to find the right time until now."

"Is this the first time you're meeting your grandfather?" Zaid asked.

"Oh, no," Adam shook his head. "Grandpa visited us several times in San Francisco. When he retired last year, Layla and I decided that it's high time we paid a visit here."

"I didn't realize that Midan was such a large island," Layla remarked. "It seems like a tiny dot when you look at the map."

"Out of the thirty-three islands of the archipelago in the Arabian Gulf, Midan, Ghassan and Wijdan are the largest," Zaid explained. "Although each has its own government, they run certain agencies together. That's why they're called the Tri-Country States."

"You live in Crescent City, don't you?" Adam asked.

"Yes," Zahra nodded. "It's the capital city of Midan."

"Have you ever visited Ghassan and Wijdan?" Adam asked.

"Oh, yes," Zaid nodded. "We've been there several times. In fact, Mom and Dad are leaving this evening for a lecture tour in Ghassan City. Dad is head of the history department at Crescent City University and he and Mom goes on a lecture tour to a different country every year."

"That's nice," Layla said. "They've probably seen a lot of places."

From the western turret, they headed back downstairs to the library, which was next to the prayer room and Mr. Horani's study. The door of the study was closed, and Zaid guessed that Mr. Horani was probably busy at work on his memoirs. In the library, they stared in delight at the floor-to-ceiling bookshelves. Except for a table with three chairs and a wooden stepladder to get to the upper shelves, the library was filled with nothing but books of all sizes and colors.

"Why don't you stay here for a while?" Adam suggested. "Lunch is at twelve-thirty, so you can look around while Layla and I help Maymun lay the table."

"Shouldn't we be helping too?" Zahra asked anxiously.

"You can help us to wash the lunch dishes later," Layla told them.

"Of course, we'll be happy to," Zaid said.

Browsing among the books, Zaid and Zahra found that the time flew by until it was time for lunch. Mr. Horani and Aunt Hafza spoke fluent English and Zaid and Zahra truly felt a part of the family when they both requested that the teenagers address them as Grandpa and Aunt Hafza respectively. Conversation flowed as they enjoyed the hot *dolmas* – succulent vine leaves stuffed with meat. Zaid was puzzled when Mr. Horani spoke loudly to Aunt Hafza several times until Adam whispered, "Aunt Hafza's forgotten to wear her hearing aid. You may catch a bit of her Professor Calculus routine."

Zaid understood what Adam meant almost at the end of the meal when Mr. Horani said to his sister, "Hafza, did you tell Maymun what you wanted for dinner?"

"Maymun said I am thinner?" Aunt Hafza frowned, holding her arms out. "I really do not think so."

Zaid hid a grin as Mr. Horani sighed and bellowed his

question. Aunt Hafza flinched and snapped, "You do not have to shout so, Yusuf. I can hear you perfectly well."

THE CAPTAIN STOOD on the stern of his ship, The Desert Queen, as she plowed along at a jaunty clip on the high seas. The sun shone brilliantly down, drying the drops of spray that splashed onto his face. They had set sail that morning, The Desert Queen laden with rare spices, luxurious bolts of fabrics and magnificent carpets.

"Captain!" the first mate called out urgently. "We're being pursued by pirates. I've spied their skulls and crossbones through the telescope."

"How far away are they?" the captain asked, his worst fear materializing.

"About ten knots. They're moving fast."

"Pirates ahoy, pirates ahoy," the captain shouted. "Full speed ahead, mates!"

"Aye, aye, Captain!" the sailors responded as they scrambled into position. They fired the cannons several times as a warning, but it did not deter the pirate ship, which continued in close pursuit.

The Desert Queen sped along, the wind buffeting furiously at her sails. But it was no match for the smaller pirate ship, which was almost at their stern. The captain and his men watched stoically as the pirate ship drew alongside The Desert Queen. The pirates swarmed aboard, and a deadly battle ensued.

The pirate captain, a brawny giant with a bushy beard and a black patch over one eye, smiled evilly, showing rather large yellow teeth as he came at the Captain with his sword. The Captain fought valiantly with his pirate counterpart, their swords flashing furiously as they lunged and feinted and blocked and parried. As the Captain stumbled over a coil of rope and lost his balance, the pirate captain saw his chance. Lunging forward, he raised his sword with deadly intent. The Captain moved desperately aside to escape the death

blow, but the side of the sword slashed into his left arm and he cried
out as all went dark around him.

ZAID AWOKE WITH a start, his heart thumping madly and his
arm still stinging from the slash of the sword in his dream. *What
a weird dream,* he thought as his heartbeat returned to its steady
rhythm. Imagine him dreaming that he was captain of a ship!
And the pirate captain had borne a remarkable resemblance to
Mr. Ahmed!

Zaid had not expected to fall asleep so quickly. After lunch,
he and Zahra had helped Adam and Layla make quick work of
the lunch dishes before they had all come up to their rooms.
After the midday prayer, he had sat on the window seat for a
few minutes gazing into the bay. Spying a little sailboat in the
distance, he had stared at it until it disappeared beyond the
horizon. He had then picked up a book to read but had fallen
asleep with it still clasped to his chest. As he lifted the book and
sat up, he noticed a small orange-colored object lying next to
him. He stared at it in surprise. It was a dart.

"Where did this come from?" he said aloud. Suddenly, a
muffled giggle came to his ears. Scrambling up, he peered over
the bed. Crouched at the foot, he saw two identical, freckled
faces grinning up at him. One of them was clutching a dart gun
in his hand.

"Why, you little rascals," he cried. "Did you shoot a dart at
me while I was sleeping? No wonder my arm was stinging."

Before the twins could answer, they heard Adam calling,
"Hassan! Hakeem! Are you up there?"

"They're here," Zaid called out.

Adam poked his head into the room and eyed the twins
suspiciously. "What are you doing here? Layla's been looking
everywhere for you."

"Um…they sort of took a shot at waking me up," Zaid said, his sense of humor getting the better of him.

"Out with you," Adam hustled the twins out the door. "And don't you dare pull a disappearing act like this again." Pausing in the doorway, he turned back to Zaid and said, "We'll be having afternoon tea on the patio in fifteen minutes. Come join us when you're ready. And tell Zahra. I'm not sure if Layla told her."

After using the bathroom and freshening up, Zaid went and knocked on Zahra's door. She did know about afternoon tea and was in the process of getting dressed, clothes strewn all over her bed. As Zaid was about to beat a hasty retreat, Zahra said, "Wait a moment. Which outfit do you think I should wear?" she pointed to the bed.

Zaid smothered a groan. He had been trying to avoid this very trap.

"Hmm…," he said as he pretended to look, "wear the green dress."

Zahra glared at him. "If you had looked properly, you'd have known that there is *no* green dress there."

Reluctantly, Zaid turned his gaze to the bed and said, "What about that blue one?"

"No, I think the lavender one is better for the afternoon. You're no help at all," Zahra turned up her nose at him. "I pity your wife when you get married."

"I don't know why you even bother to ask me," Zaid grumbled. "Hopefully, I will have the good sense to marry someone who won't put me through this torture." Zahra stuck her tongue out at him but when she appeared on the patio ten minutes later, she was wearing a smile on her face, along with the pretty lavender dress.

They all sat down to eat at the white wicker table, which held freshly cut fruits, crumbly pastries and a large pot of cinnamon tea. Mr. Horani did not make an appearance and Adam told them that he usually had Luqman take him a light snack in the study. Gul flew onto the patio, mewling softly.

"He wants to eat with us," Hakeem said, throwing some crumbs on the ground. Swooping swiftly down, the bird pecked up the crumbs. They took turns feeding it, Zaid marveling at its ravenous appetite.

After finishing up the goodies, Adam and Layla continued the tour, taking Zaid and Zahra to the cellar next. The indoor entrance was in the kitchen, through the door that Zaid had mistook for a storage closet. Adam opened the bolt and turned on a light switch. Bright fluorescent light flooded the stairway and cellar below. It was a large area, cool and musty, and packed floor to ceiling with groceries, homemade preserves, and household supplies. A stepladder stood to one side next to a small round table.

Adam pointed to a door. "That door leads outside. It's kept open so Abbas can be able to come in. In the old days, the Captain used to keep his ship's supplies here. They would get ready for a voyage weeks in advance, stocking up on salted fish and meat, fruit preserves and barrels of water."

"A sailor's life is pretty dangerous, isn't it?" Zaid remarked, thinking about his odd dream.

"It sure is," Layla agreed. "They leave their families for a long time and are at the mercy of the sea."

After leaving the cellar from the door that led outside, they went past the patio towards the thick spread of almond trees. In the middle was a smooth, paved path.

"Abbas's cottage is behind the trees," Adam looked impishly at Zaid. "Wanna race to see who gets there first?"

"You're on," Zaid said recklessly as he rose to the challenge.

"Layla, can you start us off?" Adam requested.

Layla rolled her eyes. "By all means, run like wild beasts if you must. Okay, on your mark. Get set. Go!"

The youths pounded down the path with as much speed

as they could muster. Zaid was a good sprinter but Adam was faster. As the other boy neared the thick screen of trees, a man stepped out and ran full tilt into him, sending both of them crashing to the ground. Fortunately, Zaid was able to swerve to the side before he too met with the same fate. Adam and the strange man got slowly to their feet. The impact had knocked the breath out of them but thankfully they seemed fine. Layla and Zahra hurried forward and they all stared at the stranger. He was rubbing his left shoulder with a disgruntled look on his face. Zaid wondered who he was. He was in his late twenties, and was tall and lanky, with overlong hair, a shadow of a beard and dark, intense eyes.

"I'm sorry," Adam apologized. "I didn't expect to run into anyone here."

"You shouldn't have been running here to begin with," the man said cuttingly. "This isn't a racetrack."

Adam's face turned beet red at the admonition. Before he could make a rejoinder, Abbas stepped out from behind the canopy of trees. Behind him, Zaid caught a glimpse of a little whitewashed cottage.

"*Assalaam Alaikum*, everyone," Abbas said, impervious to the tension in the air. "I see you've met my nephew Mir. He's visiting from Crescent City. Mir, these are Mr. Horani's grand-children and their friends."

Mir nodded to them, his face unsmiling. He did not seem to be a very friendly person.

After an awkward moment of silence, Abbas asked, "Were you coming to see me?"

"Oh, no," Adam replied. "We were showing our guests around. If you'll excuse us, we'll continue the exploration."

"Yes, yes, of course," Abbas nodded. "Mir and I are going out for some groceries."

As the two men moved out of earshot, Adam said, "Whew! Mir's nephew is one mean guy."

"Well, you just knocked him down," Layla said. "What did you expect?"

"A little more graciousness for one thing," Adam grumbled. "It was an accident, but he acted like I deliberately did it."

"Well, forget about him and let's move on," Layla said. "I can't wait to show Moss Haven to Zaid and Zahra."

"Moss Haven?" Zahra queried. "What's that?"

"You'll see," Layla said mysteriously.

Behind the almond trees lay Abbas's little whitewashed cottage. To its left was an herb and vegetable garden filled with the pungent aroma of thymes and mints planted in neat rows, along with tomatoes, cucumbers and peppers. There was a rough pebbled path on the right which led to a huge grove of acacia trees with gnarled limbs and great trunks. Once they entered among the dark shelter of the trees, Adam veered right, and they walked until they came to the wall which ran around the property.

Adam drew alongside it and pointed to a door with a bolt across the top. "You see that door? It leads out to the bluffs. That's the only way to get to the cove. The other way is by boat, of course."

They continued walking until the trees thinned out to reveal an old lopsided shack covered with creepers and green moss.

"This," Layla pronounced, "is Moss Haven. Isn't it a charming little place?"

Zaid and Zahra eyed the crooked building dubiously. "Is it a storage shed?" Zaid inquired.

"Grandpa said it used to be the gardener's shack before the new cottage was built," Adam told them. "Come on, we'll show you the inside. It's in much better shape than the outside."

He pushed on the door of the shack and it swung open with a series of rusty creaks to allow them entry. They entered an average-sized room with two windows facing out front, both covered with thick green moss that blocked out the light and cast the shack in gloom. It was empty except for several worn armchairs arranged around a scratched, lopsided coffee table. Other than the bitter odor of rotted leaves and a smell of dankness, the space was surprisingly clean and dry.

"I hope there aren't any creepy-crawlies in here," Zahra looked uneasily around.

"Oh, we haven't seen any so far," Layla replied nonchalantly. "But there's a spider web hanging over your head," she pointed upwards, her eyes dancing with mischief. As Zahra scuttled hurriedly to the side, Layla chuckled and said, "I guess I forgot to mention that the spider is long gone."

"Very funny," Zahra huffed.

"Don't you think this would be an excellent meeting place?" Adam asked. "No one would bother us here."

"Meeting place for what?" Zaid asked.

"To plan how we'll search for the hidden diamond," Layla replied.

"Hidden diamond?" Zahra's eyes became wide as she looked from brother to sister. "For real? You're not pulling our legs, are you?"

"Not at all," Adam replied. "Let's meet here at eleven tomorrow. We'll tell you everything then. And remember, it's a secret."

Chapter Three

Captain Red Rafiq

ELEVEN O'CLOCK THE next day found them all gathered in Moss Haven. Zaid and Zahra were all ears as they waited for their new friends to speak.

"It all started with our great-grandfather, Captain Rafiq Horani," Adam began. "To tell you a little about him, he was born here in Midan to English parents in the days when Midan was a British protectorate. He converted to Islam as a young man and changed his name. He joined the British Royal Navy and fought on a destroyer during World War Two. After the war ended, he married Great-Grandma Saffiyah and became a sailor. Aunt Hanifa was born a year later, and Aunt Hafza and Grandpa two years after her. Eventually, the captain got his own ship and named it the Yuhanza, which is a combination of his three children's names – Yusuf, Hanifa, and Hafza. That's when he became known as Captain Red Rafiq."

Layla took up the tale. "The Yuhanza came back from its last voyage on the Night of Catastrophe. I think you both know this bit of history, right?"

Zaid and Zahra nodded soberly. The Night of Catastrophe

as it had become known, was the conclusion of a deadly coup that had taken place in Midan over half a century ago.

"To make a long story short," Layla continued, "the rebels burned the Yuhanza and murdered the Captain right here in the house that night. Grandpa, who was twelve years old at the time, found him dying in the great hall, stabbed with his own dagger. With his dying breath, the Captain told Grandpa about a diamond that he had hidden in the house. He died before he could say exactly where. Grandpa searched everywhere but never found it. Dad also searched when he was younger, but he didn't have any luck either."

"What makes you think we'll have any better luck?" Zaid asked.

"We might not," Adam shrugged. "But we're going to give it a shot. Will you help us?"

"Of course," Zaid nodded. "It sounds like great fun."

"I think it's very exciting," Zahra said enthusiastically.

"But why do you want to keep it a secret?" Zaid asked. "Wouldn't it be better if everyone helps?"

"We'd rather not tell them," Layla said. "The twins will pester us and Grandpa will probably think we're wasting our time. Besides, it's more fun looking for it in secret."

"We'll search whenever we can spare the time," Adam said. "I'd really love for us to find it before we leave."

"Where are we going to search first?" Zahra asked.

"We'll have to discuss the most likely places," Layla said. "Then we'll start searching the first one on the list."

Fifteen minutes later, after a vigorous discussion of where the diamond could be hidden, Adam said, "Okay, we'll start searching the western turret tomorrow."

THAT NIGHT, ZAID sat on the window seat in his room, cool tendrils of bay air swirling around his face. The night was rather dark, with no moon or stars and the only sounds to be heard were the muted roar of the waves crashing against the cliffs and the far-off cry of a night heron. Zaid closed his eyes and inhaled several deep breaths of the salt-tinged air.

Perhaps there's a boat crossing the bay right now, but I can't see it, he thought. He tried to conjure a picture of what the imaginary vessel looked like. *It's a small outboard motor, modern and sleek. It cuts swiftly and powerfully over the waves with hardly a sound.*

My imagination is really good, Zaid thought as he heard the faint buzz of an engine. As the sound became louder, his eyes flew open when he realized that he was hearing a *real* engine rather than an imaginary one.

"It's a real boat coming in," he murmured in surprise as he peered into the darkness. He could make out the shape of a small boat in the waters off the cove. Even as he looked, the boat entered the cove and disappeared from sight in the shadows of the cliffs. He could no longer hear its engine either. Zaid wondered what the boat was doing in the cove at this time of the night. *And stranger still, why was its lights off?* Perhaps it was in some sort of distress and was awaiting help? Puzzled, he went to bed and was soon fast asleep.

BEFORE HE HEADED down to breakfast the next morning, Zaid looked down into the cove to see if the boat he had heard last night was still there. But the cove was empty and there was no sign of it. It must have left sometime during the night. Perhaps Adam would be able to shed some light on what it had been doing there.

The two youths were the first ones down for breakfast. As

they sat eating in the dining room, Zaid said, "By the way, I saw a boat come into Bayan Cove last night."

"A boat?" Adam echoed. "What did it look like?"

"I couldn't really see much of it, but it looked like a small outboard motor. I thought it might have been in trouble because it had it lights off. When I looked out this morning, there was no sign of it."

"It was probably someone out for a joy ride," Adam replied without much interest. "From what I hear, Bayan Bay has its share of madcaps."

After finishing their meal, the youths made for the living room where Adam turned on the television. As he flipped the channels for an appropriate program, Zaid's ears pricked up as he heard the word *pirates*.

"Go back to the last channel," he told Adam.

Adam obligingly went back and they listened to the news about a ring of modern-day pirates plundering a ship in the Bayan Strait the previous day.

"Oh no, it's the pirates again," Zaid said in dismay.

"What's that about?" Adam asked.

"The modern-day pirates have been attacking and robbing ships in the Bayan Strait since we came to live here two years ago. It's been all over the news in Midan."

"That's a shame," Adam said. "I hope they're caught soon."

LATER THAT MORNING, to Zaid and Zahra's delight, they received a phone call from their parents in Ghassan City. Mr. Horani picked up the call in his study and after escorting them there, he discreetly left. This was the first time they were seeing his inner sanctum. It was a spacious carpeted room, with a row of shaded windows facing the courtyard. In the room was a file cabinet, a large oak desk and a leather swivel chair in the center. The desk held a computer, a stack of notepads and a caddy containing pens and pencils. The room was neat and scrupulously clean, proclaiming its occupant to be a man of fastidious habits. Of the memoirs he was writing, there was no sign and Zaid guessed that he must be either typing them into a computer file or had locked them away in the drawers.

Zaid put the phone on speaker before he and Zahra greeted their parents.

"How are you children doing?" Mrs. Alkurdi asked. "Are you having a good time?"

"Yes, we're doing great," Zaid said.

"It's beautiful here," Zahra said. "Layla, Adam and the twins are a lot of fun."

"How about you?" Adam asked. "How's the tour coming along?"

"Just fine," Professor Alkurdi replied. "All the conferences have been well attended. We can't ask for better than that."

"We've finally met Shaykh Sulaiman ibn Al-Khalili, the sponsor of our tour," Mrs. Alkurdi told them. "He's such a humble man, even though he's so wealthy."

"Guess where he is right now?" Professor Alkurdi chuckled.

"Where?" Zahra asked obligingly.

"In Midan," Professor Alkurdi replied. "He said he had a matter of importance to take care of there and apologized to us for leaving."

"Well then, we might even run into him," joked Zaid. They chatted for a few more minutes before Professor and Mrs. Alkurdi ended the call.

AFTER TEA ON the patio that afternoon, the teenagers sat

conversing while Hassan and Hakeem went to play with Gul in the courtyard. Soon after, Gul swooped onto the patio, mewling loudly before perching itself on the back of a chair. The bird had a small piece of paper tied to its leg, and they stared at this unusual sight.

"What on earth is that on Gul's leg?" Adam asked.

"Hassan and Hakeem must have put it there," Layla said. "Watch, they'll be giving him clothes to wear next."

Zahra giggled. "How do you know Gul's a *he* and not a *she*?"

"Hassan and Hakeem just assume the bird is a *he*," Layla grinned. "We're just going along with them."

The bird began pecking at the scrap of paper on its leg. It then looked up and gave a loud squawk.

"Noisy bird," Layla covered her ears.

"He wants the paper off his leg," Zahra said. "It must be irritating him."

"Well, let's put him out of his misery," Adam said. Cautiously, he walked up to the bird, which stared at him with its great beady eyes but stayed put as Adam gently untied the string, releasing the paper. He glanced casually at it and then did a double take.

"It has *Hassan* and *Hakeem* written on it," he chuckled in amusement. "They must be training Gul to be a carrier pigeon. Here boy," he told the bird. "Go to Hassan and Hakeem. Go to Hassan and Hakeem, boy!"

To their delight, Gul let out a piercing shriek, lifted its wings majestically in the air and disappeared over the roofline of the house.

"Gul is so smart," Zahra said admiringly.

"Yeah, he's got real bird brains," Layla quipped.

Minutes later, the twins came racing around the corner of the house and up to the patio, Gul in their wake.

"It worked! It worked!" Hakeem chortled.

"Woohoo, it worked!" Hassan raised a fist triumphantly in the air.

"Did you send us a message with Brainy Big Bird here?" Layla asked.

"Yes, we did!" Hassan replied gleefully.

"Do you intend to turn Gul into a carrier pigeon?" Adam asked.

"What's a carrier pigeon?" Hakeem asked.

"It's a pigeon that's trained to take messages," Adam replied. "In the old days, they were used a lot."

"Yes, we'll teach Gul to be just like that," Hassan vowed.

"What makes you think that a seagull will want to be like a pigeon?" Layla asked teasingly.

"Well, they're cousins, aren't they?" Hassan said.

"How do you know they're cousins?" Zahra asked.

"Anyone can tell they're cousins," Hakeem scoffed, "cause they look like each other a lot."

The teenagers burst into merry laughter at Hakeem's childish wisdom.

After the twins and their pet disappeared once again, Adam said, "Everyone ready for the search in the turret this afternoon?"

"Oh yes," Zahra said eagerly. "I'm quite ready."

"I just can't get excited about poking into dusty old boxes," Layla said with a distinct lack of enthusiasm, "but I'm ready to tackle it too."

"It will be easy with four of us doing it," Zaid said optimistically.

THAT AFTERNOON, THEY gathered in the turret and discussed how best to conduct a methodical search. They came up with a plan to divide the area into four portions, with each of them being assigned one. They would then search every trunk, box, nook and cranny of the broken furniture.

As Layla started to unpack a box, clouds of dust rose up, causing her to sneeze. *"Alhamdulilah,"* she said automatically before grumbling, "This is going to be my least favorite place to search. There's enough dust here to keep us in sneezes for the rest of our lives."

Zaid's portion was close to the window that had a view of the Bayan Woods. As he pushed a broken chair out of the way, he glanced out of the window and into the shadowy woods. A sudden movement caught his eye and he stared at the spot, wondering what it was. After a minute of looking, he decided that whatever it was had moved away.

"I just saw something move in Bayan Woods," he called out to the others. "But it's gone now."

"What did it look like?" Layla asked.

"I couldn't tell. It was just a dark shape moving."

"Maybe it's a *jinn* or a vampire bat," Adam joked and they all chuckled.

After that diversion, they turned their full attention to the search. There were sporadic bursts of conversation amid rustling papers and dragging of furniture. At one point, Layla held up a bunch of rolled-up posters. Each had a large black and white drawing of skull and crossbones. Other than that, the search yielded nothing else of interest.

ZAID WAS RAVENOUS by the time they sat down to a dinner of baked chicken served with an eggplant and chili pepper salad.

"Where's Aunt Hafza?" Zahra asked, noticing that Mr. Horani's twin was missing from the table.

Mr. Horani sighed. "I am afraid her arthritis is flaring up

again. I will take her to see Dr. Qazi after *Jumu'ah* on Friday. We will be going to the largest *masjid* in Bayan Bay, *insha'Allah*."

"Cool," Adam said. "There must be some really beautiful *masjids* in the city."

"Yes, there are several. You should be able to see most of them before you leave."

As they ate, Layla regaled their grandfather with the story of Hassan and Hakeem giving Gul a message to carry.

"Very good, boys," Mr. Horani said, his usually stern face breaking into a smile.

"We're going to have a party for him," Hassan blurted out.

"A party?" Mr. Horani raised his eyebrows. "What for?"

"So Gul's family and friends can see how smart he is," Hakeem said excitedly.

"Yes, we'll ask Maymun to make lots of cookies for them," Hassan said.

"How will you get Gul's family and friends to come to the party?" Layla asked, her green eyes dancing with amusement.

"We'll send them an…an *information,*" Hakeem declared.

"You mean *invitation,*" Adam grinned. "And how will you send the invitation?"

"That's easy," Hassan said scornfully. "We'll write it and tie it on Gul's leg."

"And then he'll take it to his family and friends," Hakeem concluded triumphantly.

In the kitchen, Maymun heard the burst of laughter from the dining room as she cleaned up. "Children's laughter," she muttered to herself. "That's what this house has been missing for too long."

Chapter Four

The Shaykh's Story

To Zaid and Zahra's amazement, the most amazing
coincidence occurred the next day after lunch. After the
meal ended, the twins were shepherded upstairs by Mr.
Horani, and Maymun and Luqman retired to their quarters,
leaving the teenagers to their task of washing and putting away
the lunch dishes. They were halfway through their task when the
doorbell rang. They all looked at one another in surprise. It was
unusual for visitors to pay a call at this time of day.

"I'll go see who it is," Adam said, carefully setting down the
plate he had been drying.

They soon heard the faint sound of voices in the great hall.
Minutes went by but Adam did not reappear. Finished with their
chore by this time, Zaid and the girls headed to the great hall
and stopped short in surprise when they saw two men seated
there. One of them was in his early thirties and had the build
of a professional boxer. The other was a thin, older man in his
mid-seventies. Both of them were wearing the traditional robe
and headdress of the region.

At that moment, Adam and his grandfather descended the

stairs. Mr. Horani greeted the newcomers pleasantly before asking, "How can I help you?"

"You will pardon us for disturbing your rest," the older man spoke in a soft but surprisingly commanding voice. "But we're in Midan for only a short time. I'm Sulaiman ibn Al-Khalili from Ghassan and this is Mustapha," he gestured to the younger man. "I am here to speak with you regarding a certain matter."

Zaid and Zahra's jaws dropped open in amazement when they heard who the older man was.

"*You're* Shaykh Sulaiman ibn Al-Khalili?" Zaid said incredulously. The next moment, he turned red with embarrassment at his uncouth behavior. Thankfully the Shaykh did not seem offended as he replied with twinkling eyes, "Indeed, I am he."

"Our parents told us about you," Zahra said bashfully.

"They met you over in Ghassan City," Zaid explained. "They're Professor and Mrs. Alkurdi."

"Professor and Mrs. Alkurdi," the Shaykh exclaimed. "Allah be praised. What a marvelous coincidence. I'm delighted to meet you."

"Professor Alkurdi and my son are dear friends," Mr. Horani explained. "Their children are meeting here for the first time."

"Ah, I see," the Shaykh nodded his head approvingly. "That is most excellent."

To think, Zaid marveled, *that I had joked to Mom and Dad about running into the Shaykh and here he is.*

"We will get you some refreshments," Mr. Horani offered.

"No, please," the Shaykh held up a hand. "We had lunch at the hotel, so don't go to the trouble."

"You will have something to drink at least," Mr. Horani said firmly.

"As you wish," the Shaykh acquiesced.

"Adam and I will get it," Layla offered.

The Shaykh chatted about Professor Alkurdi's lecture tour

until Adam and Layla returned with a jug of lemonade and a tray with two glasses. After the beverage was poured and the men had taken a few sips, Mr. Horani asked, "So, what do you wish to speak with me about?"

Shaykh Sulaiman's pleasant smile faded as he said, "I will convey to you my story and at the end of it, you can tell me if I'm in the right place or not."

"Do you want to speak with me privately?" Mr. Horani asked.

"No, no, that's not necessary," the Shaykh replied. "The young ones will find the story most fascinating, I'm sure. I don't wish to deprive them of it. To begin, I will tell you a little about myself. Ours has been an old and respected family in Ghassan for many generations. Allah has bestowed on us much wealth and property within the last several decades. As head of the family, I assure you that it's a trust which I do not take very lightly. I tell you this not as a matter of pride, but that you should understand the circumstances which has brought me here today."

"Of course, I understand," Mr. Horani said respectfully.

The Shaykh continued, "My story began fifty-eight years ago when my younger sister got lost in the desert. Most fortunately, she was found unharmed by a Bedouin tribe who quickly returned her to us. So grateful and thankful was my father that he offered the chieftains of the tribe whatever reward they desired. Not surprisingly, they asked for a well-known heirloom which had been in our family for two generations. I must point out to you that my father didn't protest or hesitate in the least to accede to this request. He agreed wholeheartedly to it and the date was fixed when it would be handed over to the chieftains."

"That was very generous of him," Mr. Horani remarked.

"That might have been so," the Shaykh replied, "but it was the bargain he willingly made. Alas, when that date arrived, to his great shock, my father discovered that the heirloom had been stolen. You can imagine the state he was in when the chieftains arrived to claim their prize, only to be told that there was no prize. They were angry and offended and out of wounded pride, refused any other compensation. Believing that my father had faked the theft in order to renege on his promise, they uttered many accusations and recriminations before they left. My father, who had been a man of great honor and integrity, was utterly cast down by their bitter words. So distressed was he by this turn of events that there was an immediate decline in his health. As he lay on his sickbed, he took a solemn pledge from me that I should trace the whereabouts of the heirloom and turn it over to the chieftains. He returned to Allah soon afterwards, and ever since his death, I have been on the quest to find the heirloom. My ardent wish is to do so before I die."

The teenagers sat with wide eyes after this compelling tale until Mr. Horani asked, "What heirloom was this?"

"It was a diamond called the Moon of Masarrah. Upon its discovery in India, it became one of the most celebrated gems of the world. After it was stolen, the newspapers made a great sensation of it. I have followed many leads over the years but without any success. It is only quite recently that the knowledge has come to me that it may have left Ghassan on a ship called the Yuhanza, captained by the famous Red Rafiq, who I believe was your father."

The teenagers exchanged startled looks at this piece of information.

"Are you saying that my father stole this Moon of Masarrah?" Mr. Horani's face had gone pale.

"Never, never, as Allah is my witness," the Shaykh replied fervently. "I know who stole the Moon. Alas, it was treachery from within the House of Al-Khalili. Certain things came to light upon the death of my uncle last year." A sad tiredness came upon the Shaykh's face. "I do not like to air the dirty clothes in public…"

"Laundry," Adam said helpfully.

"Thank you," the Shaykh nodded graciously before continuing, "I do not like to air the dirty laundry in public, but you see, my uncle revealed on his deathbed that he masterminded the theft of the Moon and gave it to an underground fence to sell. The plan was to wait a year until the hue and cry had died down before attempting to sell it. Just before the year was up, the fence's cousin broke into his safe and stole the gem, having no idea of its identity and value. When confronted, the cousin admitted to stealing it and selling it to get rid of his debts. His account of this deed was that he took the gem and stood by a jewelry store, looking for someone to buy it. He dared not attempt selling it to any place of business for fear they would discover that he had stolen it. When he saw a man about to enter the jewelry store, he stopped him and showed him the gem, telling him that his family was in dire straits and he needed to sell a family possession so they wouldn't starve. The cousin said that the man seemed convinced of his sincerity for he looked at the gem and being impressed with its cut and quality, he was willing to purchase it. But he didn't have enough money on him to pay the price that the cousin asked, so he told him to bring the gem that evening to the ship, the Yuhanza, and he would purchase it then. And apparently, he did."

The Shaykh paused here to take a few sips of lemonade before he continued. "Even though the cousin had called for a substantial amount of money, it was still not even a fraction of what the gem was really worth. The fence was very angry as you can imagine. He hastened to the docks to look for the ship, but it had already left port. The cousin was found the next day with his throat cut and the fence was arrested and sentenced to death for the murder. From that day on, the Moon vanished and was never heard of again. My uncle, fearing repercussion should his evil deed come to light, did not tell a single soul until he was on his deathbed. That is my story," the Shaykh concluded. "Now tell me," he looked imploringly at Mr. Horani, "did anyone on the Yuhanza ever mention a diamond?"

There was a long silence as Mr. Horani stared into space. Then he turned to the Shaykh and said slowly, "Yes, my father did mention a diamond." Drawing an audible breath, he said, "On the night he was murdered."

"Murdered," the Shaykh exclaimed. "Will you not tell me what happened?"

Mr. Horani's face bore a pensive expression, as if his mind was digging deep into the past. Finally, he began to speak. "My father came back from his last voyage on what came to be known as the Night of Catastrophe. As you must know, it was the culmination of several days of bloody warfare by the rebel group who had staged a coup. We knew that the Yuhanza was due to dock that evening, but that it should coincide with that ill-fated event was a terrible act of misfortune. For you see, we were warned only that afternoon by one of my mother's cousins, that the rebels were planning to come to our house that night to seize my father. He had always been a vocal critic of their politics and for this reason they resented him, especially since he was a foreigner."

"It is always politics that causes trouble among our ranks," the Shaykh murmured. "But please, carry on with your story."

Mr. Horani continued, "My mother's cousin advised us to hide in Bayan Woods that night and promised that upon the Yuhanza's arrival in port, he would send a messenger to warn my father not to go home but to join us there. So my mother gathered up some food and other essentials and her cousin helped us to pitch a tent in the woods. Several hours passed and there was still no sign of my father. It was only later that we would learn that the messenger who had been sent to warn him had been killed by the rebels and having no idea of the danger that awaited him there, my father made straight for home. By that time, my mother was so frantic with worry that she wanted to go look for him herself. Having some inkling of the harm that would have befallen her were she to be found by the rebels, I persuaded her to let me go instead. With great reluctance she agreed, and I immediately set out for the house, taking all precautions to keep out of sight. When I got there, it was dark and silent. Peeping into the window, I didn't see any of the rebels, so I lit a candle and crept in quietly. That's when I saw my father. He was lying on the floor in a pool of blood and groaning painfully. The rebels had got him after all. They had stabbed him with his own dagger and left him to die."

As Mr. Horani's voice became choked with emotion, he paused for a moment to collect himself before continuing, "My father recognized me and asked about my mother and sisters. Then he whispered to me that he had hidden the diamond in the house. That's all he was able to say before he died. My mother questioned his crewmen about this diamond but none of them seemed to know anything about it. We searched the house many times but never found the diamond he spoke of."

There was a momentous silence after Mr. Horani came to a stop. Then Shaykh Sulaiman said sorrowfully, "What a terrible tale. I have no doubt that the diamond he spoke of was the Moon of Masarrah. Do you think those rebels might have stolen it from him?"

Mr. Horani looked reflective for a moment. "It did occur to me, but I don't believe so. My father was still alive and in possession of his senses when I arrived. He wouldn't have told me that the diamond was hidden in the house if the rebels had stolen it. I firmly believe that it's still in the hiding place that my father chose for it. Short of tearing the house apart, there's no nook and cranny that I haven't searched."

"I believe what you say is correct," the Shaykh conceded. "If the rebels had stolen the diamond, the Moon of Masarrah would have turned up somewhere in the world. Such a unique and valuable stone would not have gone undetected for long. What effrontery those rebels had to kill your father with his own dagger."

"We couldn't stand to look at it again," Mr. Horani's face was filled with remembered distaste. "My mother had it wrapped in a bag filled with stones and thrown into the bay."

"So much tragedy has accompanied this stone," the Shaykh lamented. "No wonder there are those who say that it is cursed, like other famous gems."

"What other tragedy has there been?" Adam asked.

"Apparently there had been a string of deaths in India before the stone was brought over to Ghassan. The man who owned it prior to my family, was trampled to death by a horse. My great-grandfather actually bought it from his widow. Then my father took ill and died as a result of its theft. After that, both the fence and his cousin lost their lives too. Now I hear of your father's murder. It all perpetuates the myth that the stone is cursed."

"It does have an unfortunate history," Mr. Horani agreed. "I can see why it would give rise to such superstition."

"Well, it's time we take our leave," the Shaykh rose slowly to his feet, assisted by Mustapha. He shook Mr. Horani's hand warmly and said, "Thank you for telling me your tale, even though it was very painful. If ever you should find the diamond, I will be grateful if you would contact me. I am willing to pay you its present-day value. Mustapha will give you a card with my information."

Turning to the teenagers, he smiled and said, "It's been a pleasure meeting you all. I hope we meet again one day, *insha'Allah.*"

Chapter Five

Legends of Gemology

THE NEXT MORNING, the teenagers met in Moss Haven and mulled over what they had heard the day before.

"I'd never heard all the sad details of the Captain's murder," Adam said. "It's heartbreaking to hear it firsthand from Grandpa."

"Well, the Shaykh's story confirms that the diamond *was* real and not a figment of the Captain's imagination," Zaid said. "It would have been easy to think so, especially when none of his crewmen knew about it."

"I never really thought about the rebels stealing the diamond," Layla said. "What if the Captain lost consciousness right after they stabbed him and they stole it then? He wouldn't have known that they found it. Perhaps that's why the diamond has never been found."

"You mean we could be searching for something that's not even here?" Zahra said in dismay.

Adam said firmly, "Listen, the rebels came that night to seize the Captain, not to steal the diamond. They wouldn't have known that he had it. Let's assume that when they came for him, he put up a fight, but they overpowered him and then stabbed him with his dagger. The only way they would have stolen the Moon, is if they searched him and discovered it on his person. But the Captain clearly told Grandpa that he had hidden the diamond in the house. Which means that he must have done so *before* the rebels came on the scene. They wouldn't have gone looking to steal something that they knew nothing about."

"You're absolutely right," Zaid agreed. "And as the Shaykh said, the diamond would have turned up somewhere if the rebels had stolen it."

"Well, now that we've agreed that the diamond must still be in the house, I think it would be helpful if we know what it looks like," Layla said. "It's a pity none of us have cell phones with internet to look it up."

"I saw a computer in Grandpa's study," Zaid said. "Maybe we can ask him to use it."

Adam shook his head. "Grandpa's very territorial about his computer. When we first got here, I asked him if I could use it. He asked me why. After I told him I wanted to read up on seagulls, he signed on without telling me what the password was and then stood by until I had finished reading the Wikipedia results. If we tell him that we want to look up the Moon of Masarrah, he might guess that we're looking for it."

"If it's such a famous diamond as the Shaykh says, maybe we can find a photo of it at the library" Zahra said.

"That's a good idea," Layla said. "We can ask Grandpa to take us to the nearest one after *Jumu'ah* tomorrow, *insha'Allah*. He'll probably think that we want to take a look at the books."

THE NEXT DAY, after an early lunch, they all piled into the gray Toyota Land Cruiser in the courtyard and set off for the *Jumu'ah* prayer. The vehicle was an eight-seater, so there was enough room for all of them to ride comfortably to the mosque. After leaving the local roads, Mr. Horani headed onto the corniche. The curving coastal road was packed with smoothly flowing traffic heading towards the heart of the city. As they exited off the corniche, remote villas that nestled close to the bay, gave way to numerous apartment buildings and stately mansions with carved doors and arabesque windows. Rows of date palms lined the avenues, which teemed with traffic and pedestrians. The city, which earned its livelihood mainly from fishing, shipping and pearling, was rife with offices, marketplaces and schools vying for square footage.

The Bayan Bay mosque was a beautiful peach-colored edifice with two slender minarets, and a great central dome surrounded by four smaller ones. Around it was thick groves of date palms, almond and fig trees. People came from all direction, walking sedately through the wide-open gates and calling out greetings to each other. There was a slight stir as a sleek white limousine pulled up to the curb. From it emerged a teenage boy and two hawk-nosed men wearing dark suits and checkered head coverings.

"Who are they?" Adam looked at them with interest. "Royalty?"

"No, just the Ambreens," Mr. Horani said brusquely. "That is Faruq Ambreen in front, the boy is his grandson and the other man is his cousin Talal."

"They certainly know how to make an entrance," Layla remarked.

As the Ambreens came through the gates, Faruq Ambreen glanced their way. A dark look immediately came over his face and he stared at them fiercely for a few moments before turning away. Zaid was taken aback by the man's animosity. *Perhaps he does not like strangers,* he thought.

"Come, let us go," Mr. Horani ushered them forward, a tight-lipped look on his face as he stared at Faruq Ambreen's retreating back.

They followed the crowd towards the prayer area, Aunt Hafza and the girls veering right towards the women's wing while Mr. Horani and the boys headed left to the men's wing. Like Crescent City, the city of Bayan Bay boasted a diverse group of expatriates from different countries. Men greeted Mr. Horani on all sides. He seemed to be well-known and well-liked.

Zaid watched as a tall, smiling African man came up to them. He and Mr. Horani exchanged greetings and embraced with open affection.

"This is Musa," Mr. Horani introduced the newcomer.

He then introduced the boys to Musa, who showed perfect white teeth as he smiled. "You have our warmest welcome. I hope you enjoy your vacation here."

"How was your trip back home, Musa?" Mr. Horani asked.

Musa's smile fell. "Not as good as I had hoped, Yusuf. Somalia still has a lot of problems. Allah knows when true peace will ever come."

"There is much to distress us in the world today," Mr. Horani said gravely. "But we must do the best we can and put our trust in Allah. We know that ultimately, good will prevail over evil."

"True, true," Musa nodded sagely. "As we have learnt from the Qur'an, for those who do good, the reward is only good. For those who do evil, they do so at the peril of their own souls. Why don't you bring everyone around to my market after *Jumu'ah*? I have some fine mangos that came in yesterday."

"I have to take Hafza to see Dr. Qazi," Mr. Horani said regretfully. "But the children can certainly come." Turning to the youths, he said, "The library is not far from Musa's Market. You can walk over when you're done. Musa will give you the directions. I will pick you up from there."

"Okay," Adam nodded in agreement.

The *Jumu'ah* prayer was delivered by an *Imam* in a flowing black and gold robe and a perfectly fitted white turban. His sermon expounded on the favors that Allah had bestowed upon

51

all of mankind. He cited many verses from the Qur'an, especially Surah Rahman, which Zaid had memorized. *Which of the favors of your Lord shall ye deny?* Zaid repeated to himself. *Not a single one,* he thought.

After the prayer ended, Mr. Horani duly dropped them off at Musa's Market, which turned out to be just a couple of blocks away from the mosque. The market was a thriving little place packed with an after-*Jumu'ah* crowd. There were fresh fruits and vegetables, rows of canned goods, and baskets of sweets and nuts. Exotic scents from a variety of oils and incenses permeated the air around them.

After enjoying the delicious mangos offered by Musa's smiling wife, Jameelah, and thanking them for their hospitality, Adam asked for directions to the library and they set off. Both he and Layla kept a firm hold on Hassan and Hakeem as they merged into the crowd of people walking down the street.

The Bayan Bay Library was a sprawling, one-story structure painted a cheerful yellow. It too, was filled with an after-*Jumu'ah* crowd.

"We'll have to ask the librarian for help," Zaid said. "We won't be able to use the computers if we're not members and it will take a long time to find the right book."

"Why don't you and Adam go?" Layla suggested. "Zahra and I will browse around with the twins. Call us when you find something."

The librarian wore glasses and a stressed look on her face as Adam and Zaid joined the queue in front of her desk. When their turn came, Adam made his request for a book on famous gems. To their consternation, the librarian looked up from her computer and subjected them to an intent appraisal as she remarked, "Interested in gems, are you? Come to think of it, I haven't seen the two of you here before. Have you just moved into the area? You'll need to apply for library cards. What? You're on vacation? Couldn't have picked a better spot in the world. Where are you staying? Bayan House, did you say?" The librarian, who had barely let them get a word in edgewise, removed her glasses to stare at the two youths.

"*Subhanallah,*" she exclaimed. "You must be Mr. Horani's grandsons."

"I'm Mr. Horani's grandson, Adam," Adam said politely. "This is my friend, Zaid. My sister and twin brothers are around somewhere."

The librarian nodded her head. "Yes, yes. Your grandfather said there were four of you. How's your father? Ah, you didn't think I knew your father, eh? Went to school together, we did. What a shame he never came back to visit. I guess he's too busy in America. Tell him Rawan sends her salaams. Well, well. Who'd have thought?" The librarian said wonderingly as she replaced her glasses and bent over her computer.

"Gems, gems…," she muttered as she typed rapidly. "How come you boys are interested in gems?"

"Er…summer project we're working on," Adam mumbled.

"Ah," the librarian exclaimed, and Zaid was not sure if it was in response to Adam's answer or what her search had brought up on the computer screen.

"Here we go," she stabbed at the keyboard. "Legends of Gemology, fourth edition by Moallem and Peterson, published 2006 in Great Britain. Check the reference section, in aisle twenty-one."

The boys thanked the librarian and as they left the queue, one of the youths standing in line, remarked scornfully to his companion, "Who does school projects when they're on vacation? Those Americans are such idiots." The other boy snickered and both Zaid and Adam glared at them with distaste. Zaid thought the rude boy seemed vaguely familiar. Of course! He was the youth who had come to the mosque in the white limousine. *He's obviously wealthy and spoiled,* Zaid thought scornfully.

"That librarian sure is talkative," Adam muttered as they made for aisle twenty-one. "Now everyone knows our business."

"That's how it is here," Zaid grinned. "Well, let's get the book and find the girls."

A quick search soon had them pulling out a huge tome entitled *Legends of Gemology* in large gold lettering.

They found the girls reading a picture book to the twins at one of the tables in a secluded alcove. In a stroke of good fortune, there was an empty table right next to them. Adam plonked the book down on it and the girls came over, leaving the twins immersed in the picture book.

Adam flipped to the Table of Contents. "The Agra," he read, "the Dresden Diamond, the Cullinan I-Star of Africa, the Hope Diamond, the Kohinoor...there's so many of them here."

"The Moon of Masarrah," Layla whispered excitedly as her eyes moved down the page. "Here it is. Page one hundred and one."

After Adam had flipped to the page, they all stared at the black and white photograph juxtaposed next to a colored one that depicted a magnificent pear-shaped stone of a golden-yellow color, with red overtones. A small caption underneath the black and white photograph read, *Early Photograph of the Moon of Masarrah* while the caption underneath the colored one proclaimed, *Digitally Enhanced Photograph of the Moon of Masarrah.*

"I forgot that black and white photos were the norm when the Moon was discovered," Adam said. "And since its disappearance, no picture could be taken, hence the digitally enhanced one."

Even in the digitally enhanced photograph, the Moon's exquisite beauty was unmistakable and they all stared at it in awe.

"It's beautiful," Layla breathed. "No wonder those Bedouin chieftains wanted it."

"Let's read the history," Zaid said and they all leaned in closer as they began to read.

The Moon of Masarrah, an exquisite pear-shaped diamond weighing 42.23 carats and measuring 31.55 mm x 20.88 mm x 12.29 mm with 39 facets, was discovered in India sometime during the Mughal dynasty. The Moon was graded as naturally colored golden-yellow with red overtones, possessing VS1 clarity. Some gemologists have likened the Moon to the famous Hope and Dresden Green Diamonds in terms of size, clarity and intensity of color. Like the Hope Diamond and others of the same ilk, the Moon has acquired a notorious reputation for leaving a trail of tragedies after its discovery, giving rise to the usual claim that it is cursed. To add to its allure, the Moon, which was last owned by the wealthy House of Al-Khalili in Ghassan, was stolen in 1959, never to be seen again. The present ownership of the Moon remains an intriguing mystery to gemologists worldwide. Today, the Moon is estimated to be worth over ten million British pounds. Some gemologists have speculated that it may be gracing the collection of the Sultan of Brunei, who is said to have one of the largest colored diamond collections in the world. The Sultan, of course, could not be reached for comment.

"Wow," Adam whispered. "Ten million pounds. Can you believe a little stone like that is worth so much money?"

"It's incredible," Zaid said. "This book was written over ten years ago, so it may be more valuable now."

"I wish we could find it," Layla said wistfully. "Grandpa would have a very comfortable retirement."

"Well, we just have to keep looking for it," Adam said.

After returning the tome to the shelf, they sat conversing until Mr. Horani arrived and sought them out in the library. As he hustled out with Hassan and Hakeem, the teenagers hurriedly returned the picture books to the shelves before following behind. As they crossed an aisle, a man carrying a high pile of books which almost covered his face, emerged and collided with Adam. The pile of books wobbled precariously before tumbling to the floor with a loud crash. Zaid was startled to see that the man was Mir, Abbas's nephew.

A look of dismay came over Adam's face when he realized who it was. "Sorry," he apologized as he stooped down and helped Mir to gather up the fallen books.

Recognizing them, Mir's eyes darkened with displeasure. "You seem to make a habit out of this," he said to Adam as he stalked away with his armful of books.

"Fancy seeing Mir here," Layla remarked as they left the library. "I can't believe the two of you crashed into each other again."

"If he watched where he was going, it wouldn't have happened," Adam grumbled.

Back in the Land Cruiser, they found Aunt Hafza snoring gently.

"Dr. Qazi gave her a shot of medicine," Mr. Horani told them. "It has made her very drowsy."

As Mr. Horani merged into the thick afternoon traffic, he told them that they had one more stop to make before heading home. Shortly after, he pulled up in the parking lot of a shop with a colorful awning and several bicycles displayed in the window.

"Come with me," he told them. "This will not take long."

They all grinned as Aunt Hafza emitted a particularly discordant snore as they got out of the van. She shifted against the seat but did not wake up as the doors closed. Mr. Horani had left the engine running with the air on, so Zaid knew she would be napping in comfort until they returned. In the shop, they found themselves surrounded by a sea of bicycles of various colors and sizes.

"Yusuf," came a hearty cry, as a plump little man wearing a beige robe came trotting up to them.

After greetings were exchanged, Mr. Horani said, "Wali, these are the children I was telling you about."

"Honored to meet you, I am," Wali smiled widely, showing a crooked row of front teeth. "Ah, you will love the beauties I have for you. Come, come, you must see them." The teenagers looked at each other, mystified. Mr. Horani beckoned to them and they followed the bouncing Wali as he led them into a room at the back of the shop.

"Behold," Wali cried, pointing to four gleaming bicycles, as if he had waved a magic wand and conjured them up.

"They are for you," Mr. Horani told the teenagers. "I am leasing them for the duration of your stay. As you can see, two of them have carriers in the back so Hassan and Hakeem can ride with you."

The teenagers thanked Mr. Horani in delight, hardly daring to believe how fortunate they were. They examined the bikes in wonder, running their hands over the handlebars and saddles.

"Can we go for a ride now?" Hakeem hopped excitedly.

"Yes, can we go please?" Hassan implored.

"All right, all right," Mr. Horani laughed. "But only for a few minutes."

As they mounted the bikes, Hassan and Hakeem in Adam and Zaid's carrier seats, Zaid realized that it was the first time he had seen Mr. Horani really laugh.

Chapter Six

During the Storm

T HE NEXT TWO days passed uneventfully as the teenagers continued their meetings in Moss Haven and searched the turret. Monday morning brought dark, overcast skies, an extremely rare occurrence in Midan for that time of the year. The wind was howling eerily outside the house and even the clamor of the seagulls seemed subdued. When Zaid looked out of the turret, he saw dark waves lashing angrily against the cliffs, hissing and foaming against the rocks. He closed the window shut as a strong gust of wind blew into the room.

On his way to breakfast, he met Mr. Horani in the great hall.

"There is a storm brewing," Mr. Horani told him. "You children must stay inside today. It can get dangerous with the lightning."

"Okay," Zaid nodded. He had been looking forward to riding their bikes but it was out of the question now. The bikes had been delivered yesterday evening and were now stored in a shed at the side of the house. The test ride on Friday had only whetted his appetite and he longed to feel the saddle under him and the wind in his face. He grinned when he remembered how excited Hassan and Hakeem had been to ride in the carrier seats.

By the time Zaid finished his breakfast, the others had still not made an appearance downstairs. When he took his empty dishes into the kitchen, Maymun said, "Zaid, will you please do me a favor and fetch the cucumbers from Abbas. I think he's forgotten about them and I need to have them for the lunch salad. He won't be able to bring them over when the storm starts."

"Sure, I'll be happy to," Zaid said, heading out the back door.

He met Abbas along the path, carrying the missing cucumbers in a small wicker basket.

"Monstrous storm coming," Abbas rumbled in his deep voice, his bushy beard quivering.

"It sure looks that way," Zaid said as Abbas turned over the basket to him.

Maymun thanked Zaid gratefully when he returned with the cucumbers. "You all must stay inside today," she said. "It won't be safe outside when the storm comes."

"Okay, we will," Zaid promised. As he headed to the living room, he heard the sound of hammering coming from outside. Curious, he went into the great hall and opened the front door. He saw Luqman mounted on a ladder, nailing strips of wood across the bay windows.

"What are you doing?" Zaid called out.

Luqman, his face glistening with sweat, said, "I'm protecting the window panes in case the storm turns out to be a nasty one. Being this close to the bay, high winds sometimes shatter the glass. I guess you children won't be going anywhere today."

"Doesn't seem like it," Zaid said. He could see that the people of Bayan Bay took their storms seriously. In Crescent City, they usually had the mildest of rains, but he guessed being this close to the water was a different scenario altogether.

"Would you like some help?" Zaid offered.

"Oh, no, I'm almost done," Luqman assured him.

"What about the windows up in the turret?" Zaid asked. "Will they be okay?"

"Don't you worry," Luqman assured him cheerfully. "Those are gale force windows on the upper floors. You'll be safe in your turret, *insha'Allah.*"

THE PREDICTED STORM arrived just after lunch, accompanied by violent thunderclaps and crackling bolts of lightning. Sheets of rain fell heavily around the house, drumming incessantly against the windows and coursing in rivulets on the ground. The teenagers and twins spent the rest of the day playing board games, reading books and watching the local TV station, which continued to issue dire weather reports. It seemed that the storm was going to last for the better part of the night. Thus, the search for the Moon had to be suspended since Hassan and Hakeem, unable to play with Gul outside, stuck to the teenagers like glue.

Zaid went up to his room in the early afternoon and stared out of his securely locked window, mesmerized by what the storm had unleashed on the world outside. The bay was a foaming cauldron of billowing waves, dashing against the rocks in a fury. Thunder growled occasionally like a ferocious beast getting ready to spring, while long, jagged slashes of lightning cut across the leaden sky like exotic fireworks. The surrounding area was almost concealed by an eerie blanket of darkness as the rain fell like gushing waterfalls from on high.

Dinner was a quiet affair. Even the normally rambunctious Hassan and Hakeem were quiet and listless, eating their *djedjad* – chicken roasted with apricots – without much enthusiasm. Aunt Hafza, who was still battling her flare up of arthritis, stayed in her room. Mr. Horani trekked back and forth to her room to supply her with food and medication. When the teenagers asked if they could visit her, he told them that she was too befuddled at the moment to appreciate their company.

After the sunset prayer, Mr. Horani went to his study ostensibly to work on his memoirs, while the teenagers and twins settled down for an episode of *Jinns of Jeopardy*. During a commercial break, Layla went to the kitchen to get a glass of milk. Already jumpy from seeing the creepy show, she almost dropped the glass of milk when she heard a scream. It came from the open door of the cellar. *Maymun must have gone down for something and injured herself,* she thought. Alarmed, she set the glass of milk down on the counter and ran to the door of the cellar. She almost collided with Maymun, who was coming hurriedly up the stairs.

"Maymun, what happened? Did you hurt yourself?"

Maymun shook her head as she pulled out a chair from the table and sat down. She was breathing heavily and her hands trembled as she held them over her heart. Worried, Layla sped down the corridor and called out to the others in the living room.

"One of you go and get Grandpa," she said. "Something's happened to Maymun."

"I'll go," Zaid said and made for Mr. Horani's study. Moments later, he and Mr. Horani entered the kitchen where the others were gathered around a still shaken Maymun.

"What's wrong?' Mr. Horani asked in concern.

The housekeeper drew a deep breath and said, "I went down to the cellar to get a jar of jam," she pointed a trembling finger at the cellar door. "I picked it up from the shelf and turned around to come back upstairs. Then I saw it on the wall beyond. It was such a shock that I dropped the jam on the ground. It made a nasty mess, I'm afraid."

"What was on the wall?" Mr. Horani asked with a perplexed look.

"A picture of…skull…and bones," Maymun fought for breath.

The teenagers exchanged alarmed looks. It sounded like one of the posters that Layla had found up in the turret.

Mr. Horani turned irate eyes on them. "Is this someone's idea of a joke?"

There came a chorus of denials and he announced grimly, "I am going to take a look."

"Can we come with you?" Adam asked.

"Just you and Zaid," Mr. Horani replied shortly. "Layla, you and Zahra take Maymun to her room and then wait with Hassan and Hakeem in the living room."

In the cellar, Mr. Horani and the boys stared up at the picture on the wall. The thin cardboard poster measured about a square foot. It was affixed to the wall at standing height and held in place by strips of clear tape. The skull and crossbones looked especially menacing looming over them. *It's definitely one of the posters that Layla found up in the turret,* Zaid thought. He had a sinking sensation in his stomach. Who in the world could have brought it down to the cellar and taped it to the wall? He looked around in bewilderment. Besides the broken jar of jam on the ground, everything else seemed the same. The step ladder was in its usual spot next to the round table and the shelves of groceries were all intact.

"This is terrible," Mr. Horani's forehead knitted into a frown. "I remember seeing a poster like that somewhere."

Compelled by his conscience to tell the truth, Adam revealed reluctantly, "We came across a bunch of them in the western turret when we were exploring up there."

Mr. Horani looked at them sharply. "Are you sure you did not put that one up there?"

Adam's honesty had succeeded in making them prime suspects and Zaid tried not to squirm uncomfortably under Mr. Horani's penetrating stare.

"Honestly Grandpa, we didn't," Adam said earnestly. "We wouldn't do something like that."

Shaking his head in bafflement, Mr. Horani ripped the poster off the wall and tore it to shreds before turning his gaze to the sticky mess of the broken jar of jam. He sent the youths up for a mop and pail from the laundry room and soon, all that remained of the broken jar of jam was a wet spot on the cellar floor. After the shredded poster had been relegated to the garbage can and the mop and pail returned to their place, Mr. Horani and the youths went into the living room where the girls and twins were waiting in suspense.

"Did you see it? Did you see it?" Hakeem asked excitedly.

"Did it look scary?" Hassan asked.

"Be quiet," their grandfather said sternly, and the twins lapsed into silence.

Looking at them all gravely, he said, "As you have heard, and Adam and Zaid have seen, someone taped a picture of a pirate's flag in the cellar. If it was meant as a joke, then it backfired because Maymun could have died from the shock. I will ask again, did any of you do it?" He looked at each of them in turn and Zaid felt like squirming again.

Another storm of denials followed and Mr. Horani held up his hand, signaling for quiet.

"If none of you will claim responsibility, then there is nothing more to be said," he stated flatly. "I am hoping that the culprit or culprits is feeling extreme regret at such an abominable act directed towards a gentle, hardworking woman who feeds us all. Now, I suggest we all pray and go to bed. We shall see what tomorrow brings, *insha'Allah.*"

After Mr. Horani left, Layla asked apprehensively, "Was it one of the posters I found?"

"Yes," Adam said unhappily. "I can't imagine how it got there."

Layla looked suspiciously at the twins. "Did you boys have anything to do with this?"

"We didn't," Hakeem said indignantly.

"I think it was a *jinn*," Hassan said in a hushed voice. "I sawed one in our room last night."

"What nonsense," Layla scoffed. "You can't see *jinns*...not unless they take the shape of something," she amended.

"Well, there *was* one. I *sawed* it," Hassan insisted, pouting. "A great, big *jinn* going out the door. I told Hakeem about it."

"He did," Hakeem nodded. "And I heard it the night before in the closet too."

"You've been watching too much *Jinns of Jeopardy*," Zahra quoted her mother and Zaid had to smile.

"Let's hear no more about *jinns*," Adam said firmly. "You were probably dreaming and thought it was real. And make sure you recite Ayatul Kursi before you sleep, otherwise you'll have nightmares tonight."

It was a miserable group of teenagers who went to bed that night. The storm outside mirrored the one within Zaid as he lay awake, agonizing over the mystery of the poster. He knew that neither Adam nor the girls would have done it. It was not something any of them *would* do. Could it have been the twins even though they had denied it? They could have found the poster up in the turret and decided that it would be fun to put it in the cellar. It would not have been difficult for them to sneak in and use the stepladder to stick it to the wall. Zaid remained awake for a little longer until he finally fell into a fitful sleep filled with uneasy dreams.

Chapter Seven

A Visit to Ma'ab Manor

ZAID GAZED OUT the turret window the next morning to see what ravages the deluge had wrought outside. The downpour had subsided in the early hours of the morning, but the evidence left behind of its fury was very subtle. Other than the fresh smell of the air and the uncommon moisture glistening on the jagged bluffs, everything else looked the same. A bright sun shone overhead and the bay was a veritable sea of serenity, with the waves breaking almost languidly against the cliffs, as if exhausted from their frenzy of the day before. A couple of sailboats drifted lazily on the horizon and even the seagulls had resumed their usual clamor.

Everyone was in low spirits that morning, the incident of the night before casting a pall over them, especially when they went down to breakfast and saw how pale and drawn Maymun looked. It was clear that she had not slept well. There were dark circles under her eyes and lines of fatigue on her face.

"Maymun, can we help you do some chores today?" Layla said. "You look very tired."

Maymun smiled wanly. "I'll be fine after a good night's sleep. Don't you worry."

"Please believe that we didn't put that poster in the cellar," Adam said. "It's a mystery to us how it got there."

"Let's forget about that," Maymun said briskly as she placed a carafe of freshly squeezed orange juice on the island. "It was just a silly picture after all."

She probably thinks one of us did it, Zaid thought. *Who can blame her?*

While they were eating, Mr. Horani walked into the dining room, he too looking tired and haggard. After greeting them, he said without preamble, "I told Maymun to take the rest of the day off and rest. You will be spending the day at the Ahmeds. Mrs. Ahmed said that Basim will be delighted to have your company."

The teenagers digested this piece of news in silence. Under different circumstances, they would have looked forward to the visit but right now it felt too much like they were being sent away in disgrace.

As if sensing what was on their minds, Mr. Horani said, "I do not want last night's incident to spoil your vacation, so I am going to chalk it down to a badly misjudged prank and it will not be mentioned again. Now, Mrs. Ahmed is sending their chauffeur for you at eleven. That gives you about an hour to get ready. They have a nice pool, so you might want to take your swimming clothes."

By the time they left the dining room to prepare for their impending visit to the Ahmeds, Zaid had perked up a bit at the prospect of using the pool. After packing his swimming gear into his backpack, he could not help reflecting how uncomfortable it felt to be under a cloud of suspicion. *I guess we'll continue to be until the culprit is caught,* he thought glumly.

At promptly eleven o'clock, the doorbell rang. Zaid and Adam were waiting in the great hall with Mr. Horani while the girls and twins were in the living room. Mr. Horani hurried to the door and opened it. A tall man wearing a chauffeur's uniform and hat stood outside. He was in his early thirties and had a long face with a closely cut beard, deep-set dark eyes and a somewhat stiff countenance. Behind him was parked a gleaming black limousine.

"I am Nassif, the Ahmeds' chauffeur," he introduced himself after greetings were exchanged. "Are the children ready?"

"Yes, they are," Mr. Horani replied. "They'll be out in a minute."

As Nassif headed back to the limousine, the girls and twins were summoned and Mr. Horani hustled them out the door. "You all have a good time."

As they walked out to the limousine, Zaid remarked, "The Ahmeds must be very rich to own a limousine with a chauffeur."

Adam nodded. "Oh, yes. Grandpa says that they are one of the richest families in Bayan Bay. Of course, *the* richest by far is the Ambreens. They're into everything. Oil, shipping, textiles, you name it."

"Didn't some of the Ambreens come to *Jumu'ah* in that white limousine?" Zahra asked.

"Yes, they did," Adam replied. "Two men and a boy."

"We saw the boy in the library afterwards," Zaid said, remembering the rude boy.

"Yeah," Adam recalled. "He was a nasty piece of work."

The ride to Ma'ab Manor took ten minutes. When they arrived at the house, the chauffeur came out and opened the door of the limousine. He waited politely as they climbed out before driving off.

Ma'ab Manor nestled amid smooth green lawns fringed by date palms. A water fountain cascaded in the middle of the courtyard, its water glinting silver in the sunlight. The house itself was a graceful, white two-story villa with a wraparound balcony on the upper floor. Judging from the cries of the seabirds flying overhead, it was also close to the bay.

"It's a beautiful house," Layla said in admiration. "It looks so new and sleek."

Basim came hurrying from the columned entryway and greetings were exchanged.

"Welcome to Ma'ab Manor," he beamed at them. "I'm so glad you came. Come on, let's go inside."

As they entered a large living area with cathedral ceilings and long, high windows that let in lots of natural light, Mrs. Ahmed came to greet them. "It's wonderful to have you all here," she said warmly. "Basim will show you around and keep you entertained. If there's anything you need, don't hesitate to ask. Lunch is at twelve-thirty, so I'll see you then."

Basim promptly took them on a tour of the house and grounds, ending at the freeform swimming pool, which had several lounging chairs around it. A strategic grove of cedar trees provided a thick screen of privacy all around. Basim promised that they would use the pool later when the sweltering heat had abated a little. After the tour, he took them to a cool, airy den at the back of the house. A set of floor-to-ceiling windows showcased a green tract of land that sloped gently downwards, giving them a stunning view of the bay.

Before long, a shy-looking maid came to announce that lunch was ready.

"Thank you, Yasmin," Basim said.

They followed Basim to the elaborate dining room where Mrs. Ahmed was already seated. An ornate chandelier hung above a gleaming mahogany dining table and its twelve matching chairs. Zaid looked with pleasurable anticipation at the eggplant, meatballs and pasta, and the golden-red pieces of tandoori chicken served with jasmine rice. On the table were also several jugs of cold lemonade and a chocolate cake for dessert. As they seated themselves and began to eat, Mr. Ahmed walked in. Basim had told them that his father was at work but was expected home for lunch.

"*Assalaam Alaikum,* everyone," he said jovially as he sat down and began to heap food onto his plate. "So glad you could visit. Are you having a good time?"

"Yes, Basim has been showing us around," Adam replied. "I love the tennis court and swimming pool."

"You should take a dip in the pool," Mr. Ahmed told them as he forked up pasta and began to eat. "Basim would lose some of that weight if he would only cut back on ice cream and use the pool more often."

Zaid almost choked on a meatball at Mr. Ahmed's tactless remark. He thought it was rather unkind of him to embarrass Basim. The poor boy looked red in the face as he told his father, "We'll be swimming later."

"Good, good," Mr. Ahmed nodded approvingly.

After lunch and the midday prayer, they went back to the den.

"Have you been to the Mariners' Museum yet?" Basim asked, as he dug out a couple of coloring books and crayons from a storage drawer and handed them to the twins.

"No," Layla shook her head. "I think Grandpa did mention it."

"It's got a miniature model of your great-grandfather's ship on display. In fact, there are all sorts of memorabilia that they've collected from the crew of the Yuhanza. My Great-Grandfather Qasim donated a few things. He was one of the crewmen, you know."

"He was?" Adam said with interest. "We didn't know."

"He died a few years ago. I used to love listening to his stories about his voyages. He was sad that the Captain had been killed and the Yuhanza burned by the rebels. He used to say that the Captain and his ship went down the same night."

"They did, didn't they?" Layla mused. "That's very symbolic."

"By the way," Basim said as he rummaged again in one of

the drawers. "I heard that some rich shaykh came to visit your grandfather the other day."

Adam shared a look of surprise with the others. "How did you know?"

"I heard Mrs. Basri tell my mom. Her niece is a maid at the hotel where this shaykh stayed and overheard him and his bodyguard talking about visiting Bayan House. So, what did he want?" Basim asked curiously as he pulled out a game of Scrabble.

"Oh, he needed Grandpa's help with something," Adam replied guardedly.

"My dad said that he was a *very, very* rich shaykh," Basim said. "It must have been something really important."

"Grandpa wasn't able to help him," Adam said dismissively. "He didn't stay very long."

Looking disappointed that there was no news forthcoming, Basim next removed the games Battleship and Pictionary from the drawer. As he placed the games onto the carpeted floor, he said, "You know, you should visit Pasha's Playland. You'll have a lot of fun there."

"Is it a toy store or something?" Layla asked.

"No, it's an amusement park. It's the only one in Midan."

"I've heard of it," Zaid said. "We always wanted to see what it's like but we never found the time to come this far. Maybe we can check it out before we leave."

"They have some really nice rides and games," Basim said. "And I love their ice cream."

"Yeah, your dad made sure we knew how much you love ice cream," Adam grinned and Basim chuckled good-naturedly. After playing several noisy games of Scrabble, Pictionary and Battleship, Basim led them upstairs to change into their swimming clothes. They descended to the swimming pool, the boys dressed in capri pants and T-shirts while the girls wore water resistant tunics and pants with their scarves. The next hour was filled with fun as they played a few games in the water and laughed at the antics of Hassan and Hakeem who swam like fishes.

"They learned to swim when they were really young," Layla said proudly. "They took to the water like...well...like fish to water," she chuckled.

The maid, Yasmin, appeared later with refreshments. The teeenagers and twins came out of the water and sat in the comfortable lounge chairs as they sipped cold lemonade and ate chicken samosas and slices of chocolate cake left over from lunch. The youths then went to the adjacent tennis court for a game while the twins played hide and seek among the trees. The girls remained supine on the lounge chairs as they conversed.

"Grandpa won't be too happy when he hears that Mrs. Basri knows about the Shaykh's visit," Layla remarked. "I heard Maymun say that Mrs. Basri is one of the worst gossips in the city. She'll probably tell a whole lot of people about it. And then they will ask Grandpa about it."

"Well, at least they won't know why the Shaykh came," Zahra said. But her assumption would be proven wrong as they were to find out shortly.

Later that evening, they took their leave of the Ahmeds. *It turned out to be a pretty fun day after all,* Zaid thought as they piled into the limousine. The unpleasant incident of last night had receded to the back of his mind during their visit but as they headed for home, Zaid felt a little of his melancholia return. Nassif drove in silence, the limousine eating up the dark stretches of road until it entered the gates of Bayan House and drew up to the courtyard. Adam thanked Nassif, who nodded slightly and drove off. Mr. Horani opened the door for them, his face bearing a perturbed expression.

Zaid grew uneasy when he sent the twins upstairs and asked the teenagers to come to his study. They looked at one another in silent alarm as they followed him. *What had happened now?* In the study, Mr. Horani picked up an envelope from his desk and said in a strained voice, "I want to apologize to you. I was wrong to suspect you of putting up that poster in the cellar."

They stared at him in surprise until Adam said, "Do you know who did it then?"

Mr. Horani shook his head. "No, but take a look at this." He pulled out a thick, folded paper from the envelope and held it out.

Adam took the paper from his grandfather and with the others gathered around him, opened it slowly. Zaid's breath hissed out in surprise as he stared at the paper in Adam's hand. It was a poster of skull and crossbones, similar to the ones found in the turret. At the bottom, printed in large handwritten letters, it warned, *Do not look for the Moon of Masarrah or its curse will come upon you.*

"Oh, my goodness," Layla exclaimed. "Where did this come from?"

"It came with the mail. Someone must have found out why the Shaykh was here and decided to play a practical joke. They must have gotten into the cellar by the door Abbas uses and now they have sent this," Mr. Horani gestured to the paper.

"But how could they have gotten hold of the poster from the turret?" Adam asked.

"Oh, those posters are on sale at many of the curio shops by the waterfront. They're a dirham a dozen."

"Whoever put it there must have heard about the Shaykh's visit from Mrs. Basri," Layla said, going on to tell her grandfather what Basim had told them.

Mr. Horani sighed. "I don't know what they mean by this since I'm not searching for the diamond anymore. And even if I was, I wouldn't be deterred by some superstitious nonsense."

Chapter Eight

A Picnic and a Journal

A T BREAKFAST THE next morning, a remorseful Mr.
Horani suggested that they use the rented bikes to go
on a picnic in Bayan Meadow that afternoon. He went
on to tell them that Maymun had been relieved that they had
been exonerated of blame for the poster in the cellar, and that
she would be happy to prepare a nice picnic basket for them.

"That's great, Grandpa," Layla said enthusiastically. "It
looks like a lovely day for a picnic." They all expressed their
delight at the idea and Mr. Horani left the dining room with
a pleased expression, which was a change from the grim look
he had worn since the poster had been discovered in the cellar.
Later that morning, they met in Moss Haven to discuss the
implications of the warning that Mr. Horani had received. As
soon as she entered the shack, Layla burst out, "Guess what? Just
before I came here, I went up to the turret to check the skull and
crossbones posters. There had been five of them total but when
I counted them just now," she paused dramatically, "there were
only four!"

"What?" Zahra exclaimed. "How could that be?"

"Well," Adam said slowly, "it could be that the poster in the cellar didn't come from a curio shop but from the turret. And it was put there by someone who has access to the house."

"Someone who knows that we're searching for the Moon and is trying to scare us off, so they can look for it themselves," Zaid said.

"But the only people who have access to the house are Luqman and Maymun," Zahra said in bewilderment.

"They're not the only ones," Layla said. "Abbas has a key, which means that both him and Mir have access too. One of them could have done it."

"But how could they have known about the Moon?" Zahra asked in bafflement.

"That's easy," Adam said. "Abbas was in the courtyard parking his Land Rover when I answered the doorbell and let the Shaykh in that day. He could have eavesdropped by the open window at the side of the house. And he could have told Mir, who must have eavesdropped on us at the library when we were reading up on the Moon."

"I noticed that one of the books Mir dropped was titled *How to find the Hidden,*" Zaid said. "That's very suspicious, if you ask me."

"Golly, I never thought we'd have competition in looking for the Moon," Layla said. "I think it's Mir. It's hard to believe that Abbas could do such a low-down thing."

"Good men do bad things sometimes," Zaid said. "Especially when a lot of money is at stake."

"Are we going to continue the search?" Zahra asked.

"Absolutely," Adam said firmly. "No one's going to scare us away. After we come back from the picnic to Bayan Meadow, we'll continue searching in the turret."

Zahra said softly, "Maybe Abbas or Mir could have overheard us talking here at Moss Haven about looking for the Moon."

"Yikes," Layla said in dismay. "You're right. We haven't been very smart at all."

Adam scrambled over to the door, opened it and peered around outside. "No one there now," he said. "From now on, we're going to leave the door open to make sure no one comes creeping up."

THAT AFTERNOON, UNDER clear blue skies and the warm embrace of a golden sun, the teenagers mounted their bikes and set off for Bayan Meadow, laden with bags of goodies that Maymun had prepared for them. Out of the gates they pedaled and onto the roadway, Hassan and Hakeem comfortably ensconced in their carrier seats with their legs tucked under them. The little boys had been beside themselves with excitement at the prospect of a bike ride. They wore rapt looks on their faces as they chattered nineteen to the dozen and searched the air for Gul.

With a flapping of wings, the bird swooped down in front of them, hovering in the wind as it stared at them out of bright, beady eyes.

"Gul's coming to the picnic with us," Hakeem cried joyfully.

"Goodbye, food," Layla said with mock dismay. "That bird will take us for all we've got."

"I'm sure he'll find some juicy worms and tasty bugs to nibble on," Adam grinned.

"Yuck, that's gross," Layla made a face. "Don't spoil my appetite."

They rode at a leisurely pace, past verdant fields and orchards abundant with trees, and roadsides adorned with colorful patches of wildflowers which relieved the monotony of the gray and green landscape around them. Gul flapped along beside them, letting out a companionable squawk now and then as if to remind them of its presence and occasionally riding an updraft of wind to soar above their heads.

Bayan Meadow turned out to be a cosy green dell overlooking

the bay. The grass was short and well kept, with clumps of aromatic white jasmine scattered here and there. The bay was tranquil that afternoon, with gentle-cresting waves rippling across its smooth blue surface. In the distance, a few sailboats undulated on the troughs, their massive sails billowing in the wind. Overhead, the gulls and curlews were acting out their own drama, shrieking wildly as they dipped and glided in constant motion. In contrast, colorful gossamer-winged butterflies flitted quietly around the meadow, alighting every now and then on a delicate flower. Zaid noticed a conical ant hill in one corner, with an army of ants moving around like cars on a busy street. Closing his eyes, he took several deep breaths of air, which bore the scent of jasmine, flavored with salt from the bay.

"It's beautiful here," Zahra said. "So natural and peaceful. I wonder why more people aren't here."

"I guess people prefer to go to the beaches," Adam said. "It doesn't take a rocket scientist to figure out why," he added in a peeved tone. "It's because they can swim there. I suggested to Grandpa that we go one day but he nixed the idea. He said he didn't want us swimming in the bay. Honestly, he's too paranoid."

"I guess he's afraid of the dangerous undertow," Zaid said. "He didn't have any problem with us using the Ahmeds' pool."

"Well, let's eat," Layla said. "I'm starving."

Pulling out a checkered blue and white tablecloth from one of the baskets, she handed it to the youths to spread on the ground. Soon, all the food was out of the baskets and laid out invitingly on the cloth. There was a chickpea and olive appetizer with cheese balls, marinated chicken stuffed in pita bread, spicy shish kebabs and date-filled cookies with juicy purple grapes for dessert. In addition to the food, there was cinnamon tea in a flask, bottled water and mango juice.

Zaid knew that food always tasted better outdoors, and this time was no exception. They ate slowly, conversing about their school life, books and television programs. Gul got its fair share of food, with no worms or bugs materializing so far. Zaid was amused by the way the bird guarded its territory like a watchdog. When a few gulls, attracted by the smell of their food, descended upon them, Gul promptly chased them off by making threatening noises and flapping its wings menacingly.

"He's a greedy bird, is what he is," Layla said, throwing a grape to it. "He's afraid if we feed the other birds, there won't be enough food for him." Gul immediately speared the grape with its bill and downed it with a quick swallow. Then it turned to Layla and let out a series of squawks.

"It's like he understood what you said," Zahra said in amusement.

"That bird is giving me the heebie-jeebies," Layla said with a theatrical shudder. "He's too smart for his own good."

After they had eaten, Zaid sprawled full-length on the grass, watching from the corner of his eye as Hassan and Hakeem chased after the butterflies. *Those two can never sit still,* he thought. Gul had flown off as soon as it realized there was no more food to be had. *Probably gone to join his feathered friends,* Zaid thought. *Or maybe he went looking for those worms and bugs for his dessert.* The bird seemed to have a huge appetite, giving new meaning to the idiom *eat like a bird.*

With much regret, the teenagers and twins mounted the bikes to return home. *Goodbye, little meadow,* Zaid said silently. *I don't know if I'll ever see you again.*

The ride back home was at a much brisker pace. Adam was in the lead and as he turned the corner at a tree-lined crossroad, he nearly collided with another biker, who swerved swiftly to the side. Unfortunately, the biker bounced over a deep rut, depositing both him and his bike into the thick shrubbery. Horrified, they all came to a stop and watched anxiously as the fallen rider got to his feet. Zaid's eyes widened in astonishment. Of all the rotten luck, it was Mir. He and Adam really seemed to have a nasty penchant for literally running into each other.

"Are you alright?" Adam called out as Mir set his bike to rights.

"I should have known it was you," Mir scowled at him. "Are you always this careless?"

"I'm sorry," Adam apologized. "I didn't see you coming."

"You probably wouldn't see a herd of camels coming until they're about to trample you," Mir said nastily. "I guess I should count myself lucky that you're not driving a car."

Adam flushed angrily as Mir hopped on his bicycle and rode off. "What a jerk! He's got some nerve putting all the blame on me."

Layla hooted with laughter and Adam turned to glare at her.

"Sorry," she gasped. "It's just too funny."

It *was* funny and Zaid had to suppress a chuckle so as not to further offend his friend.

"Mir seems to be everywhere," Zahra said. "I guess he's not planning to return to Crescent City anytime soon."

"If he's trying to scare us away and look for the Moon himself, he'll probably stick around for as long as he can," Adam said. "But if he thinks it's going to be that easy, he's got another thing coming."

THAT EVENING, THE teenagers gathered in the turret again to continue the search. They dug through boxes, gingerly taking out one dusty item after another. Adam peered at an old magazine in his hand and read, *"How to Preserve Fruits and Vegetables.* This must have belonged to Grandma Khadijah or Step-Grandma Asma. Grandma Khadijah died when Dad was very young," he reminisced. "Dad hardly remembers her. Step-Grandma Asma was very nice though. She and Grandpa visited us eight years ago. Poor Grandpa became a widower for the second time after she died three years ago."

Layla held up a book. "Look, I've found Aunt Hanifa's journal. I'm going to keep it to read."

"Are we supposed to read someone else's journal?" Adam asked doubtfully.

"It's a journal, not a private diary," Layla clutched the book protectively to her chest, as if she expected Adam to snatch it away. "I don't think Aunt Hanifa would mind her great-niece reading it."

"Suit yourself," Adam shrugged.

Half an hour later, they called it quits.

"Nothing so far," Zaid said glumly. "But thankfully, we only have a few more boxes to finish off."

ZAID WAS GLAD to get into bed that night. His muscles were a bit sore from the bike ride. He tossed and turned, trying to find a comfortable position on the bed. At one point, he heard the faint thrum of an engine through his open window and got out of bed to look outside. The dark shape of a boat was maneuvering its way into the mouth of the cove. It was a bit larger than the last one he had seen. Just like before, it melted into the cliffs and disappeared from sight. He stared for a bit longer but there was no further movement. Returning to his bed, he fell asleep within minutes.

Chapter Nine

The Mariners' Museum

UP IN HER room, Zahra opened the door to her closet and heard a slight rustling sound. She froze in her tracks. *It must be a mouse,* she thought nervously. *I hate mice.* The rustling sound came again, louder this time and with a startled squeal, she banged the door shut and stood in the middle of the room, trembling with nervousness. She needed her clothes to get dressed and go down to breakfast but the thought of a mouse rushing out at her made her quake in her bedroom slippers. What was she to do? She could not go down in her pajamas. Maybe Layla could lend her something to wear until the mouse was caught. She only hoped that the other girl was still in her room.

Knocking on the door, she was relieved when Layla opened it.

"There's a mouse in my closet," Zahra burst out. "I'm afraid to get my clothes out. Can you lend me something to wear for breakfast?"

"A mouse?" Layla said incredulously. "Was it a large one?"

"I didn't see it," Zahra confessed sheepishly. "I just heard it."

"Well, there's only one thing to do," Layla said matter-of-factly.

"You'll tell Grandpa to bring in Pest Control?" Zahra asked.

"No, silly," Layla chuckled. "I'll go take a look."

Zahra led the way back to her room. She admired Layla's courage. Mice! Ugh! She wished that she was not so scared of the little critters.

Layla opened the door of the closet and went down on hands and knees as she peered around inside. Zahra held her breath, expecting the fearsome creature to spring out at any moment.

"No mouse there," Layla announced cheerfully as she stood up. "The sound must have come from elsewhere. I don't think there are any mice in the house."

Zahra still felt nervous. The rustling sound *had* come from the closet, she was sure of it. Maybe the mouse had run down a hole.

"Thank you, Layla," she said as she quickly pulled an outfit off the rack. "I'm sorry to be such a nuisance."

"You're welcome," Layla grinned. "I was just being a mice girl...I mean *nice* girl."

ZAID WAS IN the living room when Adam turned on the television so the twins could watch one of their favorite cartoon shows. Breaking news was in progress of another act of piracy in the Bayan Strait. A male reporter dressed in suit and tie was interviewing someone who looked to be a high-ranking official of the Midan Coast Guard and they caught the tail end of his question.

"...so difficult to catch them? It's been almost two years without any breakthroughs. How can the Coast Guard justify this lack of progress? And is it true that you have created a joint task force with the Tri-Country Bureau of Inquiries?"

The official, a trim beardless man wearing a naval uniform and hat, replied, "As we've stated numerous times in the past two years, this is a very sophisticated operation at work. They are knowledgeable and cunning, they usually have the element of surprise on their side and they operate out of a large body of water with many islands where they can lie beneath the radar. Since these waters are also shared by Ghassan and Wijdan, this necessitated the intervention of the TCBI, hence our collaboration."

"Do you anticipate a breakthrough soon?"

"With the TCBI now on board, we certainly hope so."

"Thank you, Lieutenant Abdi. We wish you and your team success."

As the television channel segued back to the cartoon, Adam remarked, "They're bringing in the big guns, huh? I hope the TCBI nails these pirates soon."

Zaid stared thoughtfully into space, a frown on his face.

Adam nudged him. "What's up? You look as if your longtime pet just died."

"I saw another boat come into Bayan Cove last night with its lights off. I was wondering if they're connected to the pirates in any way. Both times I've heard them, the window was open. I'll leave it open from now on to see if there's a pattern."

"Well, keep your window, your eyes *and* your ears open," Adam grinned. "And wake me up the next time you hear one. I would like to see it myself."

LATER THAT MORNING, the teenagers met in Moss Haven, leaving the door open to guard against any eavesdroppers.

"Well," Adam said, "we've certainly reached an exciting point in the search. We've found out that we're not the only ones looking for the Moon, and our most likely suspects are Abbas and Mir. They're probably searching in the nights when we're asleep. I suggest that we speed up the search, so they don't find the Moon before us."

"We could be spending days searching in all the wrong places," Zaid pointed out, "when it might just take them an hour in the right place."

"Well, there's nothing we can do about that," Adam replied. "We're in a free-for-all, winner-takes-all competition, whether we like it or not."

THAT AFTERNOON, AS they sifted through boxes of magazines and old newspapers in the turret, Zahra asked, "Did you start reading Aunt Hanifa's journal yet, Layla?"

"Yeah, I've read quite a bit of it. She sounded like a normal young girl at times and very grown up at other times."

"Did she say anything about the Captain's death?" Zaid asked.

"I haven't gotten that far yet. It will probably be much later in the journal. She mentions the Captain's ship a lot. I wonder if we can go to the Mariners' Museum tomorrow after *Jumu'ah* and take a look at the model."

"I don't see why not," Adam said. "We can ask Grandpa at dinner."

An hour later, they came to a stop. The search had proven disappointing yet again. No diamond was to be found in any of the boxes. The only items of interest unearthed were two photo albums, which they spent a few minutes looking at. Some of the pictures were in black and white and quite old. They were mostly of the Captain, his wife and their three children. Zaid thought that Mr. Horani looked a lot like his father. They had seemed like a close-knitted family. *Until the Captain was murdered,* Zaid thought sadly. That must have brought their happy world crashing down.

"Okay, that's it for the turret," Adam said, dusting off his clothes. "We will move on to the next place on our list, which is to go around searching the walls for any hidden nooks."

At dinner, Layla broached the subject of their visit to the Mariners' Museum.

"Excellent idea," Mr. Horani nodded in approval. "After *Jumu'ah,* we will have lunch at a nearby restaurant and then I will drop you off at the museum, *insha'Allah.* Luqman can come and pick you up at five when the museum closes. Hassan and Hakeem might find it too wearisome, so they had better remain with me."

"Is there is fee?" Adam asked.

"There is no entry fee but there is a box for donations. Hud Tabibi is the founder and curator. He is a good man and very much dedicated to the museum. He has been in rather low spirits ever since his wife died earlier this year. His father Nuh used to be a crewman on the Yuhanza. He helped Hud to run the museum until illness overcame him. He's got Alzheimer's, I am afraid. His behavior can be quite erratic at times. Give Hud my regards when you see him."

The next day, they again boarded the Toyota Land Cruiser and headed into the city. After attending the *Jumu'ah* prayer at a mosque in the vicinity of the Mariners' Museum, they went over to an Afghan restaurant for lunch. Replete from a rice and kebab meal, they set off for the museum, Zaid eagerly looking forward to their visit. He liked browsing among historical artifacts, an interest cultivated by his father. Professor Alkurdi was never more in his element than when he was among antiquities of any kind. Zaid had often observed the way his father's eyes would light up, and his face become animated whenever he was among his precious relics. He understood some of his father's enthusiasm now as they came to a stop in front of the museum.

The Mariners' Museum was located at the end of a quiet street next to a medical practice. It was a long, single story building with a small courtyard for parking. At the center of the courtyard was a shady date palm under which were two wooden benches. Zaid noted that there was just one car in the parking lot. That meant that they would pretty much have the place to themselves.

Wide mahogany doors opened into a tiled foyer with a large ship's wheel inlaid in the middle. To the left was a half-moon reception desk with a slot for donations and several stacks of brochures. A staircase going down to the lower level was to their right. Through a glass enclosed office beyond the reception desk, they saw a bespectacled man sitting at a desk, working on a computer.

As Adam placed the bills his grandfather had given him into the donation slot, the man looked up and saw them. Rising from his desk, he came towards them. After greetings were exchanged, he said, "Welcome to the Mariners' Museum. I'm Hud Tabibi, the Curator. Can I be of assistance?"

Zaid studied the man whom Mr. Horani had spoken so well of. He was tall and thin, with slightly stooping shoulders and a scholarly demeanor. His hair and beard were sprinkled with gray and there was a quiet sadness on his face, no doubt due to the recent loss of his wife.

Adam replied, "We're here to see the exhibitions. Oh, by the way, my grandfather sends his regards to you."

"Er…that's very nice of him," the curator said absent-mindedly. The teenagers looked at each other in amusement. It was apparent that Hud was being polite and did not have the faintest idea who the grandfather was.

"Can you tell us where we can find the model of the Yuhanza?" Layla asked.

That got Hud's attention. "You know of the Yuhanza?" he asked.

"Yes," Adam's eyes twinkled in amusement at the surprise he was about to spring on the curator. "Our great-grandfather was Captain Red Rafiq."

Hud looked at them in surprise. "Allah be praised," he exclaimed. "You must be Yusuf's grandchildren from America."

Adam gestured to Layla and said, "This is my sister, Layla. Zaid and Zahra are our friends."

"I'm happy to meet you," Hud said. "Ah, the Yuhanza," he went on enthusiastically. "It was a magnificent ship. My father was a longtime crewman on it."

"So you knew the Captain?" Adam asked.

Hud nodded. "Oh yes. He was a fine man. A fine man indeed. I was a young boy then, but I remember his flaming red hair and booming voice. A pity you didn't inherit that red mane of his," he looked almost accusingly at Adam.

"My twin brothers did," Adam smiled. "You won't be disappointed if you see them."

"Excellent," Hud looked pleased. "Well, go ahead and look at the Yuhanza and her memorabilia. It's located in one of the chambers at the very back."

After thanking the curator, they proceeded down the aisle into the vast hall, which was crowded with marine artifacts in glass cases. The air was thick with the scent of furniture polish and dust mite neutralizer, mingling with the aura of history that emanated from old hourglasses, compasses and lamps. Zaid studied an old *kamal*, a navigational device that in bygone days had allowed sailors to determine latitude by measuring how far the Pole Star was above the horizon.

Finally, they came to the chamber housing the replica of the Yuhanza and her memorabilia. The model ship was about ten feet tall and had the look of the traditional deep-sea *dhow* with prominent prow, square stern and three triangular sails. Across the hull, *The Yuhanza* was emblazoned in bold script. On a metal plate at the foot of the replica was inscribed the names of the ten crewmen. The only ones the teenagers were familiar with were Nuh Tabibi and Qasim Ahmed, Basim's great-grandfather.

After they had gazed their fill of the model ship, they drifted off in different directions to look at the memorabilia. The charred and blackened remnants of sail, blankets, and crockery were easily recognized as items salvaged from the burnt vessel.

"Come look at these daggers," Layla called out, her nose pressed to a glass case. They all crowded around her scrutinizing the weapons. The curved bronze daggers were identical in design with pearl-encrusted hilts. Zaid counted nine of them total. They were lying on a white satin background next to their scabbards, also adorned with pearls. The caption on the glass case read, "Ceremonial khanjars carried by the crew of the Yuhanza."

Layla pointed to one of the daggers and said, "Look at the third dagger from the left. Do you notice anything different about it?"

They stared at the *khanjar* in question. Adam said finally, "No, I don't see anything different. It looks just like the rest."

"Look at the blade," Layla entreated and obediently, they stared at the *khanjar* again.

"There's a mark on it," Zaid tilted his head as he squinted down at the *khanjar*. "It's about an inch long and carved by something sharp. It looks like the English letter *K*."

"That's it," Layla said triumphantly. "It's strange…"

She was interrupted mid-sentence by a steady, tap-tapping sound. Startled, they looked around and saw a little old man with white hair and beard coming towards them. He was carrying a thick wooden walking stick which was hitting against the tiles to produce the tap-tapping sound. Upon sighting them, he stopped in surprise and thumped his stick with a loud bang. With his other hand, he waved a fist at them.

"Black-hearted baboons," he cried out in a high, quavering voice. "Spawn of Satan. Bloodthirsty pirates. Get off my ship."

The teenagers exchanged looks of alarm as the old man bore down upon them.

"He's loony," Adam said in an undertone.

"Villains. Buccaneers," the old man screeched in a frenzy. "You're not taking my ship. I'm going to fight you to the death." Holding up the walking stick like a sword, he began slashing at the air as he moved towards them with surprising swiftness.

"Run," Adam urged and they all raced out of the room, flying past the exhibits and now empty office, and out the front door. They finally came to a stop in the courtyard, panting heavily as they tried to regain their breath. They looked back warily towards the museum but there was no sign of the old man.

"Who…in…the…world…was that?" Layla said breathlessly.

"I think we just had the pleasure of meeting Hud Tabibi's father," Adam made the connection. "Remember Grandpa telling us that his father had Alzheimer's? It has to be him."

"Poor man, he must be really sick to take us for pirates," Zahra said sympathetically.

"He must have seen my eyepatch and Adam's cutlass," Zaid grinned and they shared a light moment of humor after their scare.

"What do we do now?" Zahra asked. "He might come after us if we go back in."

"Let's have a seat and discuss what to do," Adam pointed to the wooden benches under the date palm.

After they were seated, Zaid said, "We can't go back while the old man is there. We can probably explore the area a bit before Luqman comes for us at five."

Layla said, "Before we head off, I must tell you about that dagger with the K mark on it. Aunt Hanifa wrote in her journal that the night before one of his voyages, she found the Captain cleaning his *khanjar* in the study. As she watched him, he asked her if she would like to carve her initial on it. She was delighted and said yes. Since she and Aunt Hafza's initials were the same, she said that she would put her middle initial K, which stands for Kamilah. He gave her his penknife and she carved an English K on the blade, telling him that whenever he saw it, he would remember her. I'm sure that the K we saw on the dagger was the one she made."

"That's odd," Adam mused. "Didn't Grandpa say that they threw away the Captain's dagger in the bay? How can it be the same dagger when it should be lying at the bottom of the bay?"

"It could be that the Captain's dagger got switched with someone else's dagger on the ship," Zaid said. "They were all identical, so it could easily have happened."

Layla shook her head emphatically. "The Captain would have known at once if his dagger had gotten switched and wouldn't have hesitated to get it back. He certainly wouldn't have come back from the voyage carrying the wrong dagger for Aunt Hanifa to find."

"Then what could the explanation be?" Zaid asked.

"It could be," Layla said slowly, "that he was killed by someone who had a dagger just like his."

"But only the crew of the Yuhanza had identical daggers," Zahra said with wide eyes. "Surely you don't think one of them murdered the Captain?"

There was a long moment of silence. Then Adam said, "I think it's possible. I always thought it strange that the rebels would stab the Captain with his own dagger. It would have made more sense if they had shot him."

"Why would one of his crew murder the Captain though?" Zahra asked.

"I thought about that as I was looking at the daggers," Layla said. "All sorts of ideas flew through my head. But there was only one that made sense."

"What was it?" Zaid asked.

"Think," Layla said succinctly. "What did the Captain have that someone might kill to lay his hands on?"

"The Moon," Zahra gasped out.

Adam said excitedly, "I think you're right. Grandpa said that none of the crew knew about the diamond but one of them must have found out about it, followed him home that night and murdered him so he could steal it. The Captain must have already hidden it, so the murderer couldn't find it. That's why as he was dying, he told Grandpa it was hidden in the house."

"The murderer," Layla went on, "must have taken the Captain's dagger in exchange for his own. Even if he did notice the K, it wouldn't have meant anything to him since Aunt Hanifa and the Captain were the only ones who knew about it. By the time the murderer or his family donated the marked dagger to the museum, Aunt Hanifa had long been dead."

As a worrisome thought occurred to Zaid, he said, "If the murderer was someone who knew that the stone was hidden in the house, what if he searched and found it at some point after the Captain's death?"

As they looked at each other in dismay, Adam rallied their spirits by saying, "As Shaykh Sulaiman said, the Moon of Masarrah would have turned up somewhere if that was the case. It wouldn't have been missing for so long. What's the use of having a famous stone if no one knows you have it? It doesn't make sense."

"Didn't that article we read in the library say that the Sultan of Brunei might be the secret owner?" Zahra said.

"It's all guesswork to create sensation," Adam scoffed. "Do you think Shaykh Sulaiman would have kept on searching if he thought the Sultan had it? And why would the Sultan even want to hide the fact that he had such a famous diamond?"

"I see your point," Zaid admitted.

"So the search continues," Zahra said.

"Absolutely," Adam replied.

"I wonder which of his crewmen could have murdered the Captain," Layla mused.

Adam said, "I say we embark on an investigation to find out who it could have been. What do you think?"

"Good idea," Zahra said approvingly.

"I'm with you," Zaid agreed.

"Me too," Layla nodded.

Chapter Ten

The Faithful Five

THE NEXT MORNING when they met in Moss Haven, Layla showed them the entry in the journal where Aunt Hanifa had written about carving her initial on the Captain's dagger. It read:

Dear Journal, tomorrow Papa will be going away on another voyage. I know it is foolish of me to feel sad, especially when he loves the sea so much and it is our livelihood. But we miss him awfully when he is away. Indeed, the house feels dull and empty without him. I especially feel sorry for Mama. Each time Papa goes away, I can see the light go out of her eyes, only to return when he comes back. Papa says the time will fly by so fast that before we know it, he will he home again, with lots of beautiful gifts. I asked him if he thinks of us when he is in the middle of the ocean, and he told me he does all the time.

Earlier today, I saw Papa cleaning his khanjar in the study. He said that it had gotten a bit tarnished and he needed it to look shiny and new again. It is a fine-looking weapon but could be so deadly with its sharp blade. As I admired the beautiful hilt made of pearls, Papa asked me if I wanted to carve my initial on the blade. I was delighted and told him yes. But then I realized that Hafza also has the same initial as me. I know it was a bit selfish, but I decided that I would carve the initial of my middle name, Kamilah. Papa then gave me his penknife and I carved a large 'K' in English, on it. I told him that whenever he looks at it, he would remember me. He gave me a hug and said that he did not need to look at a khanjar to remember me, that each day he wakes up he thanks Allah for his precious jewels, meaning his children. He also said that he would cherish his khanjar more than ever, and that the 'K' I had carved on it was going to be our little secret. Oh, I will miss him so!

Yusuf and Hafza play with their toys but I write in my journal. My best friend Najah laughs at me. She says that someone might steal it to read. I tell her that I do not have any dark secrets, so even if someone reads it, I will not be embarrassed. I am feeling sleepy, so I will go to bed now. I want to wake up at the crack of dawn to see Papa off. Oh, how we will miss him!

"That's so sweet," Zahra sighed. "She writes so well. "Did you come across anything yet about the Night of Catastrophe?"

Layla shook her head. "No, she wrote about there being trouble in some quarters and the fear of a civil war. She didn't write in the journal again until a year after the Captain's death. Here, I'll read it to you." She flipped through the pages until she found the entry she was looking for. Then she began to read.

Dear Journal, it has been quite a while since I took a pen to your pages. Nearly a year has passed by since our dear Papa's death. Even though the terrible grief has subsided a bit, we still miss him so much and feel his loss keenly. Indeed, during the past year, I could hardly summon the will to share my thoughts with you. The great blow that had befallen our family was so much more than any inadequate words could express. But the dark cloud of sorrow that hung over us and so shriveled our spirits gradually began to lift away little by little. I can now look back at that dark period in our lives with a measure of calm and acceptance. From a Hadith, I have learned that when a child is in the womb of its mother, the angel comes to blow the breath of life into its soul and record its life span. I understand now that Papa's time was up, and he has returned to Allah. I no longer feel bitter and angry as I did in the early days. Mama has been so wise and strong throughout this ordeal. Although it was incredibly difficult for her, she never lost faith or patience. Indeed, she was the glue that held our family together during those terrible days. She told us that she takes comfort in the knowledge that one day, we will all be united with Papa in the Garden of Paradise, providing that we have faith and live good and beneficial lives.

Layla came to a stop and closed the journal. There were a few moments of eloquent silence.

"It's so touching," Zahra wiped away a tear. "And so hateful if one of his own crewmen murdered the Captain."

Adam said, "If there are nine *khanjars* in the museum, except for the one lying at the bottom of the bay, then we have to find out which of the crewmen donated the marked one. I wonder if Hud Tabibi noticed the mark and remembers who gave it. If he can tell us that, then the mystery is solved."

Layla said, "If not, then we have to find out all we can about the men's movements that night and try to figure out who could have been the murderer. We know of Nuh Tabibi and Qasim Ahmed so far. We'll have to ask Grandpa who the others were and see if we could speak to their families. We could pretend it's because of our interest in the voyages of the Yuhanza."

"Why don't we go back to the museum tomorrow?" Zaid said. "We could take another look at the dagger and check out the artifacts that we didn't get to see."

"I'll ask Grandpa," Adam promised. "For today, we will begin searching the walls for hidden nooks. Anyone has any ideas where to start?"

"Why not start in the great hall?" Zahra said. "It's the closest spot to where the Captain was murdered."

"What if anyone sees us searching?" Layla said.

"Two of us should search while two of us act as lookouts," Zaid said.

"Okay, let's get started right away," Adam said. "There's not a moment to lose."

Back at the house, they did a quick reconnaissance of where the rest of the household was. Maymun was still busy in the kitchen preparing lunch and the twins were in the living room playing with an assortment of cars, airplanes and blocks. Both Mr. Horani's and Luqman's cars were gone from the courtyard, which meant that they were out.

"Alright, Zaid and I will start searching the great hall," Adam said. "Layla, you keep by the front door in case Grandpa and Luqman returns. Zahra, you stay in the passageway and keep an eye on Maymun and the twins."

"If you see any movements in this direction, call out our names," Zaid said.

"Okay, we got it," Layla said.

It took the youths fifteen minutes to check the walls in the great hall and determine that nothing seemed out of place. Next, the youths acted as lookouts while the girls searched the dining room. Being a smaller space, it was not long before they too indicated that there was nothing to be found.

"Well, let's move on to the living room," Adam said.

"Hassan and Hakeem are still in there," Layla reminded him. "They're playing games on their iPads now."

"We'll search anyway," Adam said. "They probably won't pay any attention to us with their eyes glued to their iPads."

It was Adam and Zaid's turn to search while the girls kept watch in the passageway. The youths were so immersed in their task that it was a few minutes before they realized that Hassan and Hakeem were watching them with great interest.

"Why are you poking at the walls?" said Hakeem.

"Are you searching for something?" Hassan asked.

"Oh no, it's the Inquisition," Adam muttered. Aloud, he said, "Don't mind us, you guys. Go on with your games."

The twins ignored Adam's directive and continued to stare at them.

Finally, Hassan said solemnly, "Are you looking for the…," he halted abruptly when Hakeem gave him a sharp nudge.

"What have you two been up to?" Adam looked suspiciously from one identical face to the next.

Just then, Layla called out, "Adam, Zaid."

The next moment, they heard Maymun's voice in the passageway.

"There you children are," she said. "Can one of you take up a lunch tray for your aunt? She's got cramps in her legs, poor thing, and your grandfather is not back yet."

"I'll take it up," Adam offered.

The search for that morning came to an end as Adam took up Aunt Hafza's tray and they all prepared for lunch. After the meal, Layla and Zahra volunteered to pick up the tray from Aunty Hafza's room, using the opportunity to pay her a brief visit. Her room was cool and dim inside, the curtains drawn close together with just a slight gap in the center to let in some light. Through it, they caught a tiny glimpse of the blue waters of the bay. Aunt Hafza was reclining against the pillows, her eyes closed. She had eaten all of her baked fish, carrots and rice, they noted. As if sensing their presence, her eyes fluttered open.

"The pain is gone now," she murmured. "But so tired…so tired."

"Aunt Hafza, can we stay with you for a few minutes?" Layla asked, bending close to the old lady's ear.

"Yes, dear," Aunt Hafza replied. "It's so nice of you girls to come."

Zahra perched on a nearby chair and Layla, after sitting at the foot of the bed, leaned over and asked, "Aunt Hafza, can you tell us about the old days when the Captain was alive and went on his voyages?"

"Those were such happy days," Aunt Hafza said with a wistful smile. "We were young and carefree and had not yet learned of the trials and tribulations of this world. We were busy with our schooling, friends and books, but we missed Papa when he was away. When he came back, we were always overjoyed because he brought back the most beautiful gifts for us. He wouldn't give them to us right away but would hide them and then leave us a clue where to find them. Sometimes, he would write the clue during his voyage so he could hide it as soon as he came home and set us on the trail right away. We used to have a lot of fun searching for both the clue and gifts."

A thought occurred to Layla and she asked, "Aunt Hafza, did the Captain bring back any gifts for you from that last voyage?"

"If he did, the rebels probably took them because we found nothing. Or he might have hidden them with the diamond he told Yusuf about. Of course, we've never been able to find *that*."

Layla and Zahra shared a look. They both thought that Aunt Hafza would be very surprised to learn that they were looking for the Moon.

"What kind of gifts did the Captain usually bring for you?" Zahra asked.

"He usually brought jewelry for Mama and for us children whatever took his fancy."

"So the Moon was definitely for Great-Grandma Saffiyah," Layla remarked to Zahra. "He must have gone to that jewelry store in Ghassan to get her a gift when he ran into the fence's cousin."

"Ah, so you've heard the Shaykh's story too," Aunt Hafza remarked. "Yusuf told me all about it. What a strange twist of fate it was. Papa must have been so pleased when he brought home the diamond. But then," Aunt Hafza's smile faded and her lips trembled as if she was about to cry, "he was murdered by the rebels."

"You were all so young when it happened," Layla remarked sympathetically.

"Yes, we were. Yusuf and I were twelve and Hanifa was fourteen. We had a hard time accepting the fact that we would never see Papa again." Sounding drowsy now, she murmured, "I thought that getting lost in the secret tunnel was the worst thing that had happened to me, but Papa's death was so much more traumatic." With those words, Aunt Hafza became quiet, her eyes closed, and her chest rose and fell evenly as she slept.

Layla and Zahra shared a look of excitement at the mention of a secret tunnel. Picking up the empty tray, Layla signaled to Zahra and the two girls tiptoed out of the room.

Once they were outside, Layla whispered excitedly, "We have to tell the boys about this secret tunnel that Aunt Hafza mentioned. I wonder where it could be?"

The boys were drying the last few dishes in the kitchen when the girls came back with the empty tray. Layla quickly told them what Aunt Hafza had said.

"I've never heard Dad say anything about a secret tunnel," Adam said doubtfully as he opened a cupboard and deposited a stack of plates. "We should ask Aunt Hafza about it when she's awake."

"Let's go to her room before we go down to afternoon tea," Layla suggested. "She'll probably be awake then."

WHEN THE TEENAGERS stopped by Aunt Hafza's room later, to their surprise, she was not there.

"She must have gone downstairs," Zahra said.

"Well, let's go find her," Adam said.

They finally found Aunt Hafza out on the patio, wrapped up to her ears in a voluminous shawl. Afternoon tea had already been laid out on the white wicker table and she was drinking a mug of tea and munching on a slice of cake as she watched Hassan and Hakeem removing a message tied to Gul's leg.

"You boys are still giving Gul messages to carry?" Adam asked. "He will soon get tired of it."

"Well, we want to make sure he doesn't forget," Hakeem said.

"He likes doing it," Hassan said. "He thinks it's fun."

Layla turned her eyes heavenward. "He likes eating the reward you give him, that's why he thinks it's fun. Now, go and wash your hands and come get your tea and cake."

Obediently, Hassan and Hakeem ran into the kitchen and washed their hands before seating themselves at the table. After they had helped themselves to the refreshments, Adam inquired, "Are you feeling well now, Aunt Hafza?"

"Wheeling bell?" Aunt Hafza queried in puzzlement. "What do you mean?"

Adam sighed in frustration. Aunt Hafza had clearly forgotten to wear her hearing aid.

He bent down close to her ear and repeated the question.

"Oh yes, much better," Aunt Hafza nodded.

"Aunt Hafza," Layla leaned over, "when Zahra and I came to your room earlier, you mentioned about getting lost in a secret tunnel. Do you remember where it is?"

Hakeem suddenly choked on his tea and began coughing. Zahra thumped him on the back as she crooned, "You poor thing. Tea went down the wrong way, did it?"

Hassan said, "That's cause he was...," the boy came to a stop as his twin pinched him. Zaid, who was the only one to observe that furtive pinch, wondered what secret the two little imps were hiding.

"Aunt Hafza, do you remember where the secret tunnel is?" Adam prompted.

"Oh, it was over at Pasha's Playland," Aunt Hafza answered, to their disappointment. "I was a little girl back then. Mama and Papa took us there to spend the day. There was a maze called the Secret Tunnel that I wanted to explore but was not old enough. When no one was looking, I snuck in. I could not read the signs, so I got lost inside. I was in there for almost two hours before they found me. It was terrifying."

"What a frightening experience," Zahra commiserated. "I would have been hysterical if something like that had happened to me."

Aunt Hafza shivered and said, "There is a bit of chill in the air now. I think I shall return inside." Gathering up her shawl, she went indoors. Minutes later, they were joined by Mr. Horani who greeted them before sitting down in the chair Aunt Hafza had vacated.

"I came to tell you that I just got off the phone with Hud," Mr. Horani disclosed as he helped himself to a slice of cake. "He was very upset that his father chased you out of the museum yesterday. Apparently, the nurse dropped the old man off while she went to run an errand. Hud needed to go down to the lower level for a few minutes, so he locked the old man safely inside the office before leaving. It looked like Nuh had a sudden flash of memory for he remembered where the spare key was hidden and used it to open the door. He must have gone to look at his old ship when he saw you all. Hud sends his apologies and hopes that you will visit the museum again soon."

"As a matter of fact, we were thinking of going back tomorrow," Adam said eagerly. "There were lots of things we didn't get to see."

"That is fine. Luqman can drop you off and pick you up later."

Seeing that they had the perfect opportunity to question Mr.

Horani, Zaid said, "Grandpa, we were looking at the ceremonial *khanjars* at the museum. There were nine of them total. I guess the Tabibis got them from the crewmen?"

"Yes, Papa had ten of them made for himself and the crew. When the Tabibis started their collection for the museum, the *khanjars* were donated by the crewmen who were still alive and by the families of those who had passed away. The only one not there is Papa's, of course."

Layla, taking the cue from Zaid, asked, "Grandpa, besides Nuh and Basim's great-grandfather, did you know the rest of the crewmen?"

"Of course," Mr. Horani answered. "But the ones I knew best were the Faithful Five."

"The Faithful Five?" Adam looked quizzically at his grandfather.

"They were the men who sailed on all the voyages of the Yuhanza. They had been closest in affection as well as age to Papa. Come wind, storm or gale, they were ever at his side. That's why Papa nicknamed them the Faithful Five."

"Who were they?" Zahra asked.

"First was Nuh Tabibi, then Qasim Ahmed, Basim's great-grandfather. You wouldn't know the others by their names, but they were Maymun, Luqman and Abbas's fathers."

"Wow, I didn't know that their fathers were crewmen on the Yuhanza too," Layla said in surprise.

"They were. Very good and loyal men they were too. In fact, all nine of the crewmen were like brothers to Papa."

Adam said, "Then it's strange that out of nine, not one of them knew that the Captain had brought back a diamond."

Looking a trifle surprised at the comment, Mr. Horani revealed, "All nine of them didn't go on that last voyage."

"So who went?" Zaid asked with interest.

"Because of the unrest caused by the rebels, my father set sail on that voyage with only the Faithful Five."

Chapter Eleven

The Marked Dagger

"I STILL CAN'T GET over the fact that only the Faithful Five sailed on that last voyage," Layla remarked glumly the next morning as they entered the courtyard of the Mariner's Museum.

"Yeah, it's hard to believe that one of the Captain's closest friends could have killed him," Adam said. "Well, at least it narrows down the list of suspects. I can't wait to find out if Hud Tabibi knows who gave that marked dagger."

"Let's speak to him after we look at the daggers and exhibits," Layla suggested.

As they crossed the courtyard and headed to the entrance of the museum, Zaid noted that unlike their last visit, there were several cars parked there. *I guess we are not going to have the place to ourselves today,* he thought.

Once more in the museum, they were greeted by a very flustered Hud, who apologized profusely to them and seemed gratified that they were visiting the museum again.

"It's okay, Mr. Tabibi," Layla said kindly. "We know your father is very ill."

"Please call me Hud," he said. "There's no need to stand on ceremony. Well, go ahead then," he waved a hand. "You know the way."

They passed by the vast hall where several visitors were viewing the exhibits. To their relief, there was no one in the chamber where the model of the Yuhanza and her artifacts were displayed. Gathering around the glass case, they gazed at the marked dagger. The letter gouged out on the blade was an unmistakable K. To leave no room for doubts, they looked again at the inscripted names of the crewmen on the metal plate.

"Well, we have our answer," Zahra said finally. "None of the crewmen's names began with a K. It *was* the Captain's dagger."

"Beyond a shadow of doubt," Layla agreed.

When they returned to the reception area twenty minutes later, they found the visitors gone and Hud bent over some ledgers in his glass-walled office. Adam knocked politely on the reception desk and the curator emerged. "Finished?" he asked.

Adam replied, "Yes, it was very interesting looking at all the different artifacts from the Yuhanza. We noticed that one of the *khanjars* had a mark on the blade that looked like an English K. Did you ever notice it and which crewman donated that one?"

"A mark that looked like an English K, you say?" Hud's forehead puckered in thought. "I might have seen it when it came in or noticed it when I was examining the displays but I'm afraid there's no way of knowing who gave that one. Perhaps my father would have been able to tell you. The artifacts from the Yuhanza were of special interest to him as you can imagine."

The teenagers tried their best to hide their disappointment.

"Are there times when your father's memory comes back?" Zaid asked.

"Well, yes. But those spells don't last for long."

"Do you think we can visit him one day when it's back?" Adam asked. "We'd love to hear about his voyages on the Yuhanza."

"I guess that could be arranged. But if he starts getting agitated, you'll have to leave for your own safety."

"Sure," Adam nodded. "We understand."

"I'll let his nurse give you a call then. What number can she reach you at?"

"Tell her to call the home number and ask for us," Adam answered.

Layla took out a small, purple spiral notepad and matching purple pen. "Hud, can you tell us how to get to your house? We'll use our bikes to ride over."

After Hud had gone over the directions and Layla had written them in her notepad, Zahra said, "Hud, you must have heard a lot of stories from your father."

Hud smiled. "Well, I've come from several generations of sailors, so I've heard my fair share of stories. Like the time my grandfather nearly got eaten by cannibals. Or the time when the men on my great-grandfather's ship turned green from eating a certain fruit on a tropical island. On one of the voyages of the Yuhanza, the men saw a lamp which the natives claimed was Aladdin's Lamp. Of course, the *jinn* was long gone by then," he chuckled. "Then there was the Mask of Beauty. Legend had it that whoever wore the Mask for an entire night would regain their youthful looks by morning."

"And did it work?" Zahra asked, fascinated.

"No one knew," the curator chuckled again. "It had such a horrible smell that no one wanted it on their face for a minute, much less an entire night."

"Did anyone ever find a buried treasure?" Adam asked.

"Ah! No sailor is worth his salt if he doesn't find buried treasure. I heard that my great-great uncle found some jewels hidden in a cave in Africa. But alas, he was chased off by headhunters. Then there was my grandfather's cousin who dug up what he thought was an ordinary piece of pottery in India.

It turned out to be a sacred relic which had been stolen from a *rajah*, an Indian king. He was almost thrown into jail for that."

Zaid finally asked the question he had been eager to ask. "Hud, did your father ever tell you about the Night of Catastrophe?"

Hud sighed. "Yes, when I was younger. He had been guarding the cargo that night on the Yuhanza when the rebels swarmed on board. He had to jump into the water to save his life. He was never the same afterwards."

"Yes, we heard Grandpa's story of what happened that night," Layla said. Boldy, she added, "He told us that before the Captain died, he spoke of a diamond he had hidden. Grandpa searched but could not find it. Did you ever hear that story?"

Hud's eyes flickered in surprise. "I've never heard that story. Well, if you'll excuse me," he said apologetically as he glanced at the clock on the wall, "I have a backlog of work to catch up on before I go to lunch." Taking the hint, the teenagers thanked him politely and left.

"So, what do you think?" Adam asked once they were outside. "Could his father have been the one who murdered the Captain? And is Hud protecting him?"

"Well, his father could have gone after the Captain that night instead of guarding the ship," Zaid speculated. "And Hud seemed in a hurry for us to leave after Layla asked about the diamond. But of course, that's not much to go on."

Layla said, "I think we need to speak to Nuh himself if his memory comes back. He's the only remaining Faithful Five. I'm sure he'll be able to tell us a lot of things."

"If Hud is protecting his father, we probably won't get the chance," Zahra said.

THEIR PLAN UPON leaving the museum was to explore the area a bit, have lunch at a nearby restaurant, and then wait outside the museum for Luqman's return at two o'clock. The teenagers spent an enjoyable hour browsing the shops in the area before moving on to the restaurant, where they ordered pizza, fried chicken with fries and mint lemonade.

As they ate, Layla said, "You know where I'd like to go next?"

"Where?" Zahra asked.

"Pasha's Playland," Layla said as she bit into her crispy fried chicken. "I'm curious to see what it's like. Especially the secret tunnel that Aunt Hafza got lost in."

"Yeah, that's a good idea," Adam endorsed. "We're in need of some fun and relaxation. I say we go tomorrow. Maybe Grandpa or Luqman can take us. The playland is miles away so we can't bike over."

"Why don't we ask Basim to go with us," Zaid suggested. "Then the Ahmeds' chauffeur can take us all."

"Basim would love that, I'm sure," Zahra said as she sipped her lemonade.

"When we get home, I'll ask Grandpa and then call Basim," Adam promised.

Upon their return home, permission was sought from Mr. Horani and promptly given for their visit to the playland. Adam then called Basim, who professed himself delighted at the prospect of accompanying them. He promised to come with the chauffeur at nine the next morning.

TIRED AFTER THEIR day's outing, Zaid fell asleep minutes after his head hit the pillow that night. He awoke much later as a sound gradually permeated his dreams. From his open window, he heard the unmistakable tone of an engine. Rubbing his bleary eyes, he sluggishly got out of bed and looked out into the bay. In the faint moonlight he saw the small, unlit vessel gliding towards the cove. Remembering Adam's request, he hurried over to the other boy's room, eager to let him see the boat for himself.

"Adam," he cried, shaking his friend's shoulder. "Wake up."

"What is it?" Adam opened his eyes and blinked up at Zaid.

"It's the boat," Zaid replied. "It's coming into the cove."

Adam bolted upright, slid off the bed and followed Zaid. The two boys stood in the dark room and gazed out the window. The boat was angling its way into the cove, the sound of its engine vibrating faintly in the silence. It approached the cliffs, melded with the darkness there and vanished from sight and hearing. The boys waited for several minutes but the boat did not reappear.

"You're right," Adam remarked. "It's very strange."

"I think they're keeping watch for the pirates," Zaid declared. "I'm sure we'll hear tomorrow of another ship being plundered."

Chapter Twelve

Pasha's Playland

T HE NEXT MORNING, to Zaid's consternation, there was no news of the pirates attacking any ship.

"I guess I let my imagination run away with me," he told Adam ruefully.

"All the same, it's kind of weird. Tell you what," Adam looked at Zaid with a gleam in his eyes, "the next time you hear that boat come in, we'll go out to the bluffs to see what's going on."

"Oh, that would be so daring," Zaid was thrilled at the thought of such an adventure.

"Yeah, it will be," Adam's eyes shone with anticipation. "As long as we're not caught in the act, of course."

Promptly at nine, Basim arrived with Nassif, the chauffeur, in tow, and the teenagers and twins bounded out to the courtyard. They passed by Luqman, who was bent over the open hood of his Honda pickup truck.

"Something wrong?" Zaid stopped to inquire.

"It's not starting," Luqman said in frustration. "I'll have to get it towed to the mechanic. Well, you all have a good time at the playland."

They piled into the limousine and were soon speeding down the corniche on the way to the playland. Conversation flowed merrily all around and soon they came within sight of their destination. Pasha's Playland nestled on acres of land surrounding Lake Rawa. Zaid could see the jumbo roller coasters reaching up towards the skies and the colorful cable cars in the shape of birds moving in slow motion above. Nassif dropped them off at the entrance, and after promising to pick them up at the appointed time, he drove off. Adam paid their entry fee with the wad of bills his grandfather had given him and they sauntered inside, armed with site maps of the playland.

"I don't see the Secret Tunnel," Layla said after scanning the map.

"Oh, that? It was closed years ago," Basim said. "Too many children were wandering inside and getting lost."

"That's what happened to Aunt Hafza," Zahra exclaimed.

The playland was a beehive of activity as people moved back and forth in steady streams, their voices and laughter mingling with the exotic strains of sounds issuing from colorful tents and musical rides. At Basim's recommendation, the first ride they decided to go on was The Spinning Star. Unfortunately, due to the age restriction, the twins could not join them. Basim sportingly agreed to chaperone them on the Carousel of Camels.

There was a long line of people waiting for The Spinning Star. At last, their turn came, and they were ushered into the enclosure to board the ride. The Spinning Star was a monstrous circle-shaped carriage with a domed roof, blue walls and red seats spaced about arm-length apart. The teenagers chose their seats, which were resting on a crisscrossing network of railway-like tracks, and buckled their seat belts in readiness. When all the seats had been filled, the door closed, and the ride began.

With a clank and a sputter, the seats began orbiting around

each other at top speed. The riders cried out in excitement as they moved back and forth and left to right. Whenever it seemed that two seats would collide, they would veer off from each other at the last possible moment. To add to the thrill of the ride, some seats were sprinkled with droplets of cool water, causing the riders to shriek out in surprise. The seats went through several patterns of movement before they slowed down and returned to their original positions, allowing their laughing riders to get off.

"That was great," Zahra said.

"You can say that again," Layla agreed.

They found Basim and the twins waiting for them at the exit.

"So, how was it?" Basim asked.

"It was awesome," Adam declared.

"I knew you'd like it," Basim nodded in satisfaction. "Do you want to get some ice cream now or later?"

"Ah, the ice cream which you *love* so much," Adam waggled his eyebrows up and down, making Basim and the others chuckle. "Definitely now."

It was while they were eating their ice cream cones that Zaid felt a prickling sensation at the back of his neck, as if eyes were boring into him. He glanced around, but they were surrounded by so many people that it was hard to pinpoint anyone in particular. After they had finished their cones, Basim suggested they go on the Perilous Passage Adventure ride next. To get there, they had to take the Eagle Express, one of the bird-shaped cable cars Zaid had noticed on their approach to the playland.

They boarded the Eagle Express at the Treetop One station. After the car was filled, it took off with a great whoosh, gliding smoothly along its cable. It was an exhilarating experience being suspended in the air, looking down at the colorful tents and rides below. At the Treetop Two station, some riders got off and others came on. Finally, the teenagers and twins got off at the Treetop Three station and followed Basim to the next ride. It was in a gigantic igloo-like structure in a cordoned-off corner of the lake.

They waited in line in a tunnel-like building with a roof at the top. Zaid was glad that they were in the shade, since it afforded them protection from the fierce rays of the sun. Ten minutes later, it was their turn to disappear into the igloo-like building. Inside, Zaid saw that they stood on a jetty, brightly lit all around. The roof of the igloo rose far above, giving the impression of being in a gigantic bubble. They boarded an enormous barge, outfitted with seats in assorted colors which contained about thirty people at a time.

The captain introduced himself and his crew of two, and gave a few precautionary instructions before the boat took off at a brisk pace down the artificially lit waters. Zaid was just beginning to enjoy himself when the captain warned that there was stormy weather ahead. The waters around them began to roil, causing the boat to tip dangerously from side to side. Passengers began to squeal as thunder boomed, lightning flashed, and a light sprinkling of rain began to fall. The boat continued swaying dangerously in the churning waters, tipping too much to one side until water gushed in to puddle at their feet.

Passengers began squealing again and the captain urgently ordered his crew to bail water. Several minutes later, the storm came to an end and the boat emerged into calm waters. But not for long. The Captain warned that a squall was on the way. Soon, they were caught up in the midst of a powerful wind that battered at the boat and blasted cold air in their faces. The wind whistled and howled eerily, sweeping the vessel in a back-and-forth motion. Zaid was thoroughly enjoying himself by the time the squall ended. Next, the Captain announced that they were going to encounter foggy conditions ahead. No sooner had he spoken when they were enveloped by a thick cloud of mist that swirled and writhed around them, reducing visibility to nil.

The passengers on the Perilous Passage Adventure ride were

nearly sucked into a whirlpool and caught in the jaws of a large sea monster before the journey of the beleaguered boat came to an end. By the time the teenagers and twins emerged from the ride, they decided that it was *the* most thrilling boat ride they had ever been on.

Since the Grotto of Voices Experience was in the same vicinity, they decided to try that out next.

"The twins are under the age limit," Basim told them. "I can take them to the Shifting Sands Safari in the meantime. The Grotto is kind of creepy," he wrinkled his nose. "Weird voices and all that stuff."

"Be warned," Layla spoke with a thick, exaggerated accent. *"Your lives are in danger. You must leave Bayan Bay at once."* The others chuckled at her funny impression of a fortune teller.

While heading to the Grotto, Zaid again felt the sensation of eyes on him but was unable to find any particular pair of eyes turned their way. The Grotto of Voices was located underground via a winding ramp. At the end of the ramp was a wooden, barn-like structure with a pair of steel doors. Above it was a sign that read, *The Grotto of Voices Experience.* To the left was an enclosed glass booth where an operator sat and to the right, several large green circles on the ground. Within each circle, was written in white letters, *Four to a Circle.* The two circles ahead of them were occupied, so the teenagers stood in the third circle as they awaited their turn.

Finally, they were in the foremost circle. The door of the Grotto slid open and the group that had been ahead of them streamed out. The operator's voice came through a speaker above them, "Next group, please enter." The teenagers hurried forward through the doors, which closed smoothly behind them. They found themselves in a dimly lit space that looked like an underground cave. Great hunks of rock with life-like flora rose before them, with a narrow, winding path in the middle. On the roof above, strange signs and symbols winked on and off, like weird eyes peering down at them. They began to walk single-file down the pathway, not knowing what to expect.

There came a sibilant whisper to their left and Zahra gave a muffled shriek as a slimy snake reared up from between the rocks, its red eyes gleaming in the dark. *"You are our prisoners now,"* it hissed. *"There is no escape."*

"Goodness," Layla giggled nervously. "It looks so real."

All around them they heard indistinct whispers as burning red and green eyes peered at them in the dark. As they passed under a skeletal tree, a raucous laugh rang out as long vines reached out towards them, twisting and turning as if to trap them. One by one, they dodged the vines and continued into the grotto. On a shelf, they saw a pile of precious stones guarded by a gigantic black scorpion that whispered menacingly, *"Touch my treasure and you will feel my stinnnng."*

Soon, they came to a stream with colorful rocks around it. The water began to foam, and several piranhas sprang to the surface, their long, sharp teeth bared hideously. *"We are huuuuuugry,"* they snarled. *"All we need is a bite to eaaaaat."*

"Ooh," Zahra gasped. "They look so scary."

As they proceeded down the path, Zaid screeched as a blood-red claw came out of a crevice and a deep voice growled, *"I will riiiiiiiiip you to shreds and scatter your bones to the winnnnnd."*

"This is so cool," Adam gave a jittery laugh. "Our feet probably trigger mechanisms underground to operate these contraptions."

Further into the cave they walked until they came to a swampy parcel of ground, in the middle of which was a large pool filled with thick, murky water. Around it was tall, waving reeds from which came the humming of insects and the croaking of frogs. There was a loud gulping sound and bubbles started to pop up on the surface of the pool. As they stared with wide eyes, a large dark shape began to rise up slowly.

There was a crackling sound from the overhead speaker, followed by a guttural snarl. Then a rasping voice said, *"Be warned. Your lives are in danger. Stop looking for the Moon and leave Bayan Bay at once!"*

The sinister warning was followed by a cacophony of wails, howls and maniacal laughter that rose to a crescendo. Stunned, the teenagers put their hands over their ears as the very air vibrated around them. Zaid felt the blood curdle in his veins as he was overtaken by a sensation of panic. The dark shape rising out of the water, coupled with the eerie echoing sounds were too much for Zahra. With a shrill scream, she turned back on the pathway and ran frantically to the door. She began to pound on it as she yelled hysterically, "Let us out, let us out."

The others ran after her and to their relief, the noise stopped abruptly. Moments later, the door opened, and the alarmed face of the operator appeared.

"Are you all right?" he asked.

"No, we're not," Zaid replied. "Someone tried to scare us in there."

"I'm sorry," the operator looked agitated. "I shouldn't have believed that man."

"What man?" Layla demanded.

"A man who said he was your uncle. He told me that he wanted to give you some good news while you were in the Grotto. We get requests like that all the time and our customers are usually happy. So I allowed him into my booth and showed him what to do. I then made a quick trip to the restroom, telling him to wait until I got back. When I returned, he was gone but I saw that he had turned on all the audios to run at the same time. When I took it off, I heard you hitting on the door."

"He was no uncle of ours," Adam said in disgust. "What did he look like?"

"Well, he was wearing a robe with head covering and dark sunshades. He had a slight beard, I think. I really didn't take much notice of what he looked like," the operator said apologetically.

"That description fits half of the men here," Layla said.

"I'm really sorry about this," the operator said abjectly. "You can go back to the Grotto if you wish. I promise, you'll enjoy it this time."

Zaid looked at Zahra's strained face and said hastily, "No, that's not necessary. You already have two groups waiting," he pointed to the green circles where several young people had been watching the proceedings with wide eyes.

As the operator strode hurriedly over to his booth, the teenagers made their way out of the Grotto and up the ramp.

"Someone was listening to us," Layla said indignantly. "He repeated the exact words I said earlier."

"You know, I had a feeling a couple of times that we were being watched," Zaid said. "It must have been our fake uncle."

"It must have been Mir," Adam said the next day in Moss Haven. "All he had to do was put on headgear and sunglasses to become incognito."

"If it was him, he sure spoiled a wonderful day," Layla said.

"I'm sorry I behaved like such a baby," Zahra said in a small voice.

"Those sounds were enough to drive anyone crazy," Zaid said. "It was a cruel thing to do."

"All that theatrics is not going to scare us away," Adam declared. "Stop looking for the Moon and leave Bayan Bay? Yeah, right," he snorted disdainfully.

"So, what's next on the agenda?" Layla asked.

"We will continue our search of the rooms on the first floor,"

Adam said. "We can try to finish the laundry room, store room and the prayer room this morning."

As they trudged back to the house, the teenagers came to a surprised standstill as they passed by Abbas's cottage. The object of their ire was sitting on a chair reading outside, his left leg propped up on a stool. Ordinarily, this would have been nothing remarkable. But what made them stop and stare was the fact that the propped-up leg was wrapped from knee to ankle in a thick bandage.

Mir turned their way and caught them gawking. "What are you doing here?" he growled.

"Oh, just taking a stroll," Adam replied breezily. Gesturing to Mir's bandage, he asked with a touch of sarcasm, "What happened? Did you run into someone *again*?"

"Don't be an impertinent young pup," Mir scowled at him.

Abbas emerged from the cottage and greeted them. "Visiting the patient?"

"We just saw him as we were passing by," Zaid said. "What happened?"

Uncle and nephew exchanged a quick look before Abbas, looking distinctly uncomfortable, replied, "He fell yesterday and cut his shin."

After politely wishing Mir a speedy recovery, they continued on their way.

"He seems to be very accident-prone, our Mir," Layla remarked when they were out of earshot.

"At least he can't blame that lamer on me," Adam said smugly.

Zaid said, "Well, I guess he couldn't have been our fake uncle at the playland if he was off injuring his leg yesterday."

"I wouldn't be too sure of that," Adam was quick to negate that thought. "He might have injured it after coming back from the playland."

Upon returning to the house, they began their search at

once. Zaid and Zahra searched the laundry room and store room while Adam and Layla kept watch. Then Adam and Layla searched the prayer room while Zaid and Zahra kept watch. As with the other areas, nothing was to be found.

"Well, it's not surprising that we've found nothing so far," Layla said. "Grandpa and Dad must have already covered these areas."

"Zaid and I will search the kitchen tonight after everyone goes to bed," Adam said. "We don't have to worry about Maymun and Luqman's quarters since that wing was a new addition to the house."

THAT NIGHT, AFTER the rest of the household had gone to sleep, the two youths crept down to the kitchen to begin their search. Zaid took the first stint while Adam kept watch in the passageway outside. In the midst of Zaid's search, Adam came hurriedly into the kitchen.

"Someone's coming," he hissed, switching off the light. "Quick, under the table." They were not a moment too soon, for they heard the heavy tread of footsteps coming into the kitchen and the light was switched on again. The youths huddled under the table, glad that the vinyl tablecloth shielded them from view. They heard liquid being poured into a glass and then the sound of drinking. After that came a satisfied grunt, then the sound of a utensil being placed in the sink. Zaid put his head close to the ground and peered up. He recognized Luqman's form moments before the handyman turned off the light and the sound of his footsteps receded in the passageway.

The youths waited a few minutes before emerging from their hiding place.

"I'll search now," Adam said. "You can keep watch."

As Zaid poked his head out into the passageway, he saw

a thin beam of light flash out from the living room. The next moment it disappeared, and all was dark again. Mystified, he whispered to Adam, "I saw a light in the living room just now, but it's gone."

"It must be Luqman," Adam whispered back. "Let's go before he catches us. We'll have to search another time."

Quietly, they crept along the dark passageway. As they passed by the living room, they caught a glimpse of a figure aiming a flashlight at the wall to the far left. Zaid smothered a gasp as he followed Adam noiselessly into the great hall and up the stairs.

"Luqman's the one searching for the Moon," Adam said indignantly once they were back in the turret. "He must have been our fake uncle from the Grotto."

"Wait a minute," Zaid cautioned. "He couldn't have gone to the playland yesterday."

"Why not?" Adam demanded hotly.

"Because his pickup truck wasn't working, and he had it towed to the mechanic. Grandpa took him after lunch today to pick it up, remember?"

The fight went out of Adam like air deflating from a balloon. "You're right. But Luqman sure *is* looking for the Moon from the look of things. He may be searching on his own or is in league with Abbas and Mir."

"It certainly seems that way."

"Meeting. First thing in the morning," Adam said, covering a yawn.

Chapter Thirteen

The Old Sailor

THE NEXT MORNING, Zaid had a quick conversation with Maymun before joining the others in Moss Haven. Adam told the girls what had transpired last night and predictably, they were shocked to learn that Luqman was searching for the Moon.

"Maybe Maymun doesn't know about it," Zahra said unhappily. Zaid understood how his sister felt. They had become rather fond of the housekeeper and were reluctant to think that she could be part and parcel of the devious scheme. And Zaid had just gotten some information from her that could further incriminate her husband.

Layla said, "If Luqman is searching for the Moon, then it must have been him at the Grotto of Voices."

"No, his car was at the repair shop," Adam said. "It had to be Mir."

"Actually, I just found out that Luqman *could* have gone to the playland," Zaid said.

"I thought you said he couldn't," Adam protested.

"Well, I had a quick talk with Maymun before I came here

and found out that Luqman borrowed Grandpa's van yesterday to go for a doctor's appointment and run several errands."

"Well, *I* spoke to Abbas before we came here," Adam said rather smugly, "and found out that Mir used the Land Rover yesterday and didn't get back until the afternoon. Which means that he *could* have gone to the playland and then cut his foot afterwards. Abbas still didn't give any details of how *that* happened. I had the feeling that he was hiding something."

"So who's looking for the Moon?" Zahra asked in confusion. "Is it Luqman or is it Mir and Abbas?"

"I think all of them are," Adam said. "They may be in league or working separately."

Through the open door, they heard the crunching of gravel and became quiet as they looked at one another. Zaid rose and went to the door just as Abbas came lumbering up.

"Thought you'd be here," he said in his deep voice. "Maymun was looking for you. She said to tell you that Nuh Tabibi's nurse called, asking to speak to you urgently."

"Okay, thanks Abbas," Adam said. "We'll be right there."

After the gardener shuffled away, Layla said excitedly, "Maybe Nuh's memory is back. And Hud has kept his promise. I had totally given up hope of that."

"Well, we shall soon find out," Zaid said. "The two crucial things we have to ask Nuh about are the dagger and the diamond. *If* he remembers about them and is willing to tell us, of course."

Back at the house, Maymun handed Adam the nurse's phone number. Picking up the cordless phone in the kitchen and turning on the speaker, he dialed the number. The nurse, who seemed a chatty woman, confirmed that Nuh was presently in possession of his faculties and they should come right away. She also invited them to stay for lunch, which Zaid thought was very nice.

"We'll be there as soon as we can," Adam promised.

"Going to visit the old salt, eh?" Maymun looked up from the potatoes she was peeling, her eyes speculative.

"Yes," Adam replied. "Can you let Grandpa know? I don't want to disturb him."

"Of course. And don't worry, I'll see to the little ones. You all have a nice time."

"Thank you, Maymun," Layla said gratefully, feeling awful for even thinking that the good-natured woman could be involved in any underhanded scheme.

After getting their bikes from the shed, Layla fished out her little purple notepad with the directions to the Tabibis' house and studied it. "It seems clear enough. We go in the same direction that we went for the picnic but keep going until we come to a fig orchard. Take the shortcut through it and go past some houses until we come out onto a road. Follow the road, and it's the first house we see."

They set off on their bikes at a brisk clip and soon approached the fig orchard, which was filled with tightly packed trees laden with ripening figs on the verge of turning purple. Getting off their bikes, they pushed them along under the shady trees as they listened to the birdcalls and the buzzing of fig wasps. Clearing the orchard, they saw a cluster of small, dilapidated villas ahead of them. A group of young boys were playing with a ball in a little clearing, talking and laughing in shrill, high-pitched voices. When they saw the newcomers, they stopped and stared at them, their ball lying unheeded on the ground.

"We have to look for a road here," Layla consulted her purple notepad. "Let's ask one of those little boys. It will be faster."

Adam beckoned to them and a skinny little boy wearing oversized clothes came forward.

"Hello, little one," Adam said to him. "What's your name?

"Miqdad," the boy smiled, showing a gap in his front teeth.

"Miqdad, can you show us where the road is?" Adam requested. As he reached into his pocket, Zaid laid a restraining hand on his friend's arm and said in an undertone, "If you give him something, all the others will come running for their share too."

Adam quickly pulled his hand out of his pocket and repeated his request. Miqdad, who had witnessed the byplay, said shrewdly, "I don't know where the road is."

"You sly little rascal," Zaid said in exasperation. "You know very well where it is."

"Okay, here's some toffee," Adam said, pulling out a small packet of brown squares. "Now tell us where the road is."

Miqdad looked at the toffees and remained silent, his eyes eloquent with disdain at the measly offering.

"Here's some candy," Zahra held out several.

"And a bar of chocolate," Layla offered.

Miqdad looked pointedly at Zaid next. Rolling his eyes, Zaid dug into his pocket and pulled out several gums. Handing them to the little rascal, he said, "Now will you tell us where the road is?"

Miqdad quickly grabbed all the booty before pointing to the left. "The road is there."

"You drive a hard bargain, Miqdad," Adam said ruefully, ruffling the boy's hair.

Miqdad smiled shyly and sped away.

"He'll make a good businessman someday, *insha'Allah*," Zaid said and they all laughed.

They set off down the road, pedaling vigorously to make up for lost time. As they rounded a curve in the coastline, they spied an attractive villa almost hidden among almond and pomegranate trees. They rode down the curving driveway towards the courtyard and after parking their bikes they walked up to the front door. Zaid rang the doorbell and moments later, the door opened and a heavyset woman wearing glasses looked out. The teenagers exchanged greetings with her and waited politely to be invited in.

"Come in, come in," she gestured to them, opening the door wider.

When they were inside she studied them through the thick lens of her glasses. "I'm Salma, Nuh's nurse. I hope you didn't have any trouble finding the place."

"One of the little fellows across from the orchard helped us," Adam told her.

"Those little ragamuffins?" Salma sniffed. "I hope you didn't give them money. It just encourages them to beg."

"Um…just candy," Adam replied.

"Hmph," Salma snorted. "I suppose that's fair enough. You do have the look of your father," she said, appraising Adam intently. "My daughter Rawan said you did. Which one is your sister?" After subjecting Layla to an intense scrutiny, which made the girl squirm a bit, Salma said, "You remind me of your Great-Aunt Hanifa. You have the same green eyes with pointed chin and dimples. She and my oldest sister Najah had been best friends. Where has the time gone?" she asked of no one in particular. "Seems like only the other day my Rawan and your father were at school together."

"Your daughter was at school with my father?" Adam asked.

"Oh, yes. It was she who told me you children were here. She saw you at the library. She's the librarian there."

"We've met her," Adam replied, sharing a knowing look with Zaid.

"You'd better go in and talk to Nuh then," Salma pointed to a closed door. "Right pleased he was to hear you were coming. He hasn't been himself for a long time. Don't know how long that's going to last. Let me know if he starts getting agitated. Hud told me what happened at the museum. Shocked to hear that, I was," she clucked. "I'll have lunch waiting for you when you're done."

"Thank you," Layla said as they headed to the door.

The door opened into a cozy sitting area with a panoramic

view of the bay visible from the open windows at the back. Nuh was lying in a recliner, his chest rising and falling gently as he dozed. At the sound of the door opening, his eyes opened, and he stared at them before getting slowly to his feet. There was no sign of recognition in his eyes as greetings were exchanged. Not that Zaid had expected to see any. The old man had been in the grips of dementia when he had chased them out of the museum and was unlikely to remember that episode.

"Sit down, sit down," Nuh said in a high, thin voice as he sat back in the recliner and gestured to several sofas. "You are all Yusuf's grandchildren?" he squinted up at them.

When Adam indicated himself and Layla, the old man stared at them for a long moment.

"Rafiq's great-grandchildren," his voice trembled with a wealth of emotion, as tears filled his eyes. "It's such an honor to meet you."

"Mr. Tabibi," Adam said tentatively, "it's very kind of you to see us."

"Oh, please call me Nuh. How can I help you?"

"We've come to ask you about the last voyage of the Yuhanza," Zaid said. "Do you remember anything about it?"

"The last voyage of the Yuhanza," the old man uttered in a quavering voice. "How could I forget it? It was the last time I sailed with my dear friend. We were just a handful and had to work extra hard, but we made it by the grace of Allah."

"Yes, Grandpa told us that only the Faithful Five and the Captain sailed on that last voyage," Layla remarked.

Nuh frowned as if in thought. Then he shook his head and said, "No, that's not right."

"What's not right, Nuh?" Zaid asked.

"It wasn't just the Faithful Five and the Captain who sailed on that voyage. There was another crewman who came with us."

Chapter Fourteen

Last Voyage of the Yuhanza

THE TEENAGERS SHARED a look of surprise after Nuh's revelation.

"Are you sure, Nuh?" Adam asked. "Grandpa told us it was just the Faithful Five and the Captain."

"Well, it wasn't so," the old man replied testily. "Rafiq and I were at the wharf getting set for the voyage when Tahir Usmani, one of the regular crewmen who had opted out of that voyage, came and begged us to take his son Iyad along. He said that Iyad's life was in danger and he must leave Bayan Bay at once. Rafiq was moved by Tahir's plea and agreed without a moment's hesitation. So Tahir gave over his ship's bag and *khanjar* to his son and that's how Iyad came to be the sixth crewman."

"You're sure this was the last voyage of the Yuhanza, Nuh?" Adam asked, reluctant to trust the old man's memory when his grandfather had told them otherwise.

"Yes, yes," Nuh replied impatiently. "It most certainly was. Iyad was no sailor but we *were* shorthanded, so no one questioned his presence there. Only Rafiq and I knew the reason why. We kept silent out of consideration for Tahir."

Adam looked meaningfully at the others. If Nuh's memory

was correct, then that meant another suspect who might have murdered the Captain.

"Tell us about Iyad," Zaid urged.

"Oh, he was quite a disagreeable man," the old man wrinkled his face in distaste. "Always bad-tempered and ready to use his fists. He was Tahir's only son and had two older sisters who coddled and spoiled him. He was married for several years until the poor woman took their daughter and fled back to her people up north. We all felt sorry for Tahir. He was getting on in years and instead of his son taking care of him, he was taking care of his son."

"But why was Iyad's life in danger?" Zahra asked.

"We never knew. Tahir would not tell us and we didn't press him."

"Is Iyad still alive?" Layla asked.

"We never saw hide nor hair of him again after we docked that night. Whoever was after him most likely killed him and buried his body someplace. Poor Tahir was a broken man afterwards. He used to wander around the docks at night looking for his son. Alas, he became almost like a lunatic before he too disappeared one night."

"Tahir disappeared too?" Zahra exclaimed.

"Yes. It must have been about three months after the Night of Catastrophe. Although they searched and searched for him, his body was never found. Everyone thought he must have fallen over the docks in the night and his body washed out into the Bayan Strait."

"So not even Iyad's mother and sisters knew who was after him?" Layla asked.

"I don't think they knew. Otherwise they would have talked, I'm sure. Only Tahir knew and *his* lips were sealed."

Finally, Zaid said, "Nuh, at the museum we saw the display of *khanjars* from the crew of the Yuhanza. One of them had a mark on the blade that looked like an English K. Do you remember seeing that one and who gave it?"

They all waited with bated breath for Nuh's answer.

"I'm afraid I don't recall seeing any mark. My eyesight started to go bad a long time ago and wearing glasses was just a nuisance. The mark wouldn't have mattered to me anyhow. The most important thing was that we had all nine of the remaining *khanjars,* except for Rafiq's, of course."

"Wait a moment," Adam frowned. "If the Captain's *khanjar* is at the bottom of the bay and Iyad disappeared on the Night of Catastrophe, then there should have been only eight *khanjars* at the museum, not nine."

"Aye, and it would have been so if Iyad's bag had not been found outside his house the next morning. Whoever must have killed him did it right outside his house. The *khanjar* and his personal belongings were still inside the bag, so we gave them all to Tahir. When we were collecting stuff for the museum, his granddaughter sent us the *khanjar.*"

"What a sad tale of father and son," Layla said. "It's a mystery that no one learned who was after Iyad."

"The only person who might have known was Jafar Ambreen. He and Iyad had been best friends."

"Jafar Ambreen?" Adam queried. "Was he related to the present day Ambreens living here in Bayan Bay?"

"Jafar Ambreen was Faruq Ambreen's father."

"Faruq Ambreen," Zahra repeated the name. "Isn't he the richest man in Bayan Bay? And wasn't he one of the men who came to *Jumu'ah* in that white limousine?"

"Yes," Zaid nodded as he remembered the look of animosity on the man's face. "That's him."

"The Ambreens," Nuh said, "were much poorer in the old days and did not have a smidgen of the wealth that they have today. If Jafar Ambreen had knowledge of what happened to Iyad, he might have passed it on to his son Faruq."

Moving on with the questions, Adam asked. "Nuh, what ports did you sail to on that last voyage?"

"Well, now," Nuh's forehead wrinkled as he searched his memory. "We were going to Yemen, so our direction was straightforward. From the Gulf, we sailed across the Strait of Hormuz. I think we may have stopped over in Bandar Abbas in Iran. Then we continued on to the Gulf of Oman and dropped anchor at Muscat…or was it Salalah?" the old man looked uncertain. "After that, we continued across the Arabian Sea until we reached the Gulf of Aden. We then crossed the Bab Al Mandib into the Red Sea and docked at Al Hudaybah in Yemen."

Zaid marveled that the old man could have almost perfect recall of their journey fifty-seven years later.

"And on the way back, did you stop at the same ports?" Layla asked. Her question made them realize that there had been no mention of Ghassan, where, according to Shaykh Sulaiman, the Captain had bought the Moon.

"No, no. On our return journey, we came straight back home. And what a horrible homecoming awaited us." The old man's face clouded over as he remembered the horror of the Night of Catastrophe.

"So you don't recall stopping over in Ghassan?" Layla asked.

"Ghassan?" Nuh looked uncertain again. "Now that you mention it, I think we went there first to pick up some cargo before heading for Yemen. I had quite forgotten about that."

The teenagers shared a meaningful look before Adam asked, "Nuh, before the Captain died, he told Grandpa about a diamond he had brought back and hidden in the house. Did you know anything about it?"

"A diamond you say?" Nuh frowned in thought. Then his brows cleared and he said, "Why, your great-grandmother Saffiyah asked the crewmen that same very question after Rafiq was murdered by the rebels. If he brought back such a gem, we had no idea. We weren't in the habit of prying into each other's business. At the time, we all thought that the rebels must have stolen it if Rafiq indeed brought one back. Or if he left it on the Yuhanza, it perished that night when the ship was set on fire. Fire…" he repeated softly. "There was so much fire. Everywhere you looked, there was fire." Nuh stared off into space, a faraway look in his eyes.

"The pirates are coming," He struggled to his feet, his eyes terrified. "They have cannons, they'll set us on fire. Get the rafts, we must leave at once." The old man's breathing escalated as he looked wildly around him. The teenagers stood up in alarm at the swift change in him.

"Layla, go and get Salma," Adam said before he and Zaid took firm hold of Nuh and set him gently back into the recliner.

"It's okay, Nuh," Zaid spoke soothingly. "The pirates are gone now."

"They'll come back," the old man whimpered. "I know they will. But you've got to stop them." He grasped Adam's arm, his mouth working. "Rafiq… you must forgive me. You trusted me, and I betrayed you." The old man's face puckered up as if he was about to cry.

Salma came hurrying into the room, Layla at her heels.

"Oh my, he didn't last too long, did he?" the nurse cast an anxious look at her patient. "There, there," she crooned, placing her hand reassuringly on his shoulder. "Take it easy now. Everything's all right." Nuh looked so much like a bewildered child that Zaid felt a great rush of pity for him even as he wondered if the old man had been the one to murder the Captain.

"His mind's gone again," Salma said. "Allah knows when it will return. I'll have to give him his medication now. Why don't you go and wash up in the meantime? Lunch is already laid out in the dining room."

A short while later, the teenagers thanked Salma and headed

out of the courtyard with their bikes. They were comfortably full from a delicious lunch of baked swordfish in sesame sauce and their only thought now was to get home and rest. They followed the same route back but there was no sign of the little 'ragamuffins' as Salma had referred to them. Zaid was not surprised since it was the time of day when everyone sought the coolness and comfort of their home, away from the relentless sun.

MR. HORANI JOINED them on the patio for afternoon tea to inquire about their visit with Nuh. Adam gave his grandfather a brief account before asking the question which was uppermost on their minds. "Grandpa, Nuh told us that there was a sixth crewman who sailed on the last voyage of the Yuhanza and that it was not just the Faithful Five."

"A sixth crewman? I'm surprised Nuh even remembered what happened that long ago."

They took turns telling Mr. Horani all that Nuh had told them about Tahir and Iyad Usmani.

"I remember Tahir as being a very nice man, much older than the rest of the crew," Mr. Horani finally said. "I vaguely recall hearing about his son's disappearance and then his. If Iyad sailed on that voyage, I have no idea. But here comes Abbas," he indicated the gardener coming up the path toward them. "Perhaps he knows. Let's ask him."

Abbas exchanged greetings with them, and Adam posed the question to him.

"It's true," the gardener rumbled. "My father always spoke about that last voyage. Tahir's son did sail with them."

AFTER AFTERNOON TEA, the teenagers met for a conference in Moss Haven.

"Iyad sounded like quite a shady character," Adam said. "He would have been the perfect suspect but I don't see how he could have killed the Captain if he himself was killed that night."

Zaid said, "I agree. It has to be one of the Faithful Five."

"I wish we could speak to Faruq Ambreen and ask him about Iyad," Layla said. "I'm sure he must have heard something from his father."

"We'll have to figure out a way to meet him," Adam said. "If he will see us."

"So what about Nuh Tabibi?" Zahra asked. "Could he have killed the Captain."

"Those last words he said was very suspicious," Adam said. *'Rafiq…you must forgive me. You trusted me, and I betrayed you.'* He could have been referring to murdering the Captain."

Zaid said, "Well, we have to question the relatives of the remaining Faithful Five and see what *they* have to say. Then we'll have to decide which of the crewmen could have been the murderer."

"We still have to continue searching for the Moon," Adam reminded them. "The time is going fast, and we still have a lot more ground to cover."

Chapter Fifteen

Basim Visits

T HE SEARCH FOR the Moon resumed the next morning after Mr. Horani and Luqman went out. Using the opportunity to search the study while its sole occupant was gone, the teenagers tapped, jabbed, poked and pried, but there was nothing to be found.

"Okay, the library next," Adam said. "We'll search the bookshelves to see if there's any hidden compartments behind the books. Zaid and I will search the upper shelves with the stepladder. You girls can do the lower shelves. I'll take the first turn up."

They got distracted by the books during their search. Every now and again they would flip through the pages of an interesting title. In the midst of their search, the doorbell suddenly rang.

"Oh, drat," Adam exclaimed in annoyance. "Who could that be now?"

"I'll go see," Zaid offered. When he opened the front door, he was surprised to see Basim standing outside.

"Hullo, *Assalaam Alaikum,*" Basim sang out.

"*Wa Alaikum Assalaam.* What a pleasant surprise to see you, Basim," Zaid smiled as he ushered their new friend in.

"I thought I would drop by to see how you all were doing, so I had Nassif bring me over. Is everyone at home?"

"Yes, they are. They're…er…a bit occupied in the library at the moment."

"I hope I haven't come at a bad time," Basim said in dismay. "I really should have called first."

"It's okay, don't worry about it. Come into the living room and I'll let the others know you're here."

In the living room, they found Hassan and Hakeem watching an episode of *The Adventures of Mahmood.*

"Hi, Basim!" Hassan and Hakeem tore their eyes away from the television long enough to greet Basim.

"Hi, boys. What's on? Oh good, *The Adventures of Mahmood.* One of my favorite shows."

"Well, make yourself comfortable," Zaid gestured towards the sofas. "I'll get the others."

When Zaid returned to the library, Zahra asked, "Who was that?"

"Basim. He came to pay us a visit."

"Darn," Adam said irritably. "I wanted to finish off this section, but I suppose we'll have to stop now." Heaving a sigh, he added, "Basim has been really nice to us, so I guess I shouldn't complain."

"It's almost time for lunch anyway," Layla pointed out. "We'll continue with the search some other time."

"We need to go wash off all this dust," Zahra looked in dismay at her grimy hands and clothes.

"Yikes, you're right," Layla glanced at her own grubby hands and apparel.

As she and Zahra went out the door, Adam descended the

ladder, clutching a yellowed sheet of paper. Handing it to Zaid, he said, "Here, take a look at this when you get a chance."

"What is it?"

"Some paper I found wedged between the pages of a book called *Diamond In the Rough*," Adam replied as he hauled the stepladder back into the corner. "I was trying to figure out what was written on it, but the words are hard to read. I guess I found a diamond after all," he grinned. "Just not the right one."

"I'll take a look at it later," Zaid said, folding up the paper and pocketing it without much interest.

As they left library, Adam said, "While Basim is here, we might as well grill him about his great-grandfather's dagger and anything he might have learned from him about the Night of Catastrophe."

AFTER LUNCH, THE teenagers quickly tackled the lunch dishes, so they could get down to the task of pumping Basim for information. The good-natured youth, who was accustomed to being waited on hand and foot at Ma'ab Manor, found it a novelty to roll up his sleeves and dip his hands in the suds. As they worked, they carried on a light banter until the last utensil had been washed and relegated to its rightful place in the cupboard. After the midday prayer, they hastened to the living room and settled on the couches as they prepared to interrogate Basim.

"Basim," Adam began. "When we visited you at Ma'ab Manor, you told us that your great-grandfather used to tell you stories when you were a young boy."

"Oh, yes. Great-Grandfather Qasim was quite a character. He started out in life with barely a penny and ended up very wealthy. His sons and grandsons have carried on the tradition as good businessmen. I hope that I can too, someday, *insha'Allah*."

Zaid said, "When we went to the museum to look at the

model of the Yuhanza, we saw the daggers that the crewmen had carried. Did your great-grandfather ever show his to you?"

"No, I didn't even know he had one until the museum opened."

"What about the Night of Catastrophe?" Layla asked. "Did he tell you any stories about that?"

"Oh yes. After Great-Grandfather Qasim got off the Yuhanza, he had a hard time getting home that night, as the rebels were everywhere. When he finally came home, he was splattered with blood and in a terrible state. All he could say was, '*I've killed him, I've killed him.*' It turned out that he had killed one of the rebels who attacked him."

The teenagers exchanged startled looks at this revelation.

Adam said, "We heard that the Captain brought back a diamond, but it couldn't be found. Did your great-grandfather ever tell you about that?"

"No, never," Basim looked interested now. "Did that rich shaykh come to ask you about that? I heard Dad telling Mom that the Shaykh has been looking for some famous diamond that was stolen from his family years ago. Does he think it was the one the Captain brought back?"

They were all left with mouths agape at Basim's astuteness. Zaid could hardly credit the fact that the chubby youth had put two and two together and come up with the right sum. Adam was the first one to recover. Choosing his words carefully so he would not lie, he said, "The Shaykh does think that it was the diamond he is looking for. But since it cannot be found, he is still searching for it."

"Poor Shaykh," Basim said pityingly. "Looking for a small diamond in this big, big world is like looking for an ant in the desert."

What would Basim say if he knew that we're looking for the Moon right here at Bayan House, Zaid wondered. *It's a pity we can't confide in him, but we can hardly tell him that we suspect his great-grandfather of murdering the Captain and stealing the diamond.*

Adam said, "Basim, have you ever heard of Iyad Usmani?"

"Iyad Usmani? I don't think so."

Zaid said, "His father had been Tahir Usmani, one of the regular crewmen on the Yuhanza."

"Yes, I've heard of Tahir Usmani. He was in some of the stories that Great-Grandfather Qasim used to tell me. But I've never heard anything about a son."

"Iyad was one of the crewmen who sailed on the last voyage of the Yuhanza," Zahra said. "Nuh Tabibi told us about him."

"Nuh Tabibi? That old geezer? I didn't think he even remembered his own name."

"His memory came back for a bit yesterday," Layla said. "His nurse called us, so we went over to visit him. He remembered the last voyage of the Yuhanza quite well. He told us that Tahir begged the Captain to take Iyad along because Iyad's life was in danger. After they came back from the voyage, Iyad disappeared that night and everyone thought he must have been killed and buried somewhere by whoever was after him."

"That's interesting," Basim looked intrigued now. "I never heard that story. Did Nuh say why Iyad's life was in danger or who must have killed him?"

"No, he didn't know," Zaid said. "That's what we'd like to know too. We heard that Iyad and Faruq Ambreen's father used to be good friends. We would like to meet with Faruq Ambreen and ask him if he heard anything from his father. It would be nice to solve that mystery."

"Meet with Faruq Ambreen?" Basim looked at them with wide eyes. "You're not joking, are you?"

"No, we're not," Layla replied. "Why, is it that difficult to see him?"

"Well, he's a very proud man and doesn't mix much with people," Basim's eyes slid away from theirs.

"So you think he will refuse to see us?" Zahra asked.

"Yes, he might think you're too presumptuous." Basim still avoided their eyes.

Looking at the youth with sudden perception, Adam said, "I think you're not telling us something, Basim. What is it?"

Looking unhappy, Basim replied, "Your grandfather won't be pleased that I told you, but there's some sort of feud between your families."

"A feud?" Layla exclaimed. "What sort of feud?"

"Well, from what I've heard, it began when the Captain bought the old fort house from Faruq Ambreen's grandfather. The Ambreens needed the money but Jafar Ambreen and the rest of the family were furious that it had been sold to someone they considered a foreigner. Ever since then, the Ambreens have held a grudge against the Horanis."

That's why Faruq Ambreen looked so hostile that day in front of the mosque, Zaid thought. *It makes sense now.*

"What fort house was this?" Layla asked. "Does it still stand?"

Basim gaped at them. "You mean you don't *know?*

"Know what?" Adam looked mystified.

"*Bayan House* was the old fort house. I can't believe that you didn't know that."

"We had no idea," Layla declared. "I guess no one thought it would be of interest to us."

"Well, I'm going to ask Grandpa more about this feud," Adam said, a determined look on his face. "It's time we learned more about the family history."

AT DINNER, ADAM made good on his promise to ask his grandfather about the feud with the Ambreens. "Grandpa," he began.

"Basim told us today that there's some sort of feud between the Horanis and Ambreens. Can you tell us about it?"

There was a sudden silence at the table as they all looked at Mr. Horani. Frowning, he said, "I wish Basim hadn't told you that. It's all water under the bridge now."

To their surprise, Aunt Hafza snapped, "Tell the children about it, Yusuf. They have a right to know. They're Horanis after all."

"I wanted to spare them all that unpleasantness," Mr. Horani retorted. "But I suppose it's no use now." *Good for Aunt Hafza,* Zaid thought. *She must be wearing her hearing aid for a change.*

By the time Mr. Horani finished his tale, the teenagers were looking wide-eyed.

Layla said, "So the Ambreens didn't just hold a grudge because of the house but also because Great-Grandma Saffiyah refused Jafar Ambreen's offer of marriage and married the Captain instead."

"That sums it up," Mr. Horani agreed.

"After Papa died, Jafar again asked Mama to marry him," Aunt Hafza revealed. "She refused him, telling him that she wanted to be reunited with Papa in Paradise and wouldn't ever marry again. He already had a wife so she knew he only wanted the house back."

"He must have been angry," Layla said.

"He practically frothed at the mouth," Aunt Hafza chuckled. "After he got rich, he demanded that Mama sell the house to him and was enraged when she refused."

"It's unfortunate that the Ambreens still feel that the house belongs to them," Mr. Horani said. "After both Mama and Jafar passed away, Faruq asked me to sell it to him, but I told him no. He asked me again when I retired and became angry when I refused."

"Well, he may get the house back in the future," Aunt Hafza

said sadly. "After you and I are gone, Adil will probably sell it to him."

"Maybe if you tell Dad not to sell it to them, he won't," Adam said.

"I will make no such stipulation," Mr. Horani said firmly. "It will place your father in a very difficult position and I do not wish that for him. They can buy it back if they wish to. It's just a house after all. The Ambreens have made it a bone of contention, but neither of us will take the house when we depart this world."

THAT NIGHT, AS Zaid got ready for bed, he felt the rustle of paper in his pocket. Pulling out the sheet of paper Adam had given him in the library, he unfolded it and held it under the bedside lamp. The paper was old and yellowed, with several English words written in a looped, cursive style. The words were faded in some places and blotchy in others, making it hard to read.

From his backpack, Zaid took out the magnifying glass his mother had given him last *Eid-ul-Fitr* and held it over the paper. Little by little, he was able to make out the hard-to-read words until he had deciphered them all. At the end of the paragraph, were the letters MA. The words seemed meaningless to him and he finally put away the paper and got into bed.

Chapter Sixteen

Midnight Quest

THE NEXT DAY was *Jumu'ah* and once again, they headed into the city. After attending the mosque close to the esplanade, and lunching at a Turkish restaurant flanking it, Mr. Horani took them to the nearby beach, much to everyone's delight. Even though there was no swimming involved, the teenagers and twins enjoyed themselves immensely.

The beach was packed with picnickers sitting under colorful umbrellas and swimmers moving back and forth from sand to surf. The wind from the bay was like a cooling balm and together with the spray that splashed upon their faces, provided a welcome relief from the intensity of the heat. Under Mr. Horani's gimlet eyes, they removed their socks and shoes and waded up to their ankles in the water. Zaid reflected how nice it was to finally dip his toes in the blue waters he had stared at so often from afar.

The next two hours passed by pleasantly. After a bumpy camel ride along the esplanade, they sat under the shade of a date palm tree and built a sand mosque, complete with domes and minarets. They laughed in merriment as the twins' minaret kept toppling down again and again because they kept making it so ridiculously tall. After buying them ice creams, Mr. Horani drove them over to the Souk Square, a series of small markets surrounding a green park where food vendors did a brisk business.

Adam and Layla were impressed by the little *souks* which carried a wide range of merchandise, all of which could be obtained at a reasonable price with some deft bargaining. Mr. Horani bought them a T-shirt each with *Bayan Bay* written on the front. Afterwards, they sat on a bench in the park and ate pita bread sandwiches washed down by mango lassi. They returned home that evening, tired but happy after such an eventful day out.

AT MOSS HAVEN the next morning, the teens discussed what they had heard from Basim on Thursday.

Adam said, "I think Basim's great-grandfather could very well have killed the Captain and claimed that it had been a rebel. He had a convenient excuse for coming home all blood-spattered."

"Well, that takes care of two of the Faithful Five," Zaid said. "We have to learn about the other three now."

"Zahra and I can speak to Maymun about her father," Layla said. "You boys can tackle Luqman and Abbas about their fathers."

"Okay, we will," Zaid agreed.

"We have to resume the search in the library," Adam said. "We still have some more shelves to cover."

Layla sighed. "You know, Aunt Hafza told me and Zahra that the Captain had them do treasure hunts with the gifts he brought back for them. He would hide the gifts and then leave a clue, which he usually made up during the voyage, and it would lead them to where the gifts were hidden. She said that they found no gifts in the house after that last voyage and that the rebels could have taken them or the Captain could have hidden them with the diamond before he was killed. I suppose he didn't have the time to leave a clue, that's why…huh!" She let out a startled squeak as Adam grabbed her arm.

"Why didn't you tell us this before?" he said accusingly. "On Thursday when we were searching the library, I found a sheet of paper with some English writing on it. It was in a book called *Diamond in the Rough*. Maybe the Captain *did* leave it as a clue."

"And why," Layla demanded hotly, "didn't you tell us about *that*?"

"I had no idea it could be a clue," Adam replied defensively. "If you had told us earlier about what Aunt Hafza said, I might have known. I gave it to Zaid to look at."

All eyes turned to Zaid. Pulling out the yellowed sheet of paper from his pocket, he said, "I looked at it on Thursday night. I was able to figure out all the words, but they seemed meaningless. I actually brought the paper to return it to you, Adam."

"Can you read what it says?" Layla asked.

Zaid unfolded the sheet of paper and read, "*Take a careful look at important events in the past, for the simple answer why one who always trifles with destiny is the main seeker of honor and glory of any tale.*'"

"It doesn't sound like a clue," Layla said in disappointment. "Maybe someone was copying poetry or something."

"There's two letters written at the end of the verse," Zaid said. "It looks like the initials MA."

There were exclamations from Adam and Layla. Then Layla said excitedly, "Are you sure the initials are MA?"

"Positive," Zaid said. "Do you know who they belong to?"

"The Captain," Adam's eyes glowed. "Before he became Muslim, he was called Michael Anderson."

"It *is* a clue from him then," Zahra said. "How wonderful."

"It sounds like a riddle that has to be solved," Layla said. "If only we can figure out what it means and find the Moon."

"I will study it a bit more and see if I come up with anything," Zaid promised.

Zahra said, "I wonder if Grandpa and Aunt Hafza would be able to figure it out."

"They might since they were used to it," Layla replied. "But let's try to solve it first. If we run out of time, then we'll ask them."

"Since we found the clue in the library, maybe the Captain also hid the Moon there," Zahra said.

"It's a possibility," Adam said. "Let's search some more when everyone's having their midday rest. I don't think I can sit still right now."

On their way back to the house, they spotted Abbas and Mir in the herb and vegetable garden. As Abbas waved to them and called out a greeting, Mir stared at them moodily. Zaid noted that he still had the bandage on his leg.

"Oh, boy," Adam said in an undertone. "Mir looks like a gathering storm."

Layla giggled and said, "I sure don't want to be in the path of *that* storm."

While the household was at rest, the teenagers made straight for the library, where they embarked on a rigorous search. Adam and Zaid took turns with the stepladder on the upper shelves while the girls searched the lower shelves. By the time they halted an hour later, to their disappointment, they had found no hidden compartments or nooks where the diamond might be hidden.

BEFORE GETTING INTO bed that night, Zaid brought out the

yellowed sheet of paper and studied it. For fifteen minutes, he concentrated fiercely on what the answer to the riddle could be but without any success. As he put away the paper, he had a niggling feeling that he was missing something he ought to be able to see. Frustrated, he got into bed and tossed and turned restlessly until he finally dozed off.

He was awakened later by the low hum of a boat. Rising off the bed, he glanced out of the window and saw the boat coming slowly towards the cove. There was no time to lose. He rushed over to the next room to rouse Adam.

"Adam," he shook the other boy. "The boat is coming into the cove."

Adam bolted upright. "This is it then," he said, his voice still thick with sleep. "We're going out to the bluffs."

The boys hurriedly got dressed in jeans, sweaters and socks, before grabbing up their sneakers and a flashlight each, which they had gotten from the storeroom in readiness for this eventuality. They ventured cautiously out of their rooms to the floor below, creeping quietly along the hallway and down the stairs. Crossing the great hall, they moved silently down the passageway to the vestibule, and out the back door. They stood for a few moments to don their sneakers and accustom their eyes to the gloom.

The sickle shape of a waxing crescent moon hung from the sky, its light barely visible through the thin mist that had crept in from the bay. It was distinctly cooler and Zaid was glad for his sweater as a stream of air blew straight into his face. The quiet stillness of the night was broken only by the wind whispering through the foliage and the far-off murmur of breaking waves. Adam touched Zaid's shoulder and the boys headed down the pathway, past Abbas's dark cottage and into the acacia grove.

To Zaid, the oft-trodden path seemed like unfamiliar territory in the dark. The acacias looked like massive giants with outstretched arms, sighing and creaking like living beings. The mist had obscured the faint moonlight and they were enveloped in a world of black and gray as they felt their way towards the wall.

"I can hardly see anything," Adam whispered. "And I'm afraid to use the flashlight in case anyone sees the light."

"We'll just have to feel our way along," Zaid said. "We should be coming to the wall soon."

The youths moved slowly forward, their hands outstretched like blind men groping their way. They bumped into a few tree trunks along the path until Adam gave a soft exclamation. "We've reached the wall. Can you feel it?"

As Zaid touched his back, he chuckled and said, "No, that's me. Here, this is it," he took Zaid's hand and placed it on the abrasive stone surface. "We've got to feel around for the door now. I hope the boat's still there and we're not too late to see it."

Zaid's fingers touched the bolt across the door. "I've found the door." As his fingers moved to open the bolt, he paused in surprise. "The door's open."

"That's strange. It was definitely locked the other day when we looked at it. Maybe Abbas used it and forgot to lock it back."

"I suppose so."

The boys went out of the door, pulled it shut behind them and stared in dismay at the fog-enshrouded bluffs. The mist swirled around them, thicker than ever, its clamminess feeling like slimy cobwebs on their faces. Even though the youths had never set foot on the steep bluffs, they knew how treacherous they could be. Now they were made even more so by the veils of vapor which hung like a spectral curtain over the bay. Taking a tumble down would be infinitely worse than running into an unyielding tree trunk.

"I can't see a blessed thing," Adam said in disgust. "If only the mist would clear, we would be able to see right down into the cove."

"Let's go down a little," Zaid suggested. "Maybe the mist will be thinner."

"Okay, but let's take it very slowly," Adam said.

The boys cautiously began to descend from the peak of the bluffs, with nothing else to guide them but their sense of touch. They were careful not to lose their handhold or footing, and this made their progress all the more painstaking. Zaid stubbed his toe on an outcrop of rock and grimacing with the pain, he gritted his teeth and continued down, gravity pushing at his body and making his legs move faster than he wanted them to. All of a sudden, the quiet was broken by the sound of an engine. Startled, Adam lost his footing and went rolling down the bluffs with a soft gasp.

Zaid stood still in dismay, his hand clutching at bare rock to keep his balance.

As the engine pulsed in the cove, Zaid stood frozen, cold icicles of fear creeping down his back. Was Adam hurt? He could be lying there unconscious and bleeding. *And it would be all my fault*, Zaid thought. *We shouldn't have climbed down. Mr. Horani will skin me alive if anything happened to Adam.* His heart thudded heavily, his breath coming in wheezing, choppy gasps. Knowing that he was on the verge of panic, he forced himself to take deep, calming breaths. *Okay*, he told himself. *Adam probably hit his head against a rock and knocked himself out. He must be lying somewhere along the way. The best course of action is to continue climbing down until I find him. I only hope he hasn't broken anything.*

As Zaid laboriously made his way downward, he heard voices blending with the sound of the engine. He paused for a moment, hugging a thick slab of rock as he peered through the fog. He saw the blurry outline of a boat with two figures sitting inside. As the boat drifted towards the mouth of the cove, he caught a glimpse of an emblem before it disappeared into the mist-enshrouded waters. Zaid was filled with bitter disappointment. They had not learned what the boat was doing in the cove and Adam could very well be lying injured with a broken leg or arm.

Zaid continued doggedly down the incline, wincing as he jabbed his head against a spike. Rubbing the now-painful little bump, he was about to continue when two hands came out from behind him and closed over his mouth. Zaid struggled against his unknown adversary, kicking him in the shin as he wrestled to break loose.

"Shh, it's *me*," came Adam's whisper. "Keep quiet. I think someone's all the way down at the bottom of the bluffs. I heard him earlier."

"Are you all right?" Zaid whispered, intensely relieved to find his friend conscious and on his feet.

"Yes. I think I'll have a bruise from your kick though."

The youths heard a slight scrabbling sound from below and Adam laid a warning hand on Zaid's arm. Whoever had been lurking at the bottom of the bluffs was now climbing up. They flattened themselves next to a rocky outcrop and listened with bated breath as a shadowy figure clambered past them minutes later, breathing heavily from the exertion.

When he was a safe distance away, Adam whispered, "Let's go now. He's too far away to hear us."

When they finally reached the top, they spied the shadowy figure entering through the door in the wall. The next moment, the door banged shut and they heard the sound of the bolt sliding home. The youths realized their predicament at once.

"Oh, no," Adam said in dismay. "Our mystery man bolted the door. We won't be able to get in."

A quick check verified that they were indeed locked out and stranded on the bluffs.

As they stood there grappling with the shock of their plight, an idea came to Zaid. "I know what we can do," he said excitedly to Adam. "You can climb onto my shoulders and reach over to open the bolt. You're a little taller than me."

"You're right," Adam said in relief. "Hope you'll be able to take my weight though."

The boys wasted no time in putting their plan into action. Zaid sat down on the balls of his feet, planting his palms firmly on the ground in front of him. Adam took off his sneakers and climbed carefully onto Zaid's shoulders, clutching at the door to steady himself. When Adam was securely in position, Zaid took a deep breath and slowly began to rise, using the wall as leverage as he strained to bear his friend's weight. His breathing accelerated, his shoulders throbbed, and the muscles in his lower leg contracted painfully as he gradually rose to standing height. Thankfully, Adam had maintained his balance and was leaning forward, his hand feeling for the bolt on the other side of the door. Zaid thought he had never heard a sweeter sound than the slight scrape of the bolt opening.

The youths hastened through the door, closing the bolt softly behind them. The mist had cleared up a little and with one thought in mind, they hurried down the path. They wanted to identify the man who had climbed up the bluffs. As they came to the edge of the acacia grove, they saw a figure opening the door of Abbas's cottage. In the faint light, they caught a glimpse of a familiar profile as the figure disappeared inside.

"Mir," Adam said fiercely. "I might have known it was him."

Back at the house, the youths helped themselves to hot chocolate in the kitchen and crept up to the turret with their steaming mugs. After they had changed out of their damp clothes, Adam came into Zaid's room, hot chocolate in hand. "Mmm. Just the drink to end a crazy night out."

"It's too bad we didn't find out what the boat was doing in the cove," Zaid lamented. "I couldn't even hear what those men were saying."

"I was further down, so I heard bits and pieces of what

they said," Adam's eyes shone. "Like, '*close call with the Coast Guard...nice haul...will bring in quite a few fishes.*'

"So they *are* working with the pirates," Zaid said excitedly. "And Mir must be working with them too, that's why he's here. Maybe they were coming to meet with him."

Adam had a queer look on his face. "They may be. But I could swear I saw that boat coming *out* of the cliffs."

"Out of the cliffs?" Zaid said in puzzlement. "What do you mean?"

"I think there's an opening in the cliffs that the boat goes through and hides in."

"You could be right," Zaid mused. "It seems to disappear out of sight every time I see it."

"We should go down to the cove tomorrow when everyone is resting and look for that opening."

"Okay," Zaid nodded. "That time is good as the tide won't be in yet. I still can't believe that Mir is working with the pirates. He must have cut his leg on the bluffs going down to meet them. I wonder if Abbas is in the gang too."

"I'm sure we'll soon find out," Adam replied darkly.

Chapter Seventeen

Troublesome Twins

Iɴ Moss Hᴀᴠᴇɴ the next day, the girls were astounded to hear of the boys' adventure out on the bluffs.

"So," Adam concluded, "We'll be going to look for that hidden opening when everyone's having their midday rest."

"I'm not surprised in the least about Mir," Layla declared. "He's been acting very suspicious."

"It's too bad if Abbas is also working with the pirates," said Zahra. "It would be a shock to your Grandpa."

"Well, we don't know for sure if he is," Zaid said. "But it's possible seeing that they are uncle and nephew."

"We should come down to the cove with you," Layla said. "We could help you to search for the opening."

Adam shook his head. "The bluffs are really dangerous to climb. We can't risk you girls getting hurt. Grandpa's wrath will know no bounds."

Unable to deny the wisdom of her brother's words, Layla relented and said, "Alright, but you be careful too."

Zaid said, "I caught a glimpse of an emblem on the side of the boat. It was a circle, with two interlocking chains in the middle. Perhaps we can go to the wharf tomorrow and see if there are other boats with it and who they belong to."

"We'll have to ask Grandpa where the wharf is," Adam said. "If it's not too far away, we can bike over. I wonder if it's the same one where the Yuhanza was burnt. If so, we'll have a good reason for visiting it."

After leaving Moss Haven, they returned to the house and was greeted by a loud commotion.

"...NOT TO LET THAT BIRD IN THE HOUSE," Mr. Horani's voice was bellowing from the kitchen.

"I NEARLY GOT HIM," one of the twins shouted.

"THE PIE, THE PIE," Maymun shrieked. "It's pecking the pie."

"Yikes, Gul's in the house," Layla exclaimed in dismay.

The teenagers sped inside and met pandemonium. Mr. Horani, Luqman, Maymun, and the twins were racing about the kitchen chasing after Gul, who was flying above their heads screeching for all it was worth as it tried to evade the mob of humans after it. The bird made a sudden beeline for the door leading into the passageway, its band of chasers at its wing tips. The scene was so comical that Zaid could not help grinning as he and the others entered the fray.

They all followed the bird as it flapped along the passageway, renting the air with shrill screeches as it flew past the living and dining rooms and into the great hall.

"SOMEONE OPEN THE FRONT DOOR," Mr. Horani called out. "LET IT FLY OUT."

Adam hurriedly ran to open the door. After some clever maneuvering, they finally managed to corner the bird and it flew out of the door with an earsplitting screech.

"Allah be praised," Maymun threw her hands up in the air. "That bird is like a whirlwind."

"A bird of prey more like it," Luqman muttered as he and Maymun left the great hall.

"Don't let that bird come inside the house again," Mr. Horani said sternly to the twins before stomping off to his study.

"What was that bird doing in here?" Layla put her hands to her waist and scowled down at the twins, who wore chagrined looks on their faces.

"He was hungry," Hakeem mumbled.

"We wanted to give him a snack," Hassan said.

Adam stared at the twins in exasperation. "There's dirt on your hands and clothes. What were you doing? Rolling on the ground?"

"We were trying to dig up some worms for Gul," Hakeem muttered.

"Oh, gross," Layla looked revolted.

"We couldn't find any, so we brought him in the house to give him some food," Hassan said.

"Hello, there's a whole ocean with fishes for him to eat," Layla said. "You've got to stop spoiling him. He's a bird, he has to go catch his own food."

"Go upstairs and clean up for lunch," Adam ordered, and the twins marched off with sulky faces.

Tired from their morning adventures, the little boys were cranky and fidgety at lunch, squabbling with each over petty little things and having to be reprimanded by their grandfather and siblings several times. Halfway through the meal, one spilled his mango juice while the other knocked over his glass of water.

"What's the matter with you guys?" Adam said. "Can't you just eat your food?"

"I'm not hungry," Hakeem said petulantly as he pushed aside his plate.

"Me too," Hassan said, dropping his spoon onto his plate with a loud clatter, making poor Aunt Hafza jump.

"That is enough," Mr. Horani said firmly. "The two of you will go to your room at once and stay there until dinner."

Downing their heads and scrunching up their faces, the twins marched out of the dining room.

Layla sighed. "I don't know why they're being so difficult today."

"A quiet afternoon in their room ought to cure them of it," was their grandfather's answer.

After peace reigned once more at the table, Adam said, "Grandpa, we'd like to visit the wharf where the Yuhanza was burnt. Is it very far away from here?"

Looking a bit surprised, Mr. Horani replied, "It's about three miles or so. I can drive you over if you would like. When do you want to go?"

"We were thinking of going after lunch tomorrow," Layla replied. "And we'd like to bike over if we can. It would be nice to see a little bit more of the area."

"It will take you a little over an hour. I will write out the directions for you this afternoon. It's very straightforward."

AFTER LUNCH AND the midday prayer, the youths prepared to go out to the bluffs while the girls tackled the lunch dishes.

"When should we expect you back?" Layla asked.

"In an hour or so," Adam replied as he and Zaid headed out the back door of the kitchen, sneakers in hand. "That should give us enough time to look."

Eagerly, the youths headed into the grounds, passing by Abbas's quiet cottage as they made for the door in the wall. Again, they found it unbolted and looked at each other.

"It must be Mir," Zaid said in resignation. "Well, let's go see what he's up to now."

They were soon standing on the peak of the craggy bluffs, gazing down at the raw beauty of the treacherous incline and the majestic cliffs that rose protectively around the cove. The sun was directly overhead, striking fiercely down upon the bluffs and radiating furnace-like waves of heat around them. They saw a faint blur of movement below and watched as a man clad in swimming trunks and a short-sleeved vest walked with a limping gait onto the rocky strip of beach. Taking cover behind an outcrop of rock, the youths stared down at the moving figure.

"It *is* Mir," Adam hissed. "What could he be doing down there now?"

"Maybe he's covering up the tracks of the pirates," Zaid answered.

"If so, he has lousy timing," Adam grumbled. "Let's wait for a bit and see if he leaves."

The youths huddled against the rocky outcrop as they kept their gaze trained on Mir. To their frustration, all he did was walk along the beach, peering up at the cliffs. He then went to the water's edge and washed his hands before lowering himself onto a boulder in the center of the beach. Pulling out what looked like a brown paper bag and a bottle of juice from a small knapsack on the sand, he opened the bag and began to eat.

"I don't believe this," Adam uttered in disgust. "He's having a picnic as cool as a cucumber while we stew up here."

"Well, we can't go down until he leaves," Zaid said. "Maybe we should wait in Moss Haven. We can come back in fifteen minutes."

"That's a good idea," Adam said. "Let's get out of this baking heat."

BACK AT THE house, the girls were drying the last set of dishes when Maymun appeared in the kitchen.

"I have to knead the dough to make bread for dinner," she

said as she began opening cupboards. "Those rascal boys left you to do the dishes alone, did they?"

"Oh, we let them off the hook this time," Layla said. "They had something to take care of."

"Well, I'm glad that they've been helping out," Maymun chatted as she washed her hands and began to pour flour into a bowl. "Somehow, men always feel that it's women's work doing the dishes. Luqman eventually started to help me but he always grumbled about it. That's why I made sure that my two boys did their share along with my three girls. My father never thought it beneath his dignity to help out. I remember him washing piles and piles of dishes without complaining."

The girls looked at one another as the same idea occurred to them. It was the perfect opening to ask Maymun about her father.

"Maymun," Layla began. "Grandpa told us that your father was one of the Faithful Five."

Half an hour later, the girls headed upstairs. As they walked down the hallway, Layla said, "I'll go see how Hassan and Hakeem are doing. Hopefully, they're sleeping like little lambs."

Zahra was surprised when Layla came to her room moments later, a bewildered look on her face. "The boys aren't in their room," she said. "I can't believe they snuck out. Grandpa will be furious. I have to go look for them."

"I'll come with you."

After looking in the courtyard, on the patio, and in all the rooms downstairs, the twins were still not to be found.

"Where could they be?" Layla was beginning to look alarmed.

"Maybe they're hiding in their room. Let's check under the bed and in the closet."

The girls made their way back upstairs and into the boys' room. It was furnished with two twin beds and a beautiful antique dresser. A common feature of all the rooms on that floor was a long, built-in closet with a single door in the middle. Kneeling on all fours, Zahra poked her head under the beds, while Layla opened the closet door and sat down on her haunches as she peered under the racks of clothes. Zahra nearly banged her head on the bed frame when she heard Layla give a muffled cry. Pulling her head hurriedly out from under the bed, she saw that the other girl had almost disappeared into the closet, with only her heels visible.

"Come look what I found," she told Zahra in a dazed voice as she backed out of the closet.

Curious, Zahra crawled in and it was her turn to be amazed. At the left of the closet, a huge trapdoor lay slightly wedged open with a sneaker to prevent it from closing. Opening the door wider, she could make out a flight of stairs going down. "It's a hidden stairwell," she breathed out.

"Yes, and the boys must have gone down it. Allah knows what's down there."

"Oh, no, what are we going to do?"

"I'm going after them. And I'll knock their silly heads together when I find them," Layla said fiercely.

"I should come with you," Zahra said, although the thought of going down that dark hole filled her with dread.

"No, you have to tell Adam and Zaid where I've gone when they return."

"Oh, right."

"I'll need a flashlight. I think there's a couple downstairs in the storeroom."

"I'll get one," Zahra offered, glad to do something. "I'll be right back."

Within minutes, Zahra was back in the room with the flashlight, out of breath after running up the stairs. She handed the flashlight to Layla, who immediately turned it on and beamed it down the dark entrance.

"Give me fifteen minutes down there," she said. "If we're not back by then, bring out the search party." Layla spoke lightly, but Zahra could hear the nervousness in her voice.

"Be careful," Zahra whispered. The next moment, Layla vanished from sight.

MEANWHILE, ADAM AND Zaid, not fully recovered from their adventure last night, had dozed off in Moss Haven while waiting for Mir to return from the cove. Zaid awoke first, groaning with dismay as he looked at his watch and saw that they had been sleeping for almost an hour. He nudged Adam, who sprang up and looked disoriented for a moment before realization dawned.

"I can't believe we dozed off," he looked disgruntled. "Well, let's go see if the coast is clear now."

To their annoyance, the gate remained unbolted, which meant that Mir was still on the beach. As they stood behind the outcrop of rock and gazed down below, they saw him. He had obviously taken a swim for he was emerging from the water, his clothes dripping wet. He sat down on the boulder again, pulling out a bottle of water from his knapsack.

"Of all the irritating nuisances," Adam fumed. "We'll have to forget about going down today. Mir probably plans to spend the rest of the afternoon acting like a beach bum."

"Yes, we've already used up an hour. The girls will become worried if we don't show up soon."

Back at the house, all was quiet as the youths headed upstairs. They were surprised to see Zahra standing in the doorway of the twins' room. Looking relieved to see them, she beckoned them into the room and closed the door.

"I'm so glad you boys are back," she burst out. "I've been so worried."

157

"What's going on?" Adam stared around the empty room. "Where's Hassan and Hakeem?"

Quickly, Zahra told them of the twins' disappearance, the discovery of the hidden stairwell in the closet and Layla going in search of the twins.

"A hidden stairwell?" Adam said in disbelief. "I'm not dreaming, am I?"

"No, you're not. Layla's been down there fifteen minutes," Zahra wrung her hands nervously. "She said to bring out the search party if they're not back by now."

"I'm going down," Adam said as he kneeled down and crawled into the closet.

"I'm coming with you," Zaid told him, stooping to the ground and following his friend.

In the closet, Adam removed the sneaker jammed in the trapdoor and stared at the stairs leading down. "There's a bolt to close the door from the inside so no one can get in," he said, running his hands around it. "And some type of lock to keep it closed on the outside." Releasing the door, it closed slowly, blocking the stairwell from sight.

Peering from behind, Zaid said, "It's a great hiding place. If the twins hadn't left the sneaker there, no one would have found it. How will you get it open again?"

Adam ran his hands around the surface. "I can lift it open with my fingers. It's not fully closed. Let's see if I can still open it when it's closed all the way." Shoving the door down with his fist, they heard a clicking sound as it closed tightly. Adam then ran his hand around the surface and shook his head. "I'll need something sharp and thin to pry it open. I can't feel the seams at all."

"I'll get you the scissors from my room," Zahra offered.

However, Adam was unable to get the door open again with the scissors. Frustrated, he banged on the door and it almost hit him in the face as it sprang open.

"It must be a magnetic lock that springs open when you hit it," Zaid said. As he handed back the scissors to Zahra, she said, "You will need flashlights to go down. It's very dark."

At that moment, they heard a scrabbling sound.

"Layla, is that you?" Adam called out as he opened the trapdoor wide.

"Yes," A muffled voice came from below and they all sighed in relief. As Adam and Zaid retreated from the closet, there came the sound of feet walking up the hidden stairwell. Zahra's eyes widened in sudden realization at the sound, just as one of the twins emerged, carrying a flashlight. The other twin popped out, followed by a disheveled Layla, who had a remnant of cobweb stuck to her scarf.

"Are you alright?" Adam asked anxiously.

Layla nodded and said with breathless excitement, "The boys found a stairwell that goes all the way underground. There's a bunch of tunnels down there. I couldn't believe my eyes when I saw them."

"That's fantastic," Adam exclaimed. "We have to check them out," he said to Zaid who nodded enthusiastically.

"It was *them* I heard in the closet that morning," Zahra said, turning to Layla. "Remember when I thought there was a mouse in my closet? It was the boys in the stairwell. My closet is right next to theirs, that's how I heard them. They've known about that stairwell since then."

"So, that's your secret, huh?" Adam said to the twins. "How did you find that stairwell anyway?"

"We were playing hide and seek one day," Hakeem began. "I crawled into the closet to hide and then I felt something go *click* under me."

"That must have been the trapdoor closing," Adam said. "Which meant it had not been fully closed."

"We wanted to know why it made that sound, so we got a flashlight and looked," Hassan continued. "We didn't see anything so we started to hit it. Then it opened and we found a big hole with stairs going down."

"We decided to go down to see if we could find any treasure," Hakeem went on as the teenagers shared a look of comical amazement.

"First, we sawed a big room in front of us," Hassan told them. "But we got scared that the *jinn* might be there, so we came back."

"Tell them what you did today," Layla prompted.

"After Grandpa sent us to our room today, we didn't want to sleep," Hakeem said, "so we went down the stairs again. We knew we had to be brave 'cause the *jinn* might still be down there."

"So we read Ayatul Kursi and told the *jinn* not to harm us 'cause we're the servants of Allah, like they do in *Jinns of Jeopardy*," Hassan reported proudly.

"Good Lord," Adam muttered under his breath.

"Then we walked to the back of the big room and saw more rooms that were long and dark," Hakeem narrated. "We went into one of them to see if we could find any treasure there but we saw nothing."

"We were coming back to the big room when we heard Layla calling us," Hassan could hardly wait to tell his piece.

"Thank Allah," Layla spoke fervently. "I stood in the big room and called out to them because I didn't know which of those tunnels they had gone in. I almost went crazy wondering where they were."

"You won't tell Grandpa, will you?" Hassan asked anxiously.

"He will be mad at us again if you do," Hakeem said apprehensively.

"Listen, boys," Adam said gravely. "We're not going to tell Grandpa. We'd like to see what's down there too. But you're not to go down by yourselves again, okay? You could get lost and hurt and then we'll all be in big trouble."

Hassan and Hakeem, glad to be off the hook, beamed at their older brother.

"Okay," Hakeem nodded. "We won't go down by ourselves."

"And we won't tell Grandpa if you go," Hassan promised.

Zaid and Zahra grinned at this smart maneuver while Adam and Layla rolled their eyes.

Eyeing the specks of dust on the twins' hands and clothes, Layla said, "You boys need to go wash your hands and change your clothes." Catching sight of herself in the dresser's mirror, she said, "Eek, I have to go do the same."

Zaid said to Adam, "The twins' room is almost directly above the left wing on the first floor. The stairwell must be hidden in the wall between the prayer room and library or between the library and study."

"Yes, it must be somewhere in that area," Adam agreed. "It's not very wide so it doesn't take up a lot of space. Let's check it out and see if we're right."

Chapter Eighteen

The Hidden Stairwell

L AYLA WASHED HER hands and changed her scarf before joining Zahra and the youths downstairs as they examined the left wing. After measuring the proportions of each room and their distance apart in the corridor outside, they concluded that the stairwell was located in the wall between the library and the study.

"It's so cleverly hidden," Zahra marveled as they stood in the library. "You can't even tell it's there. I wonder why it was built in the first place."

"This used to be a fort house," Layla said. "It was probably built as a hideout for the family in case of a surprise attack. Grandpa and Dad have never mentioned anything so they probably don't know about it."

"Maybe Grandpa knows and hasn't told anyone," Adam said. Much later, he would find out how wrong he had been.

"I can't wait to take a look," Zaid said with great anticipation.

"Me too," Adam said. "We could go down tonight and use strings to guide us in the tunnels, so we won't lose our way."

"By the way," Layla said. "Did you boys find anything in the cove?"

Adam snorted and said, "Just Mir having a picnic by himself."

Layla giggled and said, "Well, he certainly knows how to entertain himself."

"We fell asleep in Moss Haven while we waited for him to leave," Zaid confessed sheepishly. "He was still there when we woke up, so we decided to come back."

"Hmm, sleeping on the job," Zahra said teasingly. "Maybe Layla and I should have gone with you after all. *We* made good use of our time here though. We had an interesting conversation with Maymun."

"What did she say?" Adam asked eagerly.

"She told us that her father, Noor Al-Razzaq, usually had true dreams of future events," Zahra relayed to them. "She said that before the Yuhanza left on her last voyage, he dreamt that the Captain was going to die. He had no idea how or when it would happen, but he was very anxious during the whole journey."

"Did he tell anyone about his dream before or after the voyage?" Adam asked.

"After," Zahra replied. "He never spoke about his dreams before they happened."

"Very convenient I must say," Adam said skeptically. "Did she say anything else?"

Layla related, "She said that if he had known that the rebels were planning to seize the Captain that night, he would have stayed with him. When he returned home, he suddenly had a premonition that the Captain was in danger. Although he was tired from the journey and afraid to leave the house, he set off for Bayan House. When he got there, he found that his dream had come true. The Captain lay dead and little Yusuf was crying his eyes out."

Zaid said, "Or it could have happened this way – after killing the Captain, he started searching for the Moon. When little Yusuf arrived, he hid and then pretended to be the first one to arrive."

"Why don't you guys tackle Luqman and Abbas and see what *their* fathers had to say?" Layla suggested. "Then we'll have to figure out which of the five of them could have been the murderer."

"All right," Adam nodded. "We'll do that after we have afternoon tea. Let's meet in Moss Haven after that."

As they gathered in Moss Haven that afternoon, Layla asked, "Well, what did you boys find out from Luqman and Abbas?"

Zaid said, "I spoke to Luqman while he was washing his car in the courtyard. He told me that his father, Salman Alameen, was a huge, muscular man who acted as the Captain's bodyguard. If he was keeping an eye on the Captain, Salman could have seen when the Captain bought the Moon from the fence's cousin, and decided to steal it. I learned also that he went straight home from the wharf on the Night of Catastrophe and only heard of the Captain's death the next morning. I learned nothing else of interest."

"What did *you* learn from Abbas?" Layla turned to her brother.

"I spoke to him in the vegetable garden," Adam replied. "Thankfully, he was alone, and Mir wasn't lurking around. He told me that his father, Sajjid Abdullah, was the ship's purser. That meant he was responsible for keeping all the important papers and valuables on the ship. It could be that the Captain gave Sajjid the Moon for safekeeping, that's how *he* might have known about it and decided to steal it. After the Yuhanza docked, he also went straight home."

Layla said, "The question is, of the five suspects, who was the most likely one that murdered the Captain?"

There was a long silence as they all pondered upon what they had learned so far.

Finally, Adam said, "I think it was Qasim Ahmed, Basim's great-grandfather. Coming home blood-spattered was very suspicious."

Zaid said, "I think it was Noor Al-Razzaq, Maymun's father. Claiming that he had a dream that the Captain was going to die and being the first one to arrive on the scene, seems too convenient."

"And I," Layla declared, "think it was Nuh Tabibi. When he lost his senses, he spoke about betraying the Captain's trust."

Last of all, Zahra said, "I think it was Abbas's father. Since he was the purser, the Captain must have given him the diamond to keep and that's when he decided to steal it."

Having reached an impasse in their deductions, the teenagers were at a loss for words.

"This," Adam pronounced at last, "is harder than I thought it would be. I guess they all seemed equally likely to have murdered the Captain. Unless we learn something new, we're stuck."

"We've had no luck finding the Moon either," Layla said gloomily. "It would be great if we could come up with the Moon *and* the murderer." Turning to Zaid, she asked, "Nothing yet on that clue the Captain left?"

Zaid replied disconsolately, "No, none so far."

"Can you read it again?" Adam requested. "Maybe something will pop out at us."

"I left it in the drawer upstairs," Zaid said. "But I can read it from memory. It says, *Take a careful look at important events in the past, for the simple answer why one who always trifles with destiny, is the main seeker of honor and glory of any tale.*"

They spent several minutes taking apart the words but

the answer to the riddle still remained elusive. Next, the boys discussed what to take on their underground foray while the girls studied the directions to the Bayan Bay Wharf, which Mr. Horani had handed to them during afternoon tea.

"It looks like a long ride," Zahra said. "But it's all for a good cause."

"That's the spirit, sister," Layla grinned, her dimples making deep chinks in her cheeks. "Those pirates have met their match."

ADAM AND ZAID bided their time that night, waiting to make certain that Mr. Horani was asleep before embarking on their adventure. In Zaid's backpack were the items they had gathered earlier. There were two fat balls of string, extra batteries for the flashlights, pencil and paper, a pair of small scissors, and a hammer with a few nails. Quietly, they stole over to the twins' room and found Layla and Zahra waiting to see them off. Hassan and Hakeem were lying in their beds, wide awake and back to their old selves after their time-out.

"Do you want us to go with you?" Hassan asked. "We could show you the way."

Smothering a chuckle, Adam said smoothly, "Not tonight, sport. Grandpa might look in on you if he gets up and then we'd all be in big trouble."

"He already came to see us," Hakeem reported.

"Yes, he did," Hassan piped up. "He hugged us and said he hoped we would behave better in the futer."

"Hear, hear," Layla murmured. "And it's *future*, not *futer*."

"Okay, we're ready," Adam said, opening the closet and turning on his flashlight.

"Be careful," Zahra said.

"We will," Zaid promised as he finished putting on his

sneakers and slung the backpack over his shoulders. "I guess we'll see you all in the morning."

Zaid's heart began a rapid tempo as he crawled through the trapdoor and followed Adam down the hidden stairwell. He kept his flashlight trained on the brown stone stairs, which were narrow but had enough room for a single person to move comfortably down without getting stuck. An earthy, musty smell came to his nose and the flashlights penetrated the gloom to reveal a network of spider webs hanging suspended over the stairway.

"We've reached the bottom," Adam whispered, his voice sounding thick and muffled. A moment later, with a slight bump, Zaid's sneakers crunched against gravel. They had entered the big room that the twins and Layla had described. It was really a large chamber, made of the same brown stone that the house was made of, but crumbling in some places. The floor was also of the same material, but was severely cracked and uneven. Adam swept his flashlight in wide arcs at the back and they saw the tunnels that Layla had told them about. There were four of them, branching away in different directions.

"Which one should we try first?" Zaid asked.

"Let's start with the one on the left."

"Okay, I'll get the string out."

The boys quickly worked to hammer a nail into the wall before securing the beginning of the string to it. Zaid took hold of the ball, which unraveled slowly as they moved forward and entered the tunnel. The tunnel was a little wider than the stairway and was constructed with the same material as the chamber. It was lumpy and uneven under their feet, and they had to proceed cautiously. Soon after, it came to an end.

"Strange that it doesn't lead anywhere," Adam said.

Zaid's keen eyes spotted what looked like a rusty handle on the wall. "There's a door," he aimed the flashlight at the handle. "It must lead somewhere."

The door was made of solid rock, so the boys were prepared to do a little tugging. To their surprise, it opened easily inward to reveal several horizontal bars of wood placed evenly apart. Peering through the bars, they saw a large room, which looked and smelled familiar.

"It's the cellar," Adam exclaimed, as he saw the store of dry goods and bottled preserves. "This door is cleverly hidden by the shelves built across it. Wow, this is cool."

"Let's see where the other tunnels lead to," Zaid said eagerly.

Closing the door, the boys retraced their steps. This time, they chose the rightmost tunnel and with Adam holding the ball of string, they set off. This tunnel looked the same as the first one but after a few minutes had elapsed, they realized that it was longer. The air smelled danker and there was a creeping chilliness that made goosebumps break out on their skin. Presently, they encountered a solid wall. Again, there was a rusty handle, which told them that a door was attached to it. Yanking on the handle, they opened the door and stepped out onto a rock ledge. They were confronted at once with cool air and moonlight.

"It's Bayan Cove," Adam exclaimed.

Sure enough, they were staring directly into the cove, with the cliffs rising like deformed giants on either side. The door had been carved out from the face of the bluffs, and like the one in the cellar, was ingeniously hidden.

"It's amazing," Zaid said. "This tunnel leads straight out to the cove. No climbing down the rocky bluffs."

"This would have been the perfect opportunity to look for that hidden passage in the cliffs," Adam said. "But it's too dark and those pirates could arrive at any moment and catch us."

"The tide's in too," Zaid pointed his flashlight at the roiling waters at the base of the ledge. "The current does look very strong. We'll have to search when the tide's out."

"I think we can do it early one morning," Adam said as he closed the hidden door. "And if we must go into deeper water, we can walk with some rope and hitch ourselves to a rock, so we don't get swept out."

"Do you realize," Zaid said excitedly, "that if I hear that boat coming into the cove, we can use the tunnel to get down here quickly?"

Chapter Nineteen

At the Wharf

ZAID AND ADAM were the last ones down to breakfast the next morning. As they sat eating in the dining room, Layla walked in with the cordless kitchen phone in her hand.

"Basim's on the line for you, Adam," she said, her eyes alight with curiosity. "Put it on speaker so I can listen," she whispered in his ear.

Taking the phone from her, Adam turned on the speaker. After he and Basim exchanged greetings, Basim said, "Adam, I hope I'm not calling too early, but I just had to tell you what happened yesterday."

"What happened?" Adam obligingly asked.

"We ran into Nuh Tabibi outside the supermarket."

Layla rolled her eyes while Zaid wondered why Basim thought that running into Nuh was anything out of the ordinary.

"Was that all?" Adam looked longingly at his half-eaten omelet and toast.

"Oh no, it's what he did that I'm calling you about."

It was Adam's turn to roll his eyes. "Duh. We already know

he could be a little loony sometimes. Did he wallop someone with his walking stick?"

As Layla hastily covered a giggle, Basim chuckled and said, "No, no, nothing like that."

"Well, what was it then?"

Basim said hurriedly, "Well, Nassif drove me and my Mom to the supermarket. When we arrived there, he got out of the car to open the door for us. Nuh and his nurse happened to be passing by at the same time."

"And?" Adam prompted.

"Well, Nuh stood in front of Nassif, staring at him. Then he said the strangest thing."

"What did he say?" Adam asked, his as well as his fellow listeners' interest piqued now.

"He said, *'Iyad, where have you been? Tahir was looking everywhere for you.'*"

"Woah, he really said that?"

"Oh, yes. Nassif was embarrassed by the attention. You know how stiff and proper he is. He politely told Nuh that he wasn't Iyad and got back into the car. I had to tell you since we were talking about this Iyad person the other day."

"Was there anything else?"

"No, that's all."

"Okay, thanks for telling us."

After hanging up the phone, Adam turned to Zaid and Layla. "Well, what do you think of *that*?"

"I would have paid money to see Nassif 's face," Layla giggled. "Maybe he resembles Iyad."

"Or Nuh's just confused," Zaid said. "Remember, he took *us* for pirates."

LATER, IN MOSS Haven, the youths told the girls of their discoveries last night and predictably, they were amazed. Layla then told them that she had finished reading Aunt Hanifa's journal last night. "It ended on a very mysterious note. Let me read it to you. It says:

Dear Journal, I have an exciting secret to share with you but it will have to wait another time. I have not told Hafza and Yusuf as yet because I am afraid that they would blurt it out at the first opportunity. I want to keep the knowledge to myself a bit longer for it is so very thrilling. I will tell you more when I visit you next but right now I am very tired, so goodbye until I open your pages again.

"As you can see," Layla continued, "there are still a lot of blank pages left in the journal. It's strange that she never wrote in it again."

"Maybe she started a new one," Zaid said.

"Then we should have found it in the turret," Layla pointed out.

"She probably got too busy and couldn't find the time," Adam said.

"I wonder what her exciting secret was," Zahra said.

"Me too," Layla said. "I hate unsolved mysteries. Maybe I'll ask Aunt Hafza about it before we leave."

Zaid then produced the riddle from the library and Adam took it from him and read it slowly. *"Take a careful look at important events in the past, for the simple answer why one who always trifles with destiny is the main seeker of honor and glory of any tale."*

They spent some time diligently examining the words and coming up with different meanings. But it was to no avail and the riddle remained as baffling to them as before. As they left Moss Haven, Zaid still had that niggling feeling that he was missing something obvious.

LATER, AS THEY prepared to leave for the Bayan Bay Wharf, Mr. Horani came to their rescue when Hassan and Hakeem, after learning that they were not included in the trip, began to make a fuss.

"We want to come with you," Hassan whined. "It's boring here by ourselves."

"We'll be good, we promise," Hakeem said cajolingly.

Mr. Horani intervened then and told the twins firmly, "It is too far away for you to ride in the carrier seats. You will find it hot and would not enjoy it at all. Go up to your room now and have your nap."

Sulkily, the twins went upstairs as the teenagers donned hats and headed out the door with their water bottles. Under cloudless blue skies and a blazing yellow sun, they rode out of the gate and onto the roadway, which wound downwards like a twisting gray ribbon amid the trees. Despite the heat, it was a beautiful day for a ride, and judging from the triumphant cries of the gulls skimming over the bay, it was a good day for fishing too. Zaid could just picture them, wings outstretched, gliding in the wind before swooping swiftly down to spear their scaly prey. *I wonder if there are enough fish in the bay to feed all those ravenous birds*, he thought to himself.

Adam took charge of the directions as they rode across high and low tracts of land, green and blooming with color in some places, and stark and austere in others. Finally, they spotted the wharf in the distance. Unlike Bayan Cove, which was clasped in the bosom of the rugged bluffs, the wharf was located on a softer, greener coastline. As they drew nearer, they saw boats of all shapes and sizes clustered together, bobbing gently at their moorings as if in a slow dance. Around them sailors, fishermen, and longshoremen milled about, clad in head coverings and hats to shade them from the sun. A slight breeze wafted in from the bay, flavoring the air with a pungent odor of fish, oil, and paint.

"Let's dismount and walk from here," Adam called out.

Hitching their bikes alongside a railing, they climbed the steps onto the wooden wharf which jutted out far into the bay. Moored on both sides were a multitude of boats. Zaid recognized the design of the *shu'ai* and the *boum - dhows* that were traditional to the region. Among them were a few wooden *badans*, still popular around the Gulf. Most of the boats however, were modern in design with gleaming chrome and sleek, streamlined shapes.

Zahra pointed to a gorgeous white motor yacht anchored next to a drab-looking *dhow*.

"Isn't that yacht beautiful," she said admiringly. "It looks like a graceful swan. I'd love to go for a ride in one someday, *insha'Allah*."

"That one looks like the Yuhanza," Layla pointed to a stately *dhow* with distinctive triangular sails. "Oh, it must have been a terrible sight to see the Yuhanza going up in flames that night. The crewmen must have been so upset that both the Captain and his ship were gone."

"Except for the murderer," Zaid remarked.

"Well, let's look for that emblem," Adam urged. "You still remember what it looks like?" he asked Zaid.

"Yes, it's right in here," Zaid tapped his forehead.

"Can you do a sketch of it?" Layla suggested as she wiped sweat from her brow. "We can help you to look."

"That's a good idea but I don't have anything to sketch with," Zaid replied regretfully.

"Not to worry," Layla said as she whipped out the small purple notepad and pen, handing them to Zaid. "You can use these."

With a few quick strokes, Zaid sketched the outboard motor

boat and the interlocking chains engraving he had glimpsed on the side of it. He then held it out to the others.

"That's pretty good," Adam said admiringly.

"He's very talented," Zahra said proudly. "He has a lot of drawings at home."

"Oh, I just dabble a bit," Zaid said modestly. "Well, let's get started before we get fried in the sun."

They agreed to take a section of the wharf each and search for fifteen minutes. If they did not come across a boat with the emblem within that time, they would stop the search and move on. Zaid began searching his section, noting that some of the boats had popular names like *Fawziya*, *Johara*, and *Lulwa*. His eyes soon began to water from the glare of the sun, but he had yet to sight any boats with the emblem. After the fifteen minutes were up, they gave up the search.

"Well, none of the boats here seem to have that emblem," Adam said. "We'll probably have to try one of the other wharves."

"Why not ask someone here about the emblem," Layla suggested.

"There are two sailors in that boat over there," Zahra pointed to their left. "We can ask them."

The two sailors, bearded and disheveled, were caulking the deck of a small fishing boat. They looked up with mild curiosity as the teenagers approached.

"Excuse me," Zaid said politely, holding up his sketch. "We're looking for a boat with this emblem. Have you seen it before?"

The two men squinted up at the sketch.

"Looks like a crest," the first one finally said.

"Seems sort of familiar," the second one remarked, stroking his beard thoughtfully. "I do believe it's the crest the Ambreens use on their boats."

"The Ambreens' crest?" Zaid queried with interest. "Are you sure?"

"That's what it looks like, my boy," the second sailor said as he wiped the sweat off his forehead and went back to his caulking.

"How come we didn't see any boats here with it?" Layla asked.

"That's not surprising," the first sailor chuckled.

"Why not?" Adam asked.

"Because, son," the second sailor grunted as he tamped down on the caulking, "them Ambreens have their own shipyard and wharf."

"Really?" Zahra said. "Where?"

"If you follow the curve of the bay that way for about two miles," the first sailor pointed a callused finger, "you'll soon come to it."

After thanking the men, the teenagers, tired and sweating from their first ride but filled with the thrill of the chase, quickly mounted their bikes and set off for the Ambreen's shipyard and wharf. When they arrived there, perspiring and wilting from the heat, they found the shipyard a hive of activity with muscular, sunburned men working at ships in various stages of construction. The wharf was at the back of the shipyard and as the teenagers passed by, the men stared curiously at them.

"Can we help you?" called out a burly man with a balding head and salt-and-pepper beard.

"We're just going to take a look around," Adam replied.

"Well, you'd better do it quickly before the boss sees you," the man warned.

"What does he mean by that?" Zahra asked as the man went back to his work.

"I guess the boss, whoever he is, doesn't like visitors," Adam replied. "Well, we'd better hurry."

The teenagers quickened their strides to the wharf and stared at the plethora of boats moored there. Zaid pulled out his sketch and they could see right away that it was an exact match of the emblem on the boats.

"It's the exact same thing," Zahra said excitedly.

"It certainly is," Layla agreed.

"WHAT ARE YOU KIDS DOING HERE?" a harsh voice suddenly bellowed behind them. Startled, they spun around to see a hawk-nosed man bearing down upon them. Zaid hastily pocketed the purple notepad, saying under his breath, "Uh oh, that must be the boss."

Raising his voice, Adam called out, "We're just taking a look around."

"You have no business being here," the man shouted roughly. "This is private property. Get moving!"

Zaid thought the man looked vaguely familiar. With his distinctive nose, protruding eyes and thick lips, he looked like a cross between an angry bird and a baleful frog. In the shipyard, everything went quiet as the men stopped their work and watched the drama unfolding before them. The hawk-nosed man turned around and with a sharp word, sent them all scuttling back to their tasks.

"He must be one of the pirates," Layla said softly. "He fits the bill—ugly *and* nasty."

As Zahra gave a nervous giggle, the man reached their side in a few quick strides and said impatiently, "Did you hear what I said. Get out of here!"

Fuming, the teenagers marched across the shipyard, and rode off on their bikes without a backward look. When they were out of sight of the shipyard, Adam called a halt in a grassy field and they sat down to rest and sip their water.

"Any of you remember seeing that man before?" he asked. "He looks sort of familiar."

"He does," Layla tilted her head to the side as she tried to remember.

"He was with Faruq Ambreen at the mosque that day,"

Zaid's brain suddenly clicked on the memory. "Grandpa said he was Faruq Ambreen's cousin, Talal."

"So that's who he is," Adam scowled. "Well, one thing's clear. If the pirates are using their boats, then it means that the Ambreens are part of the pirate ring."

Zaid cautioned, "We don't know that for sure. The pirates could be renting the boats from them. Let's gather some more evidence before we say anything."

Chapter Twenty

Underground Excursion

EXHAUSTED FROM THEIR long and strenuous bicycle ride, Zaid slept deeply that night until dawn broke. If a boat came into the cove during his hours of slumber, he certainly did not hear it.

When they met in Moss Haven later that morning, Layla had an interesting nugget of information to share with them. "I asked Grandpa this morning what date Aunt Hanifa died. After he told me, I asked him how she died. He gave me a strange look and said that she fell ill. When I compared the dates, guess what? She died just two days after her last entry in the journal."

"It must have been a sudden illness," Zaid said.

"I guess so," Layla agreed. "Because she didn't mention anything about being sick in her previous entries. I feel so sad when I think of her dying so young. She was only fifteen. And it was so soon after the Captain's death. I can only imagine how Great-Grandma Saffiyah must have grieved."

After several poignant moments of silence, Adam said, "Well, let's take a look at the riddle again."

Zaid pulled out the well-creased yellowed paper and they stared at the now familiar words.

Take a careful look at important events in the past, for the simple answer why one who always trifles with destiny is the main seeker of honor and glory of any tale.

After several attempts to figure out the answer, they gave up.

"What does it *mean?*" Layla threw up her hands in frustration. "This seems to be our only clue and we still can't make head or tail of it."

Zaid sighed and said, "I keep getting the feeling that I'm missing something."

"Well, let's continue to search the library today." Adam, ever practical, got to his feet. "Tonight, we'll explore the other two tunnels. If Zaid hears the boat later, we'll go down to the cove."

Layla surprised them all by saying, "I want to come explore the tunnels too. And don't tell me I can't," she added fiercely as Adam was about to speak.

"I wasn't going to say you can't," Adam replied mildly. "I thought you were afraid."

"Well, my curiosity is much stronger than my fear," Layla admitted.

"If Layla's going, then I'll go too," Zahra said bravely. From past experience, Zaid knew that it was futile to argue with his sister once her mind was made up. But he had to let her know what the tunnels were like.

"It's very dark and creepy down there, Zahra," he said. "Are you sure you want to go?"

"Well, I have to give it a try, don't I?" she looked at him defiantly.

THAT NIGHT, THEY all assembled in the twins' room in preparation for their exploration. To Adam and Layla's exasperation, Hassan and Hakeem insisted on going with them.

"We're going to do a lot of walking," Layla tried to dissuade them. "You'll get tired and sleepy."

"No, we won't," Hassan said mutinously.

"We're not babies, you know," Hakeem said scornfully.

"We found the stairs first," Hassan said accusingly. "You told us not to go down by ourselves and now you won't let us come with you. Every day you go into the garden too and don't take us with you."

Their list of transgressions grew as Hakeem continued indignantly, "And you went riding without us today. You can't have all the fun."

"Alright, alright," Adam threw up his hands in defeat. "You can come with us. The more the merrier. But not a word to anyone of what you've seen and heard, okay?"

Mollified now, Hassan hopped around excitedly and said, "We won't. We won't."

"If you forget, I'll pinch you," Hakeem pledged solemnly to his twin.

"So that's your technique to keep the little blurter quiet, huh?" Layla remarked. "Well, be sure to give him a nice big one if he opens his mouth to rat on us."

"I don't like you," Hassan scowled at his older sister. "You're mean."

Instantly contrite, Layla gave him a hug and said, "Oh sweetie, I'm sorry. I know you won't do it deliberately."

"What's *dilba...ratey*?" Hassan asked suspiciously, his tongue stumbling over the unfamiliar word.

Zaid, who along with Zahra, had been watching the byplay among the siblings with great amusement said, "It means that you don't say or do things to hurt or get anyone in trouble. As Hakeem said, you just forget."

Adam said impatiently, "We need to get moving or it will be midnight soon. Can you girls help the boys put on some clothes? They can't go in their pajamas."

Zaid said, "I have an idea. Why don't we split up into two groups and take a tunnel each? It will be less walking and we will finish faster."

"That's a good idea," Adam agreed. "Layla and Hakeem can come with me. You take Zahra and Hassan. We already have two balls of strings. We will need two more flashlights for the girls."

"I'll get them from the storeroom," Zaid offered.

While he was gone, the girls helped to get the twins dressed in jeans and T-shirts. When Zaid returned, they all entered the closet one by one and climbed down the hidden stairwell. For Zahra, who hated dark enclosed spaces, it was quite daunting to lower herself into the recess. With much trepidation she went down the stairwell, resolutely averting her gaze from the network of spider webs suspended overhead. Hassan and Hakeem were whispering to each other, their voices sounding distorted in the compact space. Soon, they came to the end of the stairwell and entered the large chamber.

"This is the big room we sawed," Hassan said.

Adam said to Zaid, "My group will take the second tunnel from the left. Your group can take the other one."

The youths had reeled back the string they had used previously and the ball was hanging from the nail in the wall. Quickly, they hammered another nail and affixed the second ball of string. Adam then instructed, "The group that returns first should wait here until the other group gets back. If any part of the tunnel has collapsed, or if there's flowing water along the way, return at once. All right, let's go."

With Adam and Zaid each holding a ball of string and a flashlight, they set off.

The tunnel that Adam, Layla, and Hakeem took was just like the others, except that Adam had to stoop a bit in some places where the ceiling became low. He kept to a slow, measured pace in consideration of the uneven floor and Hakeem's short legs. Finally, it ended at a short flight of stairs.

"There's no way out," Layla said. "That's strange."

"Look, there's a trapdoor up there," Adam shone the flashlight above the stairs, where a rusty metal door was built into the ceiling. "Let's see where it goes."

"I'll help you to open it," Layla said. "It might be a little rusty."

As Hakeem held their flashlights and shone it upwards, Adam and Layla climbed the stairs until they were within reach of the trapdoor. Flattening their palms against it, they heaved with all their strength. The door groaned and swung open upwards upon two hinges. Eagerly, the siblings peered out into the darkness. All they could see was an open space surrounded by trees.

"Let's go out and get some fresh air," Adam suggested. "We'll also see how far away from the house we are."

From the topmost stair, it was easy to get out through the trapdoor. One by one, they emerged and gulped in the fresh, cool air which was a welcome relief after their procession down the dusty tunnel. They were standing in a wide-open space, surprisingly free of bushes and undergrowth. On the fringes were tall trees that swayed gently in the soft wind, their branches casting waving shadows upon the ground. The stars, outlined against a sky that looked like soup broth, seemed close enough to reach up and grab, while across the distant horizon, a long swathe of white clouds slowly began to meander apart.

"We must be at the very back of the grounds," Adam said. "I can't recall seeing this area before."

His flashlight picked out several stone tablets jutting out of the ground. They were small in size and evenly spaced apart. Stooping down, he pointed the flashlight at one of them and received a shock.

"I don't believe this," he said in a hushed voice.

"What is it?" Layla asked.

"Come and look," Adam said.

Bending down, Layla stared at the stone tablet framed in the flashlight. Then she saw the words written on it and drew a sharp breath. "Oh my God, it's a graveyard."

"Yes. And Great-Grandma Saffiyah is buried under this marker. I'm sure the other markers are family members too."

Even though she knew there was nothing to fear from the dead, Layla could not help the involuntary shiver that crept down her spine. "I think we should go now."

"Let me look at one more marker," Adam said. Crossing over to the next stone tablet that lay to the left, he said in an awed voice, "The Captain is buried here."

Hesitantly, Layla took a few steps over to the tablet on the right and shone her flashlight on it. "And Aunt Hanifa is here."

Hakeem clutched Adam's hand. "I'm scared."

"There's nothing to be scared of," Adam said firmly. "Our family who died are buried here. We have to pray for them and ask that Allah make their graves spacious and filled with light, that He forgives their sins and grant them the Garden of Paradise. Do you think you can remember that?"

"Yes...I think...so," Hakeem answered falteringly.

"Okay, then let's take a minute and pray for them. Then we'll leave," Adam promised.

As they returned to the tunnel and retraced their steps back to the large chamber, Layla said, "I wonder if the others are back. Won't they be surprised to hear that we found the family's graveyard."

Upon entering the large chamber, however, they found that the other group had not yet returned.

"Their tunnel must have been longer," Adam speculated. "We'll just have to wait for them to come. It shouldn't be too long now."

"We'd better wind up the string before it gets all tangled up," Layla suggested.

THE TUNNEL THAT Zaid's group took was designed no differently than the others, and they walked slowly and carefully over the indentations beneath their feet. They had not walked very far when Hassan stopped and whispered, "Do you hear that?"

"Hear what?" Zaid asked as he and Zahra also came to a stop.

In the silence, they heard a series of faint echoes.

"What in the world is that?" Zahra asked.

"It must be the *jinn*," Hassan whispered.

"No, it's not," Zaid squeezed the boy's hand reassuringly. As the echoing sounds came again, he said wonderingly, "I believe they're voices."

"Could it be Adam and the others?" Zahra asked.

"No, they're men's voices," Zaid replied as he caught the deep timbre of the echoes.

"Who could they be?" Zahra whispered apprehensively.

"I don't know," Zaid answered. "We have to go take a look. The others will want to know who they are. It's up to us to find out."

"Yes, it's up to us," Hassan's voice was filled with importance.

In the darkness, Zahra grimaced and thought, *if it had been up to me, I would have hightailed it back to my room.*

As they continued forward, the voices rose and fell sporadically, with occasional bursts of laughter which filled the tunnel with ghastly echoes.

"I'm scared," Hassan whispered, clutching at Zahra's hand.

"It's alright, sweetie," Zahra said, squeezing his hand comfortingly even though she herself was a bundle of nerves.

As they rounded a curve in the tunnel, they saw light up ahead.

"Turn off your flashlight," Zaid said to Zahra, as he clicked his own off. They were immediately cast into gloom, save for the light ahead. "All right, let's go extra quietly now."

They soon passed by another tunnel to their right and came to a stop. Above the opening was a large X written in white chalk and they stared at this unexpected sight.

"Well, this is unusual," Zaid said in a low voice. "I wonder who put that mark there and how old it is. We'll have to explore this tunnel another time."

"Do you think the *jinn* will be in there?" Hassan whispered.

"Shush," Zahra said, taking hold of the little boy's hand. "Let's not talk about that now."

As they set off again, the light grew brighter and the voices more distinct. In front of them, Zaid saw a stone gallery with high iron railings. Inching forward, they peered cautiously between the railings and Zaid's eyes widened in amazement. Below was a large, brightly lit cavern with several men busy at work packing and unpacking boxes and crates. They conversed loudly as they worked, cracking jokes and ribbing each other with easy familiarity.

"Only one more hour to go," one of them remarked as he looked at his cell phone, "and then we won't have to come back to this hole until next week."

A hawk-nosed man came into view and Zaid was startled to see that it was Talal Ambreen, the man who had chased them away from the wharf yesterday. It was clear to Zaid that they had discovered the secret lair of the pirates and that the Ambreens were indeed part of the ring. Piles and piles of boxes and crates were stacked all around the cavern with hardly any room to spare. They had to be cargo plundered from the ships in the Bayan Strait.

Zahra gave a startled cry as she felt something crawling up

her leg. Frantically, she shook her limb, trying to dislodge the creature. Unfortunately, her cry of distress coincided with a brief lull in the conversation below. Some of the men's heads shot up as they stared around them.

"What was that?" one of them asked.

"Sounded like a scream to me," another one replied. "Coming from up there," he inclined his head in the direction of the gallery.

"Then go see what it is," Talal ordered sharply. "What are you waiting for?"

"Probably one of those fool birds came through the hidden entrance in the cliffs again," the man said in apparent disgust. "Just last week we found one of them here." Nevertheless, he started towards the gallery, apparently afraid to disobey Talal.

"Let's go," Zaid's heart hammered in his chest, terrified that they might be caught. He realized that if the man came and shone his flashlight down the tunnel, they would certainly be seen.

Frantically, they sped down the tunnel as fast as the uneven ground and Hassan's short legs would allow, Zaid holding on tightly to the ball of string in the rear. Soon they came to the tunnel marked by the large white X.

"In here," Zaid panted, and they veered into the tunnel, which curved slightly to the left, blocking them from sight. They came to a halt, Zahra and Hassan clutching nervously at Zaid as they all huddled together.

The man who had climbed the stairs to the gallery shone his flashlight down the tunnel for a couple of seconds. Zaid tensed, wondering if he would notice the thin string leading into their tunnel. To his relief, he heard the man calling out to the others below, "I don't see anything. Like I said, it must have been one of those dumb birds again. It's probably hiding in a dark corner waiting to pounce on someone. If I catch it, I'll wring its silly neck."

After the sound of his footsteps faded away, Zaid and Zahra turned on their flashlights in the tunnel where they had sought refuge.

Hassan whimpered and clutched at Zaid's hand. "Wh... what's that?" he asked shakily, pointing to the ground. Zaid swung his flashlight to where the little boy pointed and almost jumped out of his skin.

"Oh...oh...," Zahra clapped a hand to her mouth as she almost screamed again.

They were staring in the face of a grinning, crumbling skeleton!

Chapter Twenty-One

In Bayan Woods

"Yaah," Zaid exclaimed involuntarily as he stared at the gruesome sight. "Let's get out of here."

Wanting to put as much distance between themselves and their grisly discovery, they raced unsteadily out of the tunnel and back to the first one, fear and revulsion lending wings to their feet. Gradually, they slowed to a more sedate pace and at last, they entered the large chamber where they found the others waiting anxiously.

"There you are," Adam said in relief. "We were beginning to get worried."

"We saw a ghost," Hassan blurted out.

"A ghost?" Hakeem said in awe.

"Nonsense," Layla said. "There's no such things as ghosts."

"It was a skeleton," Zaid said, as he began to wind his string back onto the ball. "It was old and crumbly, so it must have been there for a long time. You wouldn't believe what else we found." He gave a quick account of their discovery of the men in the cavern and how they had ended up seeking refuge in the tunnel marked by the white X.

"Imagine stumbling upon the lair of the pirates," Adam said exultantly. "Those boats coming into the cove must be bringing the stolen booty to that cavern. Well, their swashbuckling days are numbered now."

"You guys certainly had an exciting time," Layla said a bit enviously. "*We* stumbled upon the family's graveyard at the back of the grounds. It was quite a shock."

After they returned upstairs, Adam came to Zaid's room and said, "I'd really like to find that hidden entrance in the cliffs and take a look at the cavern the pirates are using. We've got to do it soon and let the TCBI know, before the pirates attack another ship."

"Why don't we go early in the morning," Zaid suggested. "The tide won't be in yet, so we should have enough time to check the cliffs."

"Okay," Adam nodded. Looking troubled, he added, "I hope the TCBI don't think that Grandpa is involved. The Ambreens have some nerve carrying on their pirate operation right under his nose. They've probably known about these tunnels back in the days when they owned the house. No wonder Faruq Ambreen wants to buy it back."

"Don't worry," Zaid said reassuringly. "The TCBI will soon find out who the real culprits are."

AFTER THE DAWN prayer the next morning, Adam and Zaid crept furtively down to the twins' room, wearing bathing trunks and T-shirts under their clothes and carrying the backpack which held their previous supplies as well as two small towels and a change of clothing. In the storeroom, they had also found several bundles of rope tucked into a chest, courtesy of Mr. Horani's days as a sailor. Two thin but sturdy coils were now stuffed inside the backpack. In the twins' room, Hassan and

Hakeem were sprawled on their beds, their mouths open as they let out a cacophony of gentle snores.

"Look at them," Adam grinned. "They must be causing chaos in Dreamland."

"We should probably let the girls know where we're going," Zaid suggested.

"No, I don't think it's necessary," Adam dismissed the idea, which he would have much cause to regret later. "We'll probably be back before they're even awake."

As one of the twins stirred and turned over on the bed, Zaid whispered, "We'd better go before the boys wake up."

Lowering themselves into the closet, the youths descended the stairwell. In the large chamber, Adam took up one of the balls of string before he and Zaid headed straight into the tunnel that led to the cove. At the end of the tunnel, they stripped down to their T-shirts and bathing trunks before prying open the door and peering out. Cool streams of air mixed with fine spray from the bay rushed at their faces and Zaid shivered as the mist touched upon his heated skin. As they stepped out onto the rocky ledge, the sun was just rising on the horizon, spreading in an ever-widening arc across the bay and hurting their eyes with its intensity. The roar of the waves dashing against the cliffs was also more pronounced, sounding like thunder to their ears.

Throwing the two coils of rope onto the beach, the boys cautiously descended the rocky bluffs until their feet touched sand below. Taking up a coil of rope each, they picked their way across the rock-strewn beach bared by the receding tide. Pretty little shells were half-buried in the sand while the huge boulder which Mir had sat down on to have his picnic, looked remarkably like a squatting beast. The towering walls of cliffs surrounding them took Zaid's breath away with their sheer massiveness.

"I'll take the cliffs on the right and you take the left," Zaid suggested to Adam.

"Okay," Adam nodded. "Remember, we're looking for some sort of opening that a small boat can go through."

"Got it," Zaid said. "Now for the ropes. We can tie it to that boulder," he pointed to the squatting beast boulder.

The youths unraveled their coils of rope until they lay in great bundles at their feet. Then they fastened each one tightly around the boulder before walking to the water's edge, the coils of unfolding ropes wriggling like snakes behind them. After knotting the end of the ropes around their waists, they entered the water. At first it felt cold on their exposed limbs, but as they went deeper it started to feel warmer.

Zaid began examining his side of the cliffs, which was riddled with jagged crevices and wicked edges. As he probed and prodded within hand reach, he advanced more and more into the water until he was up to his knees. As they gradually became immersed up to their chests, the youths broke out into strong strokes, the currents buffeting their bodies every which way. Zaid was glad that they had decided to use the ropes and had not been foolhardy enough to take their chances against the unpredictable undercurrents. The reassuring pressure of the rope around his waist gave him confidence and he and Adam devoted the next half hour to making a thorough search of the imposing rock face.

If they had thought that finding the hidden entrance was going to be easy, they were doomed to disappointment. There was simply nothing to be seen and they were filled with dismay after setting out with such high hopes.

"It's no use looking anymore," Adam said, treading water next to Zaid. "We can't find it. That's why it's such a great hideaway for the pirates."

"Well, let's get out of here and head for the cavern," Zaid said.

They soon found that swimming against the currents was as dangerous as it was reputed to be. The water swirled and eddied around them, battering forcefully at their bodies and shoving them out towards the open bay. As Zaid clutched at his rope and began to reel himself in, he felt thankful again that they had had the foresight to come prepared or they would have been in dire straits.

After drying themselves and changing their clothes, they headed back to the large chamber, and took the tunnel leading to the cavern. They soon approached the entrance marked with the large X.

Zaid pointed his flashlight to it and said, "We saw the skeleton in there. I don't know where that tunnel leads to. We can explore it some other time."

"Absolutely," Adam agreed. "I'm really curious why it has that mark."

When they came to the gallery, they descended the three shallow steps to the cavern below.

"They must have used a generator last night," Zaid's flashlight illuminated the boxes and crates stacked in high piles around them. "It was brightly lit."

"Yes, this is definitely a hideaway for storing the stuff they steal from the ships," Adam's flashlight picked out several long, wooden tables covered with ropes, packing materials and shipping tape. There was a whole section of boxes packed and ready for shipping. They also noticed several dolleys and utility carts for moving the boxes around. To the far left, was a wooden rectangular platform. It was suspended from above by thin steel cables connected to wheels and axles.

"That looks like a pulley," Adam said. "They probably use it to lift stuff up."

As they neared the back of the cavern, they heard a lap-lapping sound.

"It sounds like someone paddling a boat," Zaid whispered.

Quickly, the boys turned off their flashlights and stood stock still. But the lap-lapping sound continued without any change of cadence and they gradually relaxed their guard.

"Let's go see what's making that sound," Adam turned his flashlight back on.

Doing the same, Zaid followed his friend to the very back of the cavern until they came to a pair of wide double doors. Pushing open the door, they emerged onto a platform with iron railings like the gallery. As their flashlights glistened on water, they realized that they were standing on a small, underground dock. The lap-lapping sound was water splashing against it.

"The boats come through the hidden entrance to this dock," Zaid said excitedly. "It's fantastic." The youths stood for a minute, listening to the desolate murmur of the waves before returning to the cavern.

Adam said, "If the pulley is used to lift stuff out of the cavern, there must be an exit nearby. Let's see if we can find it."

Sure enough, at the very back of the pulley, they found a narrow stairway.

Almost tripping on the string, Adam said to Zaid, "Let's cut the string and leave it here." Zaid hammered a nail at the side of the stairway, while Adam cut the string and twined the end to the nail. Stowing the remaining ball into his pocket, he said, "I'll take the string along just in case we need it again."

Climbing to the top of the stairway, they saw the now familiar trapdoor. Pushing it upwards, it gave way smoothly and they stepped out into a small enclosure, surrounded by tall, wild looking trees that almost blocked out the sunlight.

"We're in Bayan Woods," Adam said as he swiveled his head around.

"It does look sort of wild and scary," Zaid said, a slight shiver coursing down his back as he eyed the massive tree trunks and thick undergrowth around them. "No wonder the tunnels are such a great hideout for the pirates. No one would discover these hidden entrances."

"The pirates were probably the ones who spread those tales about *jinns* and vampire bats to keep people away," Adam said. "Well, let's take a look around before we return."

From the enclosure, they followed a rough path almost hidden among the trees. They came to a stop in a large oval clearing, with tent-like pegs poking up from the ground all around.

"Those pegs glow in the dark," Adam said. "I've seen them at an airstrip. The pirates must be using this place as an airstrip. A small helicopter can easily land and take off from here."

High above their heads, they spied one of the turrets of Bayan House.

"Look, we can see straight up to the western turret," Zaid marveled. "Remember that day I saw something move in the woods? It must have been someone standing here on the path. Well, I think we have enough evidence against the Ambreens. We should return and let Grandpa know so he can tell the TCBI."

"Yes," Adam agreed. "They only have to look at all those boxes and crates in the cavern to know we speak the truth. I hope Grandpa won't be too mad that we didn't tell him right away."

The boys retraced their steps to the rough pathway. As they neared the trees, a figure dashed out without warning and ran full tilt into them. They all fell like ninepins knocked to the ground, flailing around in an awkward tangle of arms and legs. After righting themselves, the youths stared flabbergasted at the figure beside them. It was Mir. He stared at them with incredulous eyes.

"You," he gasped. "What are you doing here?"

"Run," Adam urged as both boys struggled to their feet. "Run before he gets us." Desperately, the two friends darted in the direction of the trapdoor and ran smack-dab into two hulking brutes who stood across their path.

"What have we got here?" the first man growled as he grabbed hold of Adam.

"Two nosy boys," the second man crowed, holding Zaid's arm in a vise-like grip. "Good thing the boss had that alarm installed. Otherwise we'd never have caught these pesky kids."

"Let us go," Adam panted as he and Zaid began kicking at the men and yelling for all they were worth. A sharp fist thudded into the back of Adam's neck and he went down like a sack of potatoes. Mir entered the melee just before a hammer blow landed on Zaid's temple and he too collapsed on the ground, stars dancing before his eyes.

Zaid regained consciousness gradually. His temple ached horribly, and he groaned painfully, still seeing stars, albeit tinier ones. In a rush, he recalled what had happened. *Those men have taken us prisoners,* he thought as he peered into the unfamiliar darkness around him. There were two shapes lying next to him and he knew one of them had to be Adam. From the sensation of floating and the sound of paddling, he knew they must be on a raft.

His upper arms and torso had been bound with a rope and he felt a similar bond around his ankles. As his eyes became accustomed to the gloom, he saw that the raft was being paddled by the two men who had jumped them. They carried flash-lights pointed straight ahead. Zaid's eyes widened in sudden realization. *We're paddling down the hidden passage,* he thought. He could make out the walls on either side and smell the fetid stench of musty water.

What was more shocking though, was lying next to him and Adam, also bound, gagged, and trussed up like a baked chicken, was Mir.

Mir's eyes were open, and he was looking at them. "Wrruuuuggh," he said. "Srruarrggh."

"What did you say?" Adam asked, but it really sounded like, "Whaaadiaaay."

Mir's muffled words had a questioning ring as he spoke again. "Waahgaahdaah?"

"It's no good," Zaid said. His own words sounded like "Oohnoohgooh."

"Naaamaah," Mir shook his head and lapsed into silence.

Zaid was still in shock that Mir had been captured along with them. They had thought for sure that the other man was in league with the pirates. Obviously, his capture meant that he was not. *Well, we're all in a pretty pickle right now,* he thought. *I wonder where the men are taking us? And more importantly, what they plan to do with us?*

All of a sudden, the raft came to a stop and they saw a high wall of roughly-hewn rock before them. They watched in amazement as one of the men leaned over and pulled a lever on the wall. The rock face in front of them started to slide slowly to the side. *The hidden entrance,* Zaid thought. *It only opens from the inside.* The rock wall finally stopped moving and the raft glided smoothly out of the opening. They were now in Bayan Cove.

Paddling the raft until it was grounded on the beach, the men roughly hauled out their prisoners one by one and dragged them over to the boulder which had been the boys' lifeline that morning. With a long, thick length of rope, they strapped the prisoners side by side with their backs against the boulder and their faces towards the water. Hurrying back to the raft, they returned into the hidden passage. A minute later, the rock wall slid back into place once again.

Zaid's blood turned to ice in his veins when he realized the men's intent. *They're going to leave us tied up on the beach,* he thought in horror. *When the tide comes in, we're going to drown if we don't find a way to escape!*

Chapter Twenty-Two

Gul to the Rescue

A DAM AND MIR must have come to the same realization for they began struggling against their bonds. Zaid, squashed between the two of them, with Adam to his right and Mir to his left, also began to struggle. Though their bonds eased a fraction, they still held fast and Zaid knew it was unlikely that they would be able to break free of them. He looked sideways as Mir contorted forward and used his fingers to remove the gag from his mouth.

After taking several deep gulps of air, Mir turned to the boys and instructed, "Do as I did and remove your gags."

Zaid found that the ropes lashed around their upper arms gave their lower arms some leeway. By bending their heads downward and straining to reach up with a hand, he and Adam too were able to remove the gags and fill their lungs with invigorating air.

"What were you trying to tell us in the boat?" Adam asked Mir.

"I was telling you to try and loosen your bonds," Mir said. "You didn't understand, so I said never mind."

"What are we going to do?" Zaid's eyes darted around the desolate cove. "We will surely drown when the tide comes in."

"Try shouting," Mir ordered tersely. "And praying," he added as an afterthought.

Obediently, both boys closed their eyes and prayed silently. They waited for a lull in the waves breaking against the cliffs before they began shouting together.

"HELP! HELP! *HELP!*" they shouted at the top of their voices.

While they shouted, Mir continued to strain against his bonds, flexing his muscles and baring his teeth but to no avail. The men who had bound them were obviously sailors and knew how to tie a good knot.

Zaid knew they did not have much time left before the tide started to come in. From their position, they had a close view of the curling, white-capped waves breaking onto the beach. The water's edge was still several feet away but that would soon change with the approaching tide. The thought of being drowned made Zaid want to cry like a baby. *Surely someone will hear us yelling*, he thought. But then he remembered how remote the little cove was. No one at the house would be able to hear them and they were too far away from the sight of any passing boats. His heart sank in his chest as he thought how devastated their families would be if they all drowned.

After another bout of shouting for help, there was a sudden swish of wings and a loud squawk. A large bird landed gracefully on a nearby rock. Its plumage was white in color, with an unusual sprinkling of gray dots at the base of its tail feathers. It stared at them, its head tilted inquiringly to one side in a familiar way.

"Gul?" Adam stared at the bird. "Is that really Gul?"

The bird gave a soft squawk as it continued to stare at them. There was no mistaking it. The bird was Gul, all right. It must have heard them shouting and responded to the sound of their voices. "It's definitely Gul," Zaid smiled weakly. "He heard us."

"Is that your pet?" Mir asked. "It would be good if it could talk and take a message back."

"It *could* take a message back," Zaid said dejectedly, "if only we had pen, paper and string."

"Zaid…," Adam's voice was tense. "You were wearing those same jeans yesterday when we went to the wharf, weren't you?"

Zaid thought for a moment before replying, "Yes, I was." It seemed such a long time ago since they were at the wharf although it was only yesterday. He was not sure why Adam was asking him about clothes at this critical time. Was his friend losing his mind because of their predicament? Adam's next words dispelled that notion.

"Then please tell me," Adam implored, "that you still have Layla's notepad and pen in your pocket and that you didn't give them back to her."

Zaid's eyes widened with sudden recall. He had put the pen in his pocket after sketching the emblem and had also shoved in the notepad when Talal Ambreen came on the scene. He had forgotten to return them to Layla when they came back from the wharf. Which meant he still had them in his pocket.

"I have them," he cried jubilantly, fingering the slight bulge in his pocket. "They're still here."

"And I still have the leftover ball of string in *my* pocket," Adam said joyfully.

The next moment the boys' spirits plummeted as they realized the logistics involved in writing a message and tying it to Gul's leg.

"It will work if we're careful and Gul cooperates," Adam said, bolstering their spirits. "Try to get the pen and notepad out and I will do the same with the ball of string."

"What's going on?" Mir asked, not quite understanding what they were on about.

"My twin brothers taught Gul to carry messages tied to his leg," Adam explained. "Zaid has a pen and notepad in his pocket and I have a ball of string. We have to get it all together somehow and send a message with Gul, if he doesn't fly off."

A skeptical look flashed across Mir's face before he said, "Okay, go for it. We have nothing to lose."

Contorting his hands little by little, Zaid stretched his fingers and reached inside his pocket. But his fingers still fell short of reaching his mark. Straining with the effort and using muscles that he knew would be sore for days, he forced his arms to move further. He almost gave a shout of joy when his fingers closed over the pen and notepad. But now came the tricky part. How to get them out without dropping them onto the sand and out of reach? Clutching them firmly, he drew them out inch by inch and breathed a prayer of thanks when they rested at last on his thighs. Adam had already gotten the ball of string out and while Zaid had been occupied with his task, his friend had been diligently gnawing off a piece of string, which he now passed to Zaid.

Mir had been observing them tensely. "Be careful now," he said to Zaid. "But *hurry*," he added sharply, staring fixedly at his feet.

Zaid's gaze went to his feet also. A gentle wave had glided in, wetting his sneakers and the edge of his jeans. Even as they watched, another wave undulated in and foamed at their feet. It was the ageless ritual of the tide coming in. Hardly daring to breathe for fear that he would drop the precious items and dash their hopes, Zaid forced the fingers of his left hand to hold down the notepad while he carefully took hold of the pen. Painstakingly he wrote onto it: *Help. Captured by pirates in cove. Will drown when tide comes in. Come immediately. Zaid, Adam & Mir.*

Setting the pen down after he had finished writing, Zaid carefully tore off the piece of paper, and folded it up as best

as he could with his limited range of motion. Then he turned
to Gul, who had been sitting patiently, watching them with a
remarkable look of intelligence in its eyes.

"Come, boy," Zaid said coaxingly to the bird, lightly jiggling
the paper and string. "Take a message to Hassan and Hakeem."

The bird mewled softly and flapped its wings at the mention
of Hassan and Hakeem.

"That's right," Adam said encouragingly. "If you take the
message to Hassan and Hakeem, we'll have Maymun bake you
your own pie. Come on now."

Gul continued to eye them without moving. "Come on,
boy," Zaid said. "You've got to help us out here."

"Here," Mir pulled out a crumbly cookie in a plastic wrapper
from his pocket. "Maybe this will help," he pushed it over onto
Zaid's lap.

Gul's head tilted with interest when it spied the cookie. The
sweet inducement crumbled away its last defenses and to their
delight, the bird raised its wings and flew over to Zaid's lap and
began nibbling at the cookie. As Mir and Adam looked on with
bated breath, Zaid tied the note securely around the bird's leg so
there was no chance of it falling off while the bird was in flight.
At last, Gul was ready for its mission.

"Go to Hassan and Hakeem, boy," both Zaid and Adam
urged the bird. "Go to Hassan and Hakeem." With hopeful
eyes, they watched as Gul let out a loud squawk, raised its wings
in the air and soared over the cliffs. Their euphoria lasted until
the next wave roared onto the beach and drenched them to the
skin. Reality set in again as the minutes ticked away.

Gul won't be able to give the message if everyone's in the house,
Zaid thought miserably, his eyes staring unseeingly into the
sun-streaked bay. At this time of morning, no one would be
outside. The bird was smart, but it could not fly through walls.
And even if Maymun had the kitchen door open, after the fiasco

of its last visit, the bird would be unceremoniously shooed away if it tried to enter the house.

AT THE HOUSE, the girls and twins trooped into the kitchen, where they found Maymun busily cutting up vegetables, the kitchen door slightly ajar as usual.

"There you are," the housekeeper said. "I was beginning to wonder if you children were ever coming down for breakfast."

"Zaid and Adam haven't come down yet?" Zahra asked.

"No," Maymun shook her head as she pulled the towel off a platter of golden-brown pancakes on the island. "I guess they'll show up when their bellies start to rumble. Even Aunt Hafza beat you down this morning. She's on the patio soaking up some sun for a change."

"Aunt Hafza is up?" Layla said in surprise. "Good for her," she added, glancing out the slightly opened door.

After the girls and twins had taken their food into the dining room, Layla said, "I guess Adam and Zaid are still sleeping. They must be exhausted from our little excursion last night," she added conspiratorially.

"Can't say I blame them," Zahra mumbled, still looking bleary-eyed and groggy. "Though it's not like Zaid to get up so late. He's usually an early riser."

"I saw them go into the closet this morning," Hassan spoke in a hushed voice. "Hakeem said I was dreaming 'cause *he* didn't see them."

"Hakeem is right," Zahra said. "The dream must have made you think it was for real."

"They'll probably show up any moment now," Layla said, forking up a chunk of pancake and popping it into her mouth. "And they'll be as hungry as hunters. If they had gotten down here first, there would have been hardly any pancakes left. Mmm, Maymun does make the most yummy pancakes."

OUT ON THE patio, Aunt Hafza was wrapped up like a mummy in her voluminous shawl even though it had begun to warm up. She had fallen into a light doze, tiny snores bubbling out of her half-opened mouth. When Gul landed on the patio, it directed a loud squawk her way, but Aunt Hafza was deaf to the world since she was not wearing her hearing aid. The bird tilted its head to the side, as if considering its next move. Then with a slight flap of its wings, it alighted on the chair next to her head and let out a piercing squawk. That did the trick.

Aunt Hafza erupted out of her chair with a shriek and stared wildly around her.

Seeing Gul perched on the chair, she said shakily, "Allah have mercy."

Maymun poked her head out the kitchen door and called out, "Hafza, are you okay? I heard you scream."

"Oh, it's just this tiresome bird screeching in my ear," Aunt Hafza replied irritably. "I'm alright."

After Maymun withdrew from the door, Aunt Hafza pointed an accusing finger at Gul and said wrathfully, "You… you…*brazen bird*. What do you mean by scaring me like that?"

Gul mewled softly and began pecking at the paper tied to its leg. Aunt Hafza continued to eye it in great annoyance. She had been enjoying a pleasant little nap until the bird had seen fit to jolt her awake. She was ready to return to that nap if the bird would just fly away. But it was pecking at the paper tied to its leg in a most vexing manner. She knew that the paper had to be the twins' doing. She vaguely remembered seeing them untying a similar one from the bird's leg one afternoon when she had been out on the patio. Apparently, the creature meant to stay put until she removed the paper. What was its name? Dul? Or was it Bul? Aunt Hafza frowned in thought. She could not recall what name they called the bothersome bird.

"Come here, Bul," Aunt Hafza said nervously as she reached out towards the bird. "I'm just going to remove that paper, so don't get any ideas of foul play…although I think *you* must be up to some *fowl* play," she chuckled girlishly, in a rare moment of good humor." Keeping a wary eye on its bill, she slowly untied the piece of paper from the bird's leg as it waited patiently. "There now," she said, waving the paper back and forth. "Are you satisfied now? Off you go then. Shoo!"

But the bird refused to leave. To Aunt Hafza's annoyance, it remained stubbornly perched on the chair. As she would relate to everyone later, it stared almost angrily at her. Then it gave a rude squawk.

"You *feathered fiend*," Aunt Hafza glared at the bird. "What now? You want me to read it too?" She glanced disinterestedly at the paper in her hands. The words might as well have been written in Greek since she was not wearing her reading glasses. Gul squawked again and Aunt Hafza decided that she had had enough.

"All right, you *scrawny buzzard*," she said, getting irritably to her feet. "I'll take this to Hassan and Hakeem. And I'll make sure they know of your appalling behavior," she added severely as she flounced indoors, past a startled Maymun. Espying the girls and twins in the dining room, she gave a triumphant cry before marching up to the table.

"Here," she said, thrusting the piece of paper indignantly onto the table. "That bird of yours, Dul or Bul, or whatever its name is, brought this. It made a horrendous racket in my face and woke me up. Then it wanted me to remove that paper you boys tied to its leg," she directed an irate look at the twins.

"We didn't tie that paper," Hakeem protested, looking surprised.

"Wasn't us," Hassan denied too, eyeing the paper curiously.

"Then I guess Gul must have tied it to himself," Layla said sarcastically. Her eyes widened as she recognized the purple-tinted paper. "Wait a minute," she exclaimed. "That's paper from my notepad." Snatching it up, she opened it and quickly scanned it. Turning pale, she scrambled to her feet.

"The pirates have captured the boys and tied them up in the cove," she cried out. "They'll drown if we don't reach them in time."

"Oh, no," Zahra looked horrified. "Hassan was right. They *did* go down the stairs. What are we going to do?"

"I'm going to tell Grandpa," Layla rushed out of the dining room. "He'll have to go down to the cove to rescue them."

Aunt Hafza, who had heard the girls clearly, stood rooted to the spot for a few moments before she hurried towards the kitchen. Layla returned with her grandfather, who was wearing a stunned look on his face as he rushed down the passageway and into the storeroom. He emerged with a bundle of ropes and a sheathed knife just as Aunt Hafza appeared in the passageway with Maymun, Luqman and Abbas in tow. By the grave look on the servants' faces, it was apparent that Aunt Hafza had told them what had happened. No words were necessary as the two men followed Mr. Horani across the vestibule to the back door, the girls and twins behind them.

Zahra came to a stop in the middle of the vestibule and said, "Wait. There's an easier way to get to the cove."

"Yes, yes," Layla nodded eagerly. "Grandpa, you have to come upstairs with us."

"What are you talking about?" Mr. Horani looked at his granddaughter as if she had gone mad. His eyes turned suddenly suspicious as he asked, "This is not some weird game, is it?"

"No, no, it's not…it's in the closet…we have to go down the stairs," Layla babbled incoherently. "Zahra, get the flashlights from our rooms."

As Zahra sped off, Mr. Horani said in confusion, "I thought you said we have to go upstairs."

"Yes, we have to first go up and then down," Layla said, darting down the hallway. "There's a hidden stairwell that goes underground and to the cove. Come, I'll show you."

The bewildered adults followed Layla and the twins up the stairs and to the twins' room where Zahra was waiting in the doorway with the flashlights. Aunt Hafza was breathing hard and looking rather pale. Casting an anxious look at his sister, Mr. Horani directed Maymun to take her to her room. Aunt Hafza did not protest, and the two women proceeded down the hallway to the opposite wing.

Layla quickly opened the door of the closet and told the astounded men, "Follow me."

IN THE COVE, the treacherous waters had crept insidiously over the beach and the prisoners were now immersed up to their collarbones. There were no more cries for help as their throats were on fire, and they could no longer summon the strength to raise their voices above the thundering of the waves. To take their minds off their ordeal, Mir had shared a few things about himself, which had gone a long way in explaining his erratic behavior.

"Do you think the bird took the message?" he asked Zaid and Adam now.

"I'm sure he did," Adam gasped, as a powerful wave splashed water onto his face.

Even if Gul managed to get someone to see the message, it might be too late, Zaid thought wretchedly as he blinked the salty water from his eyes. A few minutes more and there would be no escape or help for them when the waters finally rose over their heads.

As they continued to shiver and contemplate their wretched fate, the water crept up almost to their chins.

It was then that they heard their names being shouted. Their heads jerked up, joy flooding their beings as they realized that help had arrived at last. *Praise be to Allah,* Zaid thought, before he joined Adam and Mir in calling out to their rescuers.

Mr. Horani, Luqman, and Abbas climbed off the rock ledge and began wading in the quickening current towards the prisoners. The men worked swiftly, using the knife to cut them free of their bonds and helping them to stand up. The water was almost to their upper thighs, but the current was strong and swift, threatening to knock them off their feet in their weakened state. The men kept them upright and steady as they towed them over to the ledge.

Zaid and Adam soon realized that their rescuers had used the underground tunnel to get to the cove. *The girls must have told them about it,* Zaid thought dimly. When time was of the essence, it *was* the fastest and easiest way to the cove after all.

The girls and twins were standing by the entrance of the tunnel, looks of anxiety on their faces.

"Adam! Zaid!" Layla cried out in relief. "Are you okay?"

"Yes," Adam smiled wanly. "Thank Allah you reached us in time."

They all trudged silently back through the tunnel to the large chamber and up the hidden stairwell into the twins' room. Luqman, Abbas and Mir headed immediately out the door while Mr. Horani stood next to the closet, looking dazed. The teenagers and twins stared warily at him, waiting for the inevitable reckoning. Zaid felt a surge of guilt that he and Adam had brought such distress to their host. It must have been a nasty shock for him to learn that they had been captured by the pirates when they were supposed to have been sleeping in their beds.

As his grandfather remained silent, Adam glanced nervously

at him and said, "I guess we should go and change out of these wet clothes."

Mr. Horani seemed not to have heard him as he murmured to himself, "This was her room. She must have found the stairwell and used it to get there. She was always looking at the water and wishing she could swim there. And she said nothing to us."

"Who are you talking about, Grandpa?" Layla asked, looking with concern at her grandfather.

Mr. Horani blinked and seemed to come out of his reverie.

"Your Great-Aunt Hanifa," he replied, his eyes filled with sadness. "She drowned in the cove."

Chapter Twenty-Three

The Moon at Last

TODAY IS DESTINED *to be a day of shocks,* Zaid thought after Mr. Horani's startling revelation. Pulling himself together, Mr. Horani said to the youths, "You had better go and change out of those wet clothes. I will have Luqman bring up a tray of food for you. Get some rest and I will see you both in my study at two o'clock."

As he and Adam headed up to the turret, Zaid sighed in relief that they were being given a temporary reprieve from the reckoning. A few minutes to two, the youths headed apprehensively to Mr. Horani's study. After bidding them to be seated, he looked at them sternly for a long moment.

"Mir told me what's been going on," he said heavily. "I don't know how you boys discovered those tunnels and I don't have the heart to scold you for exploring them. However, I *am* very displeased that you kept it a secret and took it upon yourself to investigate what was rightfully the task of adults. You acted very rashly and unwisely and placed yourselves in great danger. You might have drowned there today. One family member drowning there was enough...," his voice broke and Zaid saw the sheen of tears in his eyes.

"We had no idea Aunt Hanifa drowned in the cove," Adam said in a small voice. "We thought she died of some illness."

"That's what Mama wanted everyone to believe," Mr. Horani sighed. "Hanifa's drowning in the cove was such a mystery, you see. She didn't leave the house through a door or window because they were still bolted from the inside when we found that she was missing. And she couldn't have gone through the door in the wall because I had seen with my own eyes that it had been bolted and there had been no one else living here besides Mama and us. After we found her body in the cove, I was sent to fetch Mama's cousin who was a doctor; the same one who had helped us on the Night of Catastrophe. Mama pleaded with him to give a verdict of death due to sudden illness because she feared if the police found out that Hanifa had drowned under such circumstances, it would lead to a lot of unpleasant suspicions. Things were much laxer in those days, so he agreed. That stairwell in the closet explains so much…," Mr. Horani's voice trailed off.

"Was that why you didn't want us swimming in the bay?" Adam asked.

"Yes, but I couldn't tell you why," Mr. Horani looked regretful. "Mama made us promise not to tell a single soul that Hanifa drowned in the cove. I suppose the need for secrecy is gone now."

"We were exploring one day and found Aunt Hanifa's grave in the grounds," Adam said. "We didn't know the family was buried here."

Mr. Horani looked a trifle surprised. "I suppose it never occurred to me or your father to mention it. It was Papa's idea to use that space there. Abbas is the one who keeps it clear of weeds and bushes."

There came a knock on the study door and Layla burst into the room, a frightened look on her face.

"Aunt Hafza's having an asthma attack," she cried. "She can hardly breathe."

"Where is she?" Mr. Horani sprang to his feet, his face turning pale.

"In her room," Layla answered. "Zahra heard her coughing. When we went to check on her, she was wheezing really badly, and the inhaler doesn't seem to be helping her."

"All the excitement has been too much for her," Mr. Horani shook his head. "I'll have to take her to the hospital." Turning to Adam, he said, "Tell Maymun and Luqman to meet me by the car."

Minutes later, they all watched worriedly as Mr. Horani helped Aunt Hafza down the stairs and through the front door. She was still gasping and wheezing horribly and several times she broke out into dry, hacking coughs that made her twist up in agony. In the courtyard, Luqman already had the Toyota up and running.

After seating Aunt Hafza in the car, Mr. Horani turned to the teenagers and twins who had followed them out into the courtyard. "Luqman and Maymun are coming with me to the hospital and Mir and Abbas have gone into town to meet with the TCBI. I want you all to stay inside the house until we come back, okay? Promise me you won't go into the tunnels."

"We promise," they all pledged solemnly.

"Poor Grandpa," Layla said as they returned inside and gathered in the living room. "It's been a difficult day for him and it only keeps getting worse."

"A day destined for shocks," Zaid murmured.

"You should have told us where you were going this morning," Layla said reproachfully to the youths. "If Gul hadn't brought that message, I don't even want to think what might have happened."

"That bird is a hero," Zahra declared.

"Yeah, he is," Hassan agreed.

"We knew that ever since we got him," Hakeem beamed, proud of their pet.

"I'll have to ask Maymun to bake him his own pie," Adam grinned, telling the girls and twins of his promise on the beach.

"Gul will enjoy that," Zahra smiled. "He will be in bird heaven when he gets a whole pie to himself."

"I wonder what Grandpa's going to do about the tunnels," Layla remarked.

"Probably seal them of," Zaid said regretfully. "They've caused nothing but trouble."

"I can't believe Aunt Hanifa drowned in the cove and we never knew about it all these years," Adam said. "I guess it's the Horani's version of a skeleton in the closet." He went on to tell the girls some of the details his grandfather had told them in the study.

"Well, we now know what Aunt Hanifa's exciting secret was," Layla said sadly. "That was her first and last swim in the cove."

They all lapsed into silence, vividly imagining a young girl crying out in terror as she battled against the cruel currents that ended her life that fateful day. Zaid and Adam, having firsthand knowledge of those dangerous undertows, had an idea of how she must have felt.

Zahra finally broke the silence to ask, "How come Mir's the good guy all of a sudden? Wasn't he supposed to be working with the pirates?"

"He had us fooled, all right," Adam shook his head ruefully. "He's actually with the TCBI."

"Does that stand for *The Country's Best Idiots?*" Layla asked drolly.

Adam chuckled and said, "Well, that *idiot* was the one who cleared Grandpa when the TCBI suspected him of being in league with the pirates. It seemed that the Coast Guard received a tip-off about Bayan Cove and their main suspects were Grandpa, Luqman and Abbas. Mir was chosen to investigate since his uncle lived here and the pirates wouldn't suspect him of spying on them. Being a newly married man, he was unhappy that he had to leave his wife and tell his uncle a lame story about doing research here, that's why he was so bad-tempered. He had cleared Abbas of suspicion by the time he took a tumble on the bluffs and hurt his leg but he pretended that it would be embarrassing if anyone found out, hence the secrecy. The real reason of course was that Grandpa was still a suspect and Mir didn't want him to know that he had been going out to the bluffs."

Zaid continued, "That night when Adam and I went out to the bluffs, Mir was finally able to clear Grandpa of suspicion when he heard those men in the boat laughing about using Grandpa's property right under his nose. Mir also saw the emblem on the boat and knew that it belonged to the Ambreens. It wasn't until we were captured together that he learned about the tunnels and the cavern. He also thought that we were annoying kids who would get in the way of his investigation. He apologized to us, of course."

"Poor man, it must have been hard to leave his wife," said Zahra, ever quick to forgive and forget. "No wonder he was always moody."

"So how did you all manage to get captured together?" Layla asked.

Zaid briefly related their adventure that morning. "So, when Mir heard a helicopter taking off from Bayan Woods last night, he went to investigate this morning. He was looking around when he heard those men coming. As he was running to hide from them, he ran into us. We thought he was with the pirates, so we ran away from him and straight into the pirates. Mir came to our rescue, but the pirates overpowered us," he concluded.

"I'm hungry," Hassan suddenly whined.

"Me too," Hakeem said. "So hungry, I could eat a house."

"You mean a *horse,* silly," Layla corrected. "Not that you'll be eating one anytime soon," she laughed. "Come on, let's raid the kitchen. It will soon be time for afternoon tea anyway."

Zaid felt a sudden stirring in his brain. *I wonder,* he thought to himself. *Could it really be? No, I don't see how it could…yes, yes, he could have heard it wrong. If he did, then that changes everything!*

"Zaid?" Adam interrupted his rumination. "Are you alright? You look sort of feverish. You're not getting sick, are you?"

"No, no, I'm not," Zaid said as he stood up. "I'll be right back." He rushed out of the living room and up to the turret, where he grabbed the sheet of yellowed paper from the drawer, certain that he had found the missing link which had eluded him so far. He worked diligently for some minutes, until he gave an exclamation of satisfaction. Grabbing a pen, he underlined several words on the paper before rushing back downstairs where he found the others seated at the dining table, tucking into meat pie and macaroons.

"Zaid, are you sure you're okay?" Adam asked, his mouth full of pie. "You took off like a bat out of hell just now."

"I had a hunch, so I went to get the riddle," Zaid explained. "I think I've solved it."

"You have?" Layla exclaimed in delight. "What is it?"

"Well, I first got the hunch when you corrected Hakeem just now," Zaid said. "I thought, what if the Captain told Grandpa that the diamond was hidden in the *horse,* but Grandpa heard it as *house?* When I studied the words again, it confirmed my idea. It wasn't really a riddle, but a hidden message."

"But how could it be a horse?" Zahra asked in puzzlement.

"Well, read the underlined words," Zaid said. "You'll notice that it's every fourth word."

They all stared at the words on the paper.

Take a careful <u>look</u> at important events <u>in</u> the past, for <u>the</u> simple answer why <u>one</u> who always trifles <u>with</u> destiny is the <u>main</u> seeker of honor <u>and</u> glory of any <u>tale</u>.

Layla then read aloud, *"Look in the one with main and tale."*

"I see what you mean," Adam said thoughtfully. "If the

Captain meant *horse,* then the hidden message is right on the mark because main and tale are homophones with mane and tail, which is found on a horse."

"And there *was* a horse in the house," Layla said excitedly. "Just not a real one."

"That's what I thought," Zaid nodded. "It has been there since Grandpa was a young boy. We should check it out."

"You mean that old rocking horse upstairs?" Zahra exclaimed incredulously. "You think the Moon is hidden in it?"

"Well, the message points that way," Zaid replied. "I think it's a wonderful stroke of good fortune that it wasn't thrown out long ago. Imagine if the Moon is really hidden in it."

"What moon are you talking about?" Hakeem asked.

"Yes, what moon?" Hassan demanded.

"We've been searching for a treasure too, just like you," Layla told them. "It's a famous diamond called the Moon of Masarrah and it could be that Great-Grandfather, Captain Rafiq, hid it in the old rocking horse upstairs."

"Really?" both boys said in unison, their eyes opening wide.

"Yes, really," Adam nodded solemnly.

"Why didn't you tolled us?" Hakeem said. "We would have helped you to search for it."

"Well, we thought that four of us looking was enough," Layla said diplomatically.

"No fair," Hassan grumbled. "If you had told us, we would have found it for you."

"Well, you can help us search the old horsey for it," Adam promised. "Zaid and I will bring it down to the living room."

Minutes later, the youths entered the living room carrying the old rocking horse.

"Make way for Old Bashir, Bringer of Glad Tidings," Adam cried out.

After setting the old horse down in the middle of the living room, Zaid's certainty wavered as he stared at the disfigured old relic. It had once been covered in plush brown fabric which had become faded and moth-eaten over the decades. The stirrup and reins had long rotted off, while the leather saddle was worn and tattered. Its wooden rockers were cracked and broken in several places, causing it to tilt unevenly to one side. *It's almost a joke to think that this pitiful old toy would conceal a legendary diamond,* Zaid thought.

"Okay, everyone," Adam instructed. "Gather around and let's see if Old Bashir has been hiding a huge secret all these years."

The teenagers and twins got down on all fours as they began a detailed examination of the horse. But they found no crack or crevice large enough to hide a diamond.

"Well, there goes *that* theory," Layla sighed.

"Maybe the horse eated up the treasure," Hakeem remarked.

"Yeah, open his mouth and see," Hassan urged, grabbing the muzzle of the misshapen toy and forcing its jaws apart. To their surprise, there was a clicking sound and the jaws parted wide to reveal metal hinges on each side and a dark, hollow cavity for the mouth.

Layla said, "Let's see if anything's inside the mouth."

Adam inserted a hand into the opening. Looking disappointed, he pulled it out and said, "Nothing's there."

"The horse must have swallowed up the treasure," Hassan said. "You got to pull it out from its tummy."

"Well, let's see if my hand can go down its tummy," Adam said.

Cautiously, he pushed his hand into the horse's mouth little by little until his wrist disappeared. His eyes widened.

"I feel something," he cried out. In breathless excitement, they watched as he carefully pulled out his hand. He clutched a black oilskin pouch.

"Open it," he told Layla, his voice tense with suspense as he handed her the pouch.

With slightly trembling hands, Layla pulled apart the drawstring, turned the pouch upside down and shook it lightly. The contents spilled out onto the wooden floor and they all caught their breath in wonder. Next to two exquisite, gold filigree bracelets, and an intricate brass carving of a ship, a dazzling stone winked up at them. Like the simulated photo in *Legends of Gemology*, it was a golden-yellow, pear-shaped gem which glowed with bits of luminescent red lights.

"The Moon at last," Adam breathed, his voice filled with awe as he picked up the stone and ran his fingers over it.

Chapter Twenty-Four

Bones and Bravery

"YOU BOYS ARE geniuses," Layla laughed joyfully, kissing Hassan and Hakeem noisily on their cheeks. She then picked up the carving of the ship and the gold filigree bracelets. "Well, we've found all the missing gifts that the Captain brought back. The carving must have been for Grandpa, the bracelets for Aunts Hanifa and Hafza and the Moon of course, for Great-Grandma Saffiyah."

Caught up in the excitement of their discovery, no one noticed a panel in the wall sliding noiselessly aside. Neither did they see the figure that emerged, a look of greedy possession in his eyes.

"Give me that." The growled command was so unexpected that the teenagers and twins spun around in alarm, staring uncomprehendingly at the man pointing a gun at them, and the wide-open wall panel behind him.

"Nassif," Zahra gasped as they all gaped in shock at the Ahmeds' chauffeur.

"Give me the diamond," Nassif demanded again, grabbing hold of Hassan and pointing the gun at the little boy's head. "Or I'm going to put a bullet in this little imp's head."

"Let him go," Adam said fiercely as Hassan scrunched up his face in fear.

"Then give me the diamond," Nassif said silkily.

With a look of fury, Adam reluctantly held out the Moon. Nassif snatched it from him and stared at the diamond with a covetous look of wonder on his face.

"We're going to get it back from you, don't think we won't," Adam said furiously.

"Don't be a sore loser," Nassif mocked him. "I warned you not to look for it in the first place."

"So, you were the one trying to scare us away," Zaid said accusingly.

"Yes," Nassif chuckled. "I had a great time at the playland. I guess I should be grateful that you didn't listen to my warnings. Otherwise I wouldn't have gotten my hands on this little beauty," he caressed the stone. "I've searched all over the house but never thought that it would be hidden in that hideous old rocking horse."

"You've been searching the house?" Layla asked disbelievingly.

"Oh, yes," Nassif smirked. "From the tunnels, I've used this secret panel and the hidden stairwell upstairs to look around. One of these little brats saw me one night as I was going out their door, so I had to be extremely careful after that."

"*You're* the *jinn*," Hassan cried out. "I sawed you. And Hakeem heard you."

"We saw you here one night too," Zaid said, recalling the figure with the flashlight in the living room. "We just didn't realize it was you."

"You must have been the one who put that skull and cross-bones poster in the cellar," Layla said. "It all makes sense now."

Suddenly, the doorbell rang and Nassif stood stock still in surprise at the unexpected interruption. As the bell pealed again, he put the diamond in his pocket and said menacingly, "Not a sound from any of you."

The bell rang once more before it became silent. Zaid thought that whoever had rang it must have left when there was no response.

"Okay, I want everyone inside the passage *now*," Nassif rapped out.

"We gave you the Moon," Adam said angrily. "You don't need to take us too."

"Oh yes, I do," Nassif insisted. "Otherwise, the moment I leave, you'll be running to sound the alarm. Now, get into the passage," he began shoving them roughly with his free hand.

Helplessly, the teenagers and twins went through the opening onto a little landing. Following after them, Nassif pulled out a powerful flashlight and closed the open panel with a soft click of the clasp. From the landing, they descended a short flight of stairs into a cramped space. Nassif opened another clasp and a panel glided open to reveal the large chamber they were familiar with. Not bothering to close back the panel, he prodded them towards the second tunnel from the right and Zaid realized that he was taking them to the cavern.

"How did you learn about these tunnels?" he asked Nassif. "Are you working for the Ambreens?"

"Clever of you to guess that," Nassif said sarcastically. "Faruq Ambreen figured that you kids would be trouble after you went looking up the Moon at the library."

"The Ambreens know about the Moon?" Zahra asked in surprise.

"Oh, yes," came the answer. "I'm so glad that they sent me over today to see what was going on. I heard there was some excitement earlier."

"They almost murdered my brother and friend in the cove," Layla said indignantly. "They will be very sorry when the TCBI comes crawling all over here," she added with relish.

"I could care less about the Ambreens," Nassif said indifferently. "I've got what I wanted and they won't see me again."

"Very loyal, aren't you," Adam sneered. "The Ambreens will soon know what a traitor they hired."

"Listen, I don't owe the Ambreens a thing," Nassif burst out angrily. "They owe *me*."

As they passed the tunnel marked with the large white X, Hassan recognized it and said fearfully, "The bones of the ghost are in there. We sawed it that night."

Nassif chuckled and said cryptically, "I was telling you that the Ambreens owe *me*. Well, in that tunnel lies the reason why."

"What do you mean?" Zahra asked.

"Those old bones in there belonged to my great-grandfather," came the surprising answer.

"Your great-grandfather?" Layla asked. "Who was that?"

"His name was Tahir Usmani. I never had the pleasure of knowing him."

"Tahir Usmani?" Zahra gasped. "But he was Iyad Usmani's father."

"So you must be Iyad's grandson," Zaid said.

"Which means that Iyad wasn't murdered on the Night of Catastrophe," Adam concluded. "He must have fled Midan. No wonder Nuh saw the resemblance."

"Well, well," Nassif said. "I didn't realize you know my family history so well."

"But everyone thought that Tahir drowned," Zahra said. "He must have gotten lost down here and died."

Nassif gave a cackle of mirth. "You kids are so stupid. Trust me, the old man didn't get lost down here."

"So how did he die here then?" Zaid asked. "And how do you even know it's his bones?"

"I know for a fact that it's his," Nassif replied. "He couldn't keep his mouth shut, that's why he ended up here."

"He was murdered?" Adam said aghast. "Your grandfather

Iyad murdered his own father? Did he murder the Captain too, so he could steal the diamond?"

"Wrong on both counts, you dumb infants," Nassif answered scornfully. "My grandfather didn't murder anyone."

"Then who murdered them?' Zaid asked.

"That's none of your business," Nassif snapped. "You're too nosy for your own good."

There was no more conversation until they reached the gallery and Nassif herded them down into the cavern.

"On the ground, all of you," he ordered, laying his flashlight onto a table and pulling on a coil of rope. *Oh no*, Zaid thought in dismay. *He's going to tie us and leave us here. I can't believe we're prisoners again.*

"You can't leave us here," Adam said furiously.

"They'll find you nosy brats sooner or later, I'm sure," Nassif replied callously. "By then, I'll be long gone."

"What are you going to do with the Moon?" Layla demanded.

"As if I'd tell you," Nassif laughed scornfully. "Let's just say that you'll never see me or the Moon ever again. Well, which one of you wants to go first?" he held out the rope. "Or should I take my pick?"

"You won't get away with this," Adam said mutinously.

"You seem to be the most troublesome of the bunch," Nassif said. "I think you'll be the first. *You,*" he barked, hurling the rope at Zaid, who flinched as it stung his bare arm. "Tie his wrists together. Do it quickly and no tricks or I'll put a bullet in you."

Sullenly, Zaid began tying Adam's wrists, trying to make the bond as loose as possible. Wholly caught up in the scene in front of them, none of them noticed the figure creeping down from the gallery, an object in his hand. Concealed by the boxes and crates lying all around, the figure crept closer and closer to where Nassif stood until he was directly behind the chauffeur. Then, with a great lunge, he whacked Nassif soundly on the back with the object, putting all his weight behind the blow. Nassif fell forward onto the ground, the gun dropping from his hand.

"Basim," They all gaped at the strapping youth and the incongruous object in his hand before they swung into action. While Zahra and Layla untied Adam, the other boys used their weight to hold Nassif down on the ground. Then Adam, the girls and the twins also entered the fray.

Nassif had recovered now and was beginning to wrestle with his captors.

"Hakeem, get the rope," Adam called out and the little boy sped forward to where the rope lay on the ground. Nassif snarled like a wild beast as he struggled desperately. Hakeem returned with the rope and Zaid grabbed it, his breath whooshing out as Nassif's knee made contact with his stomach. At last, Nassif lay securely bound, his eyes glittering murderously.

"Told you we would get this back," Adam crowed jubilantly as he removed the precious diamond from Nassif's pocket and slipped it into his own.

Zaid grinned and slapped Basim on the back. "Basim, I don't know how you came to be here, but you're a hero."

Layla laughed and said, "Thanks to you…and *Maymun's rolling pin?*" she cast a comical look at the object on the ground, "we're not prisoners anymore."

Basim beamed at everyone, his chubby face alight with pleasure.

"I don't know what *this* is all about," he gestured to the bound Nassif, "but I'm *amazed* by these underground passages," he looked around the cavern in awe.

"How did you find us?" Adam asked.

"Well, I rang the doorbell but no one opened the door. I thought maybe the bell wasn't working, so I decided to walk around to the kitchen to see if Maymun was there. As I passed by the living room, I peered in at the windows to see if any of you were in there. The curtains were open a bit and I was shocked to see Nassif pointing a gun at you and forcing you into that hidden compartment in the wall. I knew I had to help you, so after trying the back door and finding it locked, I'm afraid I had to break one of the windows in the living room to get in. I couldn't figure out how to get that hidden compartment open, so I hit it until it finally swung open. It was really dark, so I got a flashlight from the storeroom and Maymun's rolling pin from the kitchen as a weapon. I was able to follow you by the sound of your voices and finally tackle *him*," he looked disdainfully at the chauffeur.

"You chose the perfect time to visit," Zahra said happily.

"Well, I was actually coming to tell you what I found out about Nassif yesterday. As he was helping Mom to unload groceries from the car, a letter fell out of his pocket. When I picked it up to give back to him, I noticed that it was addressed to *Nassif Iyad Multani*. I decided to come over to tell you, so I asked Mom to bring me over since I couldn't get hold of *him*. I had no idea he'd be here causing trouble."

"He's Iyad Usmani's grandson," Layla told Basim.

"How come your last name is different?" Adam asked their prisoner.

"My grandfather changed it when he started his new life," Nassif said sullenly.

"Things will go easier for you if you come clean and tell us all you know," Zaid advised. "Who murdered the Captain and your great-grandfather, Tahir?"

"It was Jafar Ambreen," came the shocking answer.

"Jafar Ambreen," Zahra exclaimed. "He wasn't even on the ship. How did he know about the diamond?"

At that moment, there was a shout and the sound of running feet. A flashlight moved atop the gallery and Mir appeared, followed by Mr. Horani, Luqman, and Abbas.

"Are you children all right?" Mr. Horani asked. "After we

saw the broken window and hidden compartment, we thought the pirates must have taken you prisoners again. Who's that?" Mr. Horani's voice came to an abrupt stop as he tried to make out the bound figure in the dim light.

"It's a long story," Adam replied. "And you won't believe what we found."

Epilogue

TWO WEEKS LATER, Zaid sat on the rug in the great hall at Bayan House, gazing at the sea of faces gathered around him. Next to him were the other teenagers, the twins, and Basim. The house was ablaze with lights and filled with the merry chatter of voices all trying to speak at once. In addition to the household and employees, there were other guests present that evening.

Zaid's eyes kindled with pleasure as they fell upon his parents, Professor and Mrs. Alkurdi, who were speaking with Dr. Horani and his wife. Next to them were the Ahmeds, the Tabibis and Shaykh Sulaiman of Ghassan, Mustapha like a shadow next to him. Zaid grinned as his gaze went next to Mir, who was making sheep's eyes at his smiling wife, Sabaa. She was a pretty, petite woman who had professed herself delighted to meet them after hearing so much about them from Mir. Last of all, Zaid's eyes rested on Old Bashir, the wooden rocking horse, tucked discreetly in a corner of the great hall.

Everyone gathered there had been involved one way or another in the chain of events that had unfolded in the last few weeks. They knew little bits and pieces of what had happened but none of them knew the full extent to which events in the

227

past had impacted the present. Thus, the gathering of family and friends provided an opportunity for all the mysteries to be cleared up and all secrets to be revealed. After eating a sumptuous dinner and performing the sunset prayer, the household was now gathered in the great hall to hear many of the details which were as yet unknown to them.

Zaid came to attention when Mr. Horani began to speak.

"My dear family and friends, you have all been invited here so you can listen firsthand to the tale you're about to hear," he began. "It's not my tale to tell for indeed I play a very minor role in it all. It's the young people's tale and you will hear it from them. Adam," Mr. Horani gestured to his oldest grandson, "you can begin now."

The room became hushed as Adam began telling them of what had transpired at Bayan House since their arrival. Occasionally, he would ask the teenagers and twins to tell their parts.

Everyone looked bemused after the teenagers finished telling their tale.

"Astounding," Professor Alkurdi said. "Underground tunnels and pirates. *Subhanallah.*"

"And finding the Moon to boot," Dr. Horani said. "You children have done us proud."

To Hassan and Hakeem's delight, they were patted and complimented for their part in training Gul to carry messages and in finding the hidden stairwell. Their ingenuousness in helping to pluck the Moon out of Old Bashir's belly was also a source of much amusement.

The lighthearted comments soon gave way to more weighty matters.

"Faruq is a chip off the old block," Abbas murmured. "I would never have guessed that it was Jafar who murdered the Captain. Can someone tell us how that came about?"

Adam explained, "After questioning Nassif and Faruq, we

were able to put all the pieces together. It all began when Iyad went up north to get his wife and daughter back. After he was told by the tribe that she had divorced him, he set fire to some of their tents in anger and several people got burnt trying to put out the fires. They would have hanged him if they had caught him, that's why Tahir begged the Captain to take Iyad on that voyage. On the way to Yemen, they stopped at the Port of Ghassan for a few days to load some cargo. On the evening that the Captain bought the Moon from the fence's cousin, Iyad happened to see the Captain giving the man a wad of bills and the man giving the Captain a pouch in return. He was curious to know what was in the pouch but was unable to do so because the Captain kept it in a locked box in his cabin. He got lucky the very next day. When he went to clean the Captain's cabin, he found that the Captain had accidentally dropped his bunch of keys on the bunk. Iyad wasted no time in opening the locked box."

"Imagine his surprise," Zahra continued, "when he saw a beautiful gem inside and knew at once that it was the Moon of Masarrah. He had worked for a jeweler in his younger days and had a trained eye when it came to precious stones. After reading about the theft in all the sensational news articles in Midan, he knew that the missing stone's appearance and description exactly matched the one he now held in his hands. From that moment on, he thought of nothing else but stealing the gem for himself so he could gain wealth and power. He couldn't do it on the ship because he knew he would be caught, so he waited for a chance and got it when they reached land. When they heard of the coup, the Captain was in a hurry to get home and set off immediately on foot. Iyad's plan was to follow him, knock him unconscious along the way and steal the stone. As he set off after the Captain, he ran into no other than his best friend, Jafar Ambreen. Glad to have an accomplice, Iyad quickly told Jafar of the diamond and his plan to steal it from the Captain. Jafar agreed at once to help him."

Zaid now took up the tale and said, "The two accomplices

had just started off when the messenger who had been sent to warn the Captain came on the scene and asked where he was. Learning that Iyad had been a crewman on the Yuhanza, he told them of the message he was supposed to have given the Captain and his intention to go after him and warn him not to go home but to join his family in Bayan Woods. Since this would have interfered with their plan to steal the stone, Jafar took Iyad's *khanjar* and killed the messenger. Iyad was shocked but he still wanted the stone, so they continued after the Captain, who must have run all the way home for they didn't catch up with him at all. When they reached the house, all was quiet, with no sign of the rebels. They waited a bit to make sure that no one else came. While Iyad kept watch in the courtyard, Jafar used his head covering to make a mask for his face, and went into the house. When he saw the Captain in the great hall, all his old hatred rose up. It was then that he decided to get rid of his rival and steal the diamond at the same time. He knew that the rebels would be blamed, and no one would suspect him at all. So he killed the Captain with the bloodied *khanjar* he still carried, cleverly taking the Captain's *khanjar* so everyone would think that the Captain had been stabbed with his own dagger."

Layla continued, "While the Captain lay dying, Jafar searched for the diamond but could not find it. When he returned to the courtyard and told Iyad what had happened, Iyad became angry and that's when the two friends had a falling out and began to quarrel. Iyad said that Jafar had gone too far in killing the men and Jafar said that Iyad would be blamed for the murders since it was Iyad's weapon which had killed them. Filled with fear and panic, and still in danger from his ex-wife's tribe, Iyad took off that very night on a ship bound for Yemen. As we know, he never set foot in Midan again. As for Jafar, he cunningly placed the Captain's *khanjar* in the bag and left it outside Iyad's house. And the rest is history, as they say."

"Jafar was quite a piece of work," Maymun said

disapprovingly. "He may have gotten away with his wickedness in this world, but he will surely get his reckoning in the next."

"So, how come Tahir ended up dead in the tunnel?" Mrs. Horani asked.

Adam answered, "After he finally reached Yemen, Iyad wrote to his father and told him everything. He hoped that Tahir would be able to clear him of the murders, so he could return back to Midan. When Tahir received the letter, he was furious. He signed his own death warrant when he went to confront Jafar. Afraid that his evil deeds would be exposed, Jafar knocked Tahir unconscious and had him taken to the cavern, where he planned to kill him and hide his body. Tahir regained consciousness in the cavern and tried to make a run for it but Jafar caught up with him in the tunnel and shot him dead. When Faruq started the pirate ring, he marked that spot with a large white X and showed it to his men as a lesson for anyone who thought to betray him. Poor Tahir's remains were finally given a proper resting place in the Bayan Bay Cemetery."

"By all logic, Nassif should have hated the Ambreens," Mrs. Alkurdi commented. "Why did he become their accomplice?"

"Iyad died over a year ago," Mir interjected. "It seemed that he had redeemed himself in Yemen, gotten married to a Yemeni woman and lived a law-abiding life thereafter. After his death, when there was no longer any fear of him being accused of the Captain's murder, his grandson Nassif, who had been told the whole story and was curious about his roots, left his family in Yemen and came over to Midan three months ago. When he found out that the Ambreens were now the richest people in Bayan Bay, he came up with the idea of blackmailing them with the exposure of Jafar's crimes. So he took up a position as the Ahmeds' chauffeur," there came a contemptuous snort from Mr. Ahmed, "and waited for the right moment to confront Faruq. It was the very next night after Shaykh's Sulaiman's visit to Bayan Bay." He smiled as Shaykh Sulaiman gave a heartfelt sigh

"What happened after that?" Mr. Ahmed asked.

Layla replied, "On the night that Nassif met with Faruq, Faruq knew of Shaykh Sulaiman's visit to Bayan House and guessed that he had come in search of the Moon, which his father, Jafar, had never found. This was confirmed when he learned from his grandson, who eavesdropped on us earlier that day at the library, that we were looking for the Moon. His great fear was that we would discover the underground tunnels during our search and find the pirates lair."

Zaid said, "When Nassif met with Faruq that night and tried to blackmail him, Faruq realized that Nassif could come in very handy, so he admitted to all Jafar had done and gave Nassif some money. He then showed Nassif the underground tunnels and hidden stairwell, told him that he could search for the Moon, and to do whatever he could to stop us from searching."

"We thought that the descendants of the Faithful Five living here were the ones who were searching and trying to scare us away," Adam confessed sheepishly. Abbas and Luqman looked amused while Maymun just looked surprised.

"We also thought it had to be one of the Faithful Five who murdered the Captain," Zaid said. Turning to the curator, he said, "Hud, after your father lost his senses on the day we visited him, he grabbed hold of Adam and said, '*Rafiq…you must forgive me. You trusted me, and I betrayed you.*' Do you know what he meant?"

Hud glanced over at his father, whose face wore a customary blank expression. "He said that, did he? I'm afraid, he's always carried the burden of guilt for the Yuhanza being set on fire. He never stopped believing that he had broken the Captain's trust."

"Poor Nuh," Mr. Horani looked fondly at the old man. "He had always been one of my father's most devoted friends."

When no one asked any more questions, Adam gave the others a silent signal.

Zaid grinned and said, "Now that you've asked your questions."

"And gotten the answers," Zahra said.

"Wouldn't it be wonderful to actually lay eyes on the Moon?" Layla's dimples appeared as she smiled from ear to ear.

Instantly, excitement and anticipation charged the air in the living room.

"So, ladies and gentlemen, let me introduce you to Old Bashir, Bringer of Glad Tidings and Keeper of Secret," Adam announced as he grabbed hold of the horse. "And coming straight from the horse's mouth, we present to you the Moon of Masarrah!"

Hassan and Hakeem, beaming like the sun, opened the horse's jaws, pulled out the oilskin pouch, and handed it to Zaid with due ceremony. Zaid had been given the honor of showing the diamond to everyone because of his brilliant piece of deduction in discovering its hiding place. With great care, he opened the pouch, removed the golden-red stone within and held it out in the palm of his hand. There was an awed silence as everyone stared at the legendary diamond.

"All these years," Mr. Horani's voice was filled with great emotion, "and I never even considered that Papa said 'horse,' and not 'house.' I'm not sure I would have been able to figure out that clue. The girls were the ones who were good at that sort of thing."

"Hanifa and I became experts at Papa's clues," Aunt Hafza said nostalgically. "He would always sign them with the initials MA so we knew they were from him. Since we weren't certain that he had brought back a diamond, it never entered our heads to look for a clue." A shadow came over her face as she added sadly, "Hanifa would have loved that bracelet Papa brought back for her. I'm glad they're such a perfect fit for you girls."

Both Layla and Zahra looked at the bracelet on their wrists, still touched that Mr. Horani and Aunt Hafza had insisted that they have them.

"Well, what is to become of Old Bashir now?" Basim asked.

"I hereby decree that Old Bashir should have a new lease on life," Dr. Horani declared. "He'll be sent to the rocking horse carpenter and be given a brand-new body."

"Yes, yes!" Basim cheered along with the teenagers and twins.

Finding a teaching moment, Professor Alkurdi said, "This reminds me of the story of the Agra diamond. It was said to have been smuggled out of India and into England in the belly of a horse, which had been forced to swallow it. No doubt, the Captain must have heard of this story and used it as inspiration for his hiding place."

Shaykh Sulaiman, who had sat quietly throughout the proceedings finally spoke. "At long last," he intoned softly, a lone tear coursing down his cheek. "At long last, my search is over, and I can fulfill my promise to my father. I will forever be indebted to you," he looked at the young people in gratitude. "It would be a great honor if you all come to visit us in Ghassan."

"Adam and I would love it," Layla said enthusiastically.

"So would Zahra and I," Zaid said eagerly.

"What about us?" Hakeem asked.

"Yeah, what about us?" Hassan echoed.

"You're all invited," the Shaykh's eyes twinkled, "including your parents. I cannot promise you the excitement you've had here. But I'm sure you'll enjoy yourselves all the same, *insha'Allah.*"

And the good folks of Bayan House stayed up late in the night, marveling at the chain of events that had brought them all together.

Thank you for reading my book.
I hope it made you guess a little, laugh a little
and maybe even cry a little.

I would love to hear your thoughts.
Please email me at Zefarah@gmail.com.

Glossary

Alhamdulillah: Praise be to Allah (God)

Allah: The Arabic name for God

Assalaam Alaikum: Peace be unto you; the first greeting that Muslims say to each other

Asr: The late afternoon prayer

Ayatul Kursi: The verse of the throne: Chapter 2, Verse 255 of the Qur'an

Badan: A small type of dhow (ship)

Boum: A dhow (ship) with a tapered stern and a high prow

Dhow: An Arabic lateen-rigged ship with one or two masts

Dhuhr: The midday prayer

Eid-ul-Fitr: The festival of celebration upon the ending of the Ramadan fast

Fajr: The dawn prayer

Hadith: A report describing the words, actions and habits of the Prophet Muhammad (upon whom be peace).

Imam: The prayer leader of a mosque

Insha'Allah: If Allah (God) wills

Isha: The night prayer

Jinn: An unseen being created out of fire that can do both good and harm to mankind

Jumu'ah: The Friday prayer, required for men to be prayed in congregation

Kamal: A navigating device used centuries ago to allow sailors to determine latitude by measuring how far the Pole Star was above the horizon

Khanjar: A traditional, curved dagger of Arab origin, now popularly used as a ceremonial ornament

Maghrib: The sunset prayer

Masjid: Arabic name for mosque

Qur'an: The last Revelation of Allah (God), revealed to the Prophet Muhammad (upon whom be peace)

Shaykh: An Arabic title for a knowledgeable and/or respected person

Shu'ai: The most common type of dhow (ship) in the Persian Gulf

Souk: Market

Subhanallah: Glory be to Allah (God); a saying of Muslims to praise God

Surah Rahman: The 55th chapter of the Qur'an

Wa Alaikum Assalaam: And unto you, be peace; the return greeting for *Assalaam Alaikum*

Get Ready For Book Two:
THE SIGN OF THE SCORPION

A desert castle. An evil presence. A thirst for vengeance.

Four teenagers are about to have a vacation they'll never forget.

When Layla, her brother Adam, and their friends Zaid and Zahra, arrive at Dukhan Castle, they anticipate an exciting time exploring the mysteries of nature. They soon find themselves delving into mysteries of a different nature. A cloaked figure, spooky midnight screams, incense being burned in the eerie lookout tower, and startling secrets are just a few. The clues can only lead to one conclusion. Something sinister is simmering beneath the surface and it's just a matter of time before it breaks loose. A chance encounter with a gypsy woman begins a guessing game of intrigue, pitting the teenagers against a shadowy foe known as Al-Aqrab, the Scorpion. As danger draws closer to the castle, they must race against time to unmask the Scorpion and foil a demonic scheme of revenge.

The Sign of the Scorpion is the thrilling second book in The Moon of Masarrah Series.

Made in the USA
Monee, IL
28 March 2022